Copyright © 2008 Lynden Lewis and
Orlando Silva
All rights reserved.
ISBN: 1-4392-2470-6

Visit www.booksurge.com to order
additional copies.

To my Parents,

Thank you for opening the door to a world full of possibilities, for giving me the nudge out of the tree so I could fly, and for being yourselves so I could learn and grow. All these things I thank you both for.

                                                Orlando

To my mother,

You have always been there for me and it is because of you that I have the strength and determination to accomplish my hopes and dreams. I thank you for all you have deposited in me and for remaining strong for all these years.

You are my biggest inspiration and brightest beacon of hope.

Lynden

Special Thanks

Sehe Han

Tobias Roetsch

Derrill Hoover

Bryce Hammond

Lance Turner

Thank you all for helping us on this incredible journey.

Echoes of Tempore
Revival of Light

Table of Contents

Chapter 1: Niphiliem's Power ... 1
Chapter 2: Awakening ... 14
Chapter 2.5: Oraien vs. Atrum ... 24
Chapter 3: Purpose's Introduction ... 29
Chapter 4: Preparation of a Legend ... 42
Chapter 4.5: Ioxus vs. O'navus ... 87
Chapter 5: Hero's Beginning ... 97
Chapter 5.5: Ioxus vs. Vexus ... 112
Chapter 6: Unexpected Counterstrike ... 127
Chapter 6.5: Ioxus vs. Sendo ... 136
Chapter 7: Journey ... 144
Chapter 8: One's impact ... 170
Chapter 9: Calfieren Capital ... 184
Chapter 9.5: Blue Light vs. Red Fire ... 202
Chapter 10: Journey to the Fire Core ... 218
Chapter 11: Terrus Revenge ... 238
Chapter 12: Remedy ... 256
Chapter 13: Journey to Celeres ... 262
Chapter 14: Journey to the Far-Flying Star ... 296
Chapter 15: Capture and Seize ... 307
Chapter 16: Feldspar's Manipulation ... 313
Chapter 17: Xan's Revelation ... 324
Chapter 18: New Found Power ... 340
Chapter 18.5: Ioxus vs. Feldspar ... 344
Chapter 19: Basium ... 352
Chapter 20: Ignorant Refusal ... 370

Chapter 21: Four Paths, One Phoenix 384
Chapter 22: Enlightenment 389
Chapter 23: A New Friend 398
Chapter 24: Gathering at Space Luna 403
Chapter 25: Beckons War 413
Chapter 26: Power of the Void 418
Chapter 27: Awakens Caligus 421
Chapter 28: Awakens A'ethus 429
Chapter 29: Alpha vs. Omega 434
Chapter 30: Fraudulent Peace 442

T.I.D. Terms Information Directory 446

Chapter 1

Niphiliem's Power

The dark energia is against the light,
The light energia is against the dark,
So awakens Caligo,
So awakens the dark Caligus
So awakens Antares,
So awakens the light A'ethus,

"This poem was found on the ancient worlds of our ancestors, now desolate, ruined planets. The poem explains the everlasting conflicts of the universe: light versus darkness and stars versus black holes. Planets form around stars that can sustain life. When that star dies, so does all life in its system. Life exists where light presides, and in contrast, death exists where darkness presides. The Antares star is extremely young, large, and powerful. In-fact, it is so large that its gravity has pulled many planets away from neighboring systems thus forming the Antares Ring, the largest and the most diverse culmination of planets and civilizations in the known universe."

"Stegetons are planets surging with plasma energy. They are smaller than Natura planets yet they have a greater amount of energy. The Stegeton's plasma is harnessed through its Quarton to enable life to flourish on the planet. So, what is a Quarton? It is a massive object with mysterious symbols beautifully etched into its metal form. Although the energy of many Quartons within the Antares system has been harnessed to some degree, no civilization fully understands its true purpose. The energy is focused into the development of an atmosphere, gravity, landmass, and more. Due to its varying flow of energy, each Stegeton looks much more different than natura planets. Natura planets are the planets that have evolved naturally. They take thousands of years to produce an atmosphere with oxyg..."

-"Alright people, I'm going to pause it there. Now, these are all things that you should have learned in grade school, but just in case anybody slept through that before coming here to get your degree, does anyone have any questions about what they have seen so far?" asked Ms. Emery. In response, a student shot his arm up. "Yes, Oraien?" she said.

-"Ms. Emery, we are in the Antares star system, correct?" asked Oraien.

-"Yes, Luna is one of the many Stegetons pulled into its system. Why do you ask?" Ms. Emery replied.

Near the southern pole just above the atmosphere of Luna, a large defense satellite was moving into position. The class continued peacefully while a silent countdown within the satellite activated, determining when it would begin its attack. Its axis began tilting as ships neared Luna's space territory.

-"Well, then why would a planet like Nibiru want to attack us?" Oraien asked blatantly. Ms. Emery stared at him ferociously while whispers about the Niphiliem filled the room as the students began discussing the chilling subject.

Deep in space, an unknown fleet received a warning message with a time limit to redirect its course. Completely disregarding the message, the fleet made preparations to begin its assault. The spherical defense satellite set the reconfiguration of its panels in motion, therefore redirecting the satellites lasers to target all ships within the approaching fleet. With the panels on the front of the sphere already fixed on its targets, the mirror panels on the back began to move in random sequences. After a short while, the satellite finished its initiation into attack mode, and the panels took the shape of crystal-feathered wings, serving as laser focal points.

-"Oraien! Meet me outside!" Ms. Emery said raising her voice. Oraien let himself out of his chair and fearlessly walked across the room. When he finally made it to her desk, Ms. Emery followed behind him, making sure her aura of anger was discerned.

A minute after the countdown began, a terrifying mechanical humming noise filled the air aboard the largest ship in the fleet as its main weapon charged. Only seconds after the charging commenced, it fired directly at the engaging satellite. The satellite sent video confirmation to South Base City, the planet's heavily fortified military headquarter located on Luna's southern pole, of a large flash of light originating from the mysterious convoy now identified to be the Niphiliem forces. As the countdown was nearing its end, the satellite amassed its energy to fire. With an enormous explosion, the enemy blast annihilated the defense satellite, and the Luna planetary alarm sounded.

-"How do you know about the attack?! Oraien! Don't tell me you've been hacking into the government system again. Did I not tell you before, the abilities you have sometimes present doors that should not always be opened. Now listen to me, don't ever expose things like that to the rest of the class. I expect more from you!"

-"But Ms. Emery! This is a class one emergency. Luna is putting all it has into defense and nothing into offense, and yet the government keeps this a secret, and for what, peace? Everyone should know for their own safety. Why are we acting as if we are untouchable?" he asked firmly.

-"That's because we are. The Assembly has made sufficient preparations," she responded.

-"No, we are not. The people of Zodok thought the same thing and look wha... wait," Oraien paused and squinted his eyes suspiciously, "How do *you* know of the attack?"

Ms. Emery eyes widened but didn't allow herself to look too surprised as she quickly thought of a response.

-"In all my years here on Luna, no one has ever managed to get through our defenses, and today won't be any diff..."

~"Attention citizens of Vicero, attention citizens of Vicero," the campus intercom announced. "The Niphiliem forces have broken through our defenses. Please head to your designated evacuation areas." Ms. Emery's head jutted and a look of disbelief crossed her face. "Again, our defenses have been breached!" Suddenly silence filled the room as the planetary alarm rang in the distance.

The city of Vicero became a war zone within minutes as all alarms declared orders to evacuate. Soon, ships poured out towards the skies headed for their moon, their last hope for a safe haven. Oraien did not let shock overwhelm him as it did Ms. Emery and grabbed his belongings and yelled to his classmates, "Everyone get to the pods now!"

Oraien dashed down the hallways with incredible speed. Soon he reached the exit of the building and was flooded by the sound of distant explosions. The bright red glow in the sky was not normal during the mid-afternoon days, but Oraien figured it was the result of all the smoke from the city.

Over the city of Vicero, just above the atmosphere, the second defense satellite positioned itself to attack the unwelcomed invaders. The satellite's laser focal points opened, and the feather-like mirrors extended, ready to attack. It emerged from the north and let out an array of beams that pierced many of the ships entering Luna space territory. As soon as the Niphiliem had their artillery locked on the defense orbiter, it was immediately destroyed, causing a chaotic explosion above the atmosphere that shook the very ground of the planet.

Sudden shockwaves caused the ground to shake, and Oraien struggled to stay standing.

Soon, large debris started to fall towards the city, decimating all on which they landed. After the ground was still once more, Oraien hopped on his small magnetic-powered hover bike. His destination was soon directed when he saw downtown Vicero under attack in the distance, horrifying display of the Niphiliem destroying the myriad of ships trying to evacuate. He immediately started towards the lower level of Vicero to do what no one else seems to be doing: standing up to the invaders and protecting their home. He tried to grasp the reason behind the Niphiliem attack, and like a great spark in his mind, a single word made its way to his lips,

-"Quarton."

That was the Niphiliem's true intention: to conquer Vicero to gain the power of its Quarton. Oraien accelerated his bike and made his way through the chaotic environment full of collapsing buildings, explosions, and burning ships falling out of the sky.

Vicero was a city built on eight major support rings that kept the city off the ground. The city's layout was a pyramid, and the Luna-Quarton rested at its center. The city had three main levels. The higher level was specifically made for residence, the middle for recreation and entertainment while the bottom was strictly reserved for business offices.

Gazing into the sky levels from the lower section of the city, Oraien continued along a less dangerous path until he had no choice but to detour. Fire began to spread throughout the lower level of Vicero as the heat made its way towards Oraien. He sped past the hazardous environment, maneuvering his motor vehicle through each explosion and avoiding massive falling sections of the upper levels. He finally came to an operating elevator within a sky scrapper that stretched to the upper ground level and the sky level of the city.

Oraien hopped off of his small vehicle and into the elevator of his sky community. He punched the button that was labeled *Ground*. When the elevator doors slid open, he found himself standing before the atrium. He became sick at the sight of the countless number of bodies lying along the walls of the lobby. He began to head out but immediately stopped when he heard a helpless soul screaming. Carefully but quickly, he began to run in the direction of the excruciating scream. He cautiously peaked over the corner of a crumbling wall and saw a large figure drop a limp body.

-They just killed another person! He thought as he hid behind the wall. The Niphiliem that attacked Vicero were tall soldiers that wore uniforms of space armor adorned with silky fabrics that held each segment of armor together. They wore intimidating helmets that symbolized their ferocity and ruthlessness. Behind the wall, one of the Niphiliem placed his weapon, a plasma barrel gun, on the floor near Oraien.

His heart began to beat frantically as he tried to think of a solution. Sweat dripped from his brow and landed on the floor. His breathing sped to an almost uncontrollable rate until he heard the thud of another lifeless body. He slowly calmed himself and began to grip his fear as the thoughts of the destruction diffused into his mind. Luna was his home, and he knew that after he had come so far to stand up to the invaders, he could not cower away and betray his people. Analyzing the situation as best as he could, he remembered his mandatory combat training from his early school years. He knew that he was skillful enough to defend himself, so he let go of his fear and took one step away from his youth and one step towards the Niphiliem. Quietly, he began to sneak up behind the massive soldier for a surprise attack. However, as he almost reached the oblivious soldier, another entered the room and spotted him. Oraien leaped forward and swept his leg across the floor, tripping the monster in front of him. Oraien then grabbed the monster's arm, leaned back with his weight and thrust his legs against the creature's side, breaking his arm. The soldier who entered the room began to charge towards Oraien as he picked up a table and threw it at him. Instinctively, Oraien jumped above the table to grab it and threw it back at him.

He let his guard down, thinking that breaking the fallen soldier's arm was his final crippler, and consequently, Oraien soon found himself wrapped in the massive arm of the soldier behind him.

-"The Niphiliem show no mercy," the monster said breathing heavily. The other spoke as well,

-"You are not like the others, you actually stood against us. Who are you?" the Niphiliem soldier asked. "No matter, you will still die." The Niphiliem swung his arm with all his might and connected a blow to Oraien's head and his ribs. The bone-breaking blow to Oraien's ribs made him yell out in agony.

-"Yes, scream like the Duro you are," said the soldier with a cynical smile.

      Oraien could feel the monster's grip fading, so he waited for the next attack to attempt a parry, successfully resulting in the soldier hitting his partner. The injured Niphiliem struck the ground with a loud thump, and Oraien quickly jumped on him and twisted his neck until a sharp crack was heard. The soldier behind Oraien threw a blow that he caught from behind and swung the soldier over his head. In a desperate act of survival, Oraien grabbed the soldier's throat and dug his nails into his skin with all the strength he had left. Blood began to slide from the armor of the Niphiliem while he kicked his legs and flailed his arms through the air as he struggled for his life. With one last surge of power, Oraien pulled until he heard his opponents' neck snap and could feel the soldier's warm blood on his hands as he ripped his throat. Oraien did not let his adrenaline grip release until he felt the tall Niphiliem soldier's body fall completely still and dead.

-*What have I done*, he thought as he slowly lifted his bloody hands.

Echoes of Tempore: Revival of Light

Dust and other loose debris began to fall from the rumbling building, and Oraien, exhausted from his encounter with the Niphiliem, dragged himself against the walls until he reached the exit of the building. He finally reached the street as blood from his head slid down his forehead and into his eyes. Oraien sat down on the corner of a skyscraper, feeling his life slip away as his energy faded.

Chapter 2

Awakening

A deafening sound brought Oraien back to his senses. Strange enough, he could also feel the sound. It was a pulsing feeling that grew within him, as if his heart was approaching its limits. Oraien opened his eyes trying to find the source of this incredible feeling surging through his body. All other noises began to fade into the background; he could no longer hear the many explosions or the suffering of the men, women and children. His eyes opened and focused, to find the Luna Quarton as he peered through the many burning buildings. It seemed to be fixated on him, pulsating in resonance with his own heartbeat. It was as if nothing else existed except the Quarton and himself.

-*Luna?* Oraien questioned. In the foreign plane, Oraien was now looking at the life force of the Quarton. Darkness surrounded him, and the only source of light was the flowing blue energy of the Quarton. Oraien could see sparks of electricity sporadically flicker as he intensely studied the object before him. *It's as if the planet itself is crying, like a mother being torn apart from her precious children by an inevitable force, but it seems much more than that. It's telling me to fight, fight to protect its people.* Oraien felt the Quarton connecting with him as it pulsed with life.

- "Then give me the strength!" Oraien yelled out, "The strength to protect!"

Instantly, the pulsing began to increase its pace, and in a blinding flash of light, Oraien felt his body being infused with power like he had never felt before. When he opened his eyes again, he was back in the middle of chaos and realized that only a moment had gone by. As he stumbled to his feet, he noticed the many cryptic markings on the surface of the Quarton were glowing vigorously. Each time the symbols pulsated with light, he felt an erupting power growing from within him. Something was begging to be unleashed upon the Niphiliem, the fiends who were brutally slaughtering the people of his home.

Oraien was soon spotted by a group of Niphiliem soldiers, and they immediately began to approach him. They noticed that he was injured, so they did not take any precautions.

Rage filled Oraien's very being as he watched one of the soldiers approaching him, dragging his weapon along the ground. He was in no rush to kill Oraien, and the evil smile on the soldier's face was little more than that of a predator that had cornered his prey. As the beast lifted his weapon to finish him, Oraien's anger exploded. As a result, a sudden shockwave was created that sent the soldiers crashing into their surroundings. The shockwave instantaneously imploded back onto Oraien, and placed a metallic substance on his body. Regaining their composure, the soldiers stared upon Oraien, trembling in great fear. They knew they had found someone they stood no chance of defeating, someone who was more than capable of returning the pain they caused him and his people and someone who could and would single handedly thwart their plans of taking Luna for the sake of their own selfish reasons. The Quarton's symbols on the suit were undeniable; they had found the fifth Xextrum.

    Oraien, stunned by his new power, stood in awe and gazed at the suit that was materialized onto his body. Inscribed in the suit were markings that radiated with power, identical to that of the Quarton. The suit was an impenetrable armor that not only left him in amazement but also concern. At first glance, the armor seemed too heavy to move around freely. However, he realized that he was mistaken as he began to move. He felt incredibly light. His eyesight increased greatly and altered because of the shield covering his eyes that locked his very senses onto all targets in sight. He could feel the strength he possessed in his new form and could also feel the suit was learning and adapting to his surroundings. Taking his eyes off of his suit, he looked at the Niphiliem soldiers that were stunningly looking at him through the falling debris. Shocked and dumbfounded, only one soldier mustered the courage to speak, hoping to escape his inevitable annihilation.

-"Mercy, great Xextrum!" the fearful soldier cried out. Oraien thought about how he would answer the soldier's plea while envisioning the treatment his people had received. He then gazed into the fire that was consuming his home; all the people that he once knew and loved were now dead or forced to flee.

Looking into the eyes of the frightened Niphiliem, Oraien felt no remorse. He felt no emotion. The event had detached him from his kindness, and this day his life, and his fate, had changed within the spur of destiny. Still gazing into the soldier's eyes, Oraien's mind was set. He turned to the Niphiliem soldiers and coldly replied,

-"Mercy? There will be none."

Blasting off from his position with unprecedented speed, he connected his fist with the face of a Niphiliem soldier with such a force that it snapped the soldier's neck and sent his body flying through a wall a few meters off in the distance. He then turned in to strike the other soldier next to him with a kick that sent him smashing through a vehicle and into a shop across the street. In a prideful futile attempt to stop Oraien, the rest of the soldiers attacked in unison only to meet a swift demise.

Slowly Oraien began to understand how powerful he had become and attempted daring techniques to test himself. At first, he tried jumping and realized that he was able to leap several stories at once. Furthermore, with his great agility, he began to run along the sides of the building, defying the gravitational pull of Luna before landing on the ground again. Looking onward, Oraien spotted a group of Niphiliem chasing a few civilians on a bridge not far from his location, so once again, he began running quickly on the walls of the skyscraper. As he neared the top, he tried to jump to the bridge, but the overwhelming pressure under his feet caused the glass to break. With nothing but air to break his fall, Oraien plummeted to the surface, hitting the sides of the buildings as he fell. Pulling himself out of the small crater his impact created, he realized that he was inexperienced with his new power. But he also realized that the civilians being chased by the Niphiliem did not have the time for him to explore the limits of his new power. So, he ran along the road to rescue them but arrived too late. With even more rage growing inside of him, Oraien slaughtered the Niphiliem soldiers who were laughing at what they had done.

    Instead of fighting all the soldiers at once, he decided to take them out in waves and keep them guessing where he would strike next. Oraien used his new power to run along the sides of buildings at a speed that the Niphiliem soldiers could not see. Not wanting to focus too much on the small groups, he strategically lured them into large masses and then dashed between the soldiers, killing all in his path. After having eliminated a large number of the Niphiliem, he realized that their militia was not only land-based but also air-based. To do any major damage, he would have to work his way to the source of their origin and stop them once and for all.

Looking overhead through open spaces between buildings, he saw massive ships moving out and knew he had to stop them before they got too far. Examining his armor, he wondered if the suit possessed any weapons. He soon found himself in control of two dagger- like blades that were infused with lightning that jettisoned from his outer forearms. He retracted them and scaled his way up the buildings. With one last push off the side of the building, Oraien moved into the path of one of the smaller ships to immobilize it. Once in position to take out the incoming ship, he summoned his blades and sliced the Niphiliem soldier as well as the entire craft in half. The ship's segments continued in two different directions. Oraien observed that although the blades were short in length, once they made contact with the ship, they extended the full length of the two-manned vessel until it was completely cut in half. Oraien cut through the ship with such agility that each explosion did not occur until a few moments had passed. Immediately, he started to jump from one ship to another, slicing them into little pieces, continuously moving to the next ship before it exploded. When he managed to cut his way through the fleet, he found himself landing upon a very large building overlooking ground zero, the source of all the carnage: the massive Niphiliem war-ship.

Coming from the starship were colossal bridges designed to channel energy. They were attached to the Quarton, absorbing massive amounts of the planet's energy. The Niphiliem mother ship was now within Oraien's view, and in front of the ship were masses of soldiers lined up in formation awaiting orders to dispatch into the city and carry out their mission. The vibrant sunset made the incoming crafts seem peaceful, and the ground troops seemed as ants crawling from their colony. The air fleet alone did not alarm Oraien, but he knew making his way to the war-ship through the ground troops would be a more challenging feat.

Before Oraien jumped into action, he thought of what the best course of action would be. He decided to use fallen ships in his surroundings to throw them like disks through massive soldier clusters, literally cutting their numbers in half. Oraien jumped off his high spot from the skyscraper to the ground to begin his personal mission. While fighting for some time, a few ships came within his range. So he scaled his way up the side of a building to once again ship hop, slicing his way through them until he reached a larger ship in the center. Once aboard, he tore off the main turret and began to use it as his own firearm, shooting down many other ships in the distance and killing the many soldiers they landed on. Oraien let the turret fall once it was out of ammo and jumped into the center of the ground troops as he drew his weapons for combat. Watching the destruction of his troops, the Niphiliem commander became enraged at the incompetence of his men with only one enemy.

-"Fools!" he proclaimed, destroying the table that once stood before him. "Who is that!?" he asked furiously.

-"We're not sure, Commander Atrum. We have just received reports that large numbers of our troops are being found dead throughout the city." he regrettably replied.

-"Worthless maggots! It looks like I'll have to deal with this threat myself," he said as he stormed out of the room. Atrum was the ranking officer in charge of the invasion and did not lead lightly. His subordinates knew the wrath he would cast down upon them should they ever fail to follow his orders. Therefore, his soldiers never compromise their lives by holding back while fighting their enemy.

Without any hesitation, Oraien blasted off running in the direction of the Quarton, slicing all in his path. When he reached the base of the Quarton, he continued running full speed up the slanted figures side, building his strength to cut the bridges. Each link of energy was held in place by pods that detached from the mother ship, and each pod let out bursts of energy towards empty space. Oraien struck in an instant fluent motion, and his short blades let out a longer blade of lightning that stretched enough to fully separate the colossal connection. One after another, he repeated this action until all connections were severed. With no energy to keep them stable, each massive bridge fell back thrashing through the crowd of Niphiliem soldiers, decimating their numbers. Oraien's peripheral vision caught a glimpse of a strange soldier to his left. It was the commander, who had made his way to the Quarton in anticipation of Oraien's attempts to disable the bridges.

Chapter 2.5

Oraien vs. Atrum

-"You have caused me enough trouble, insolate warrior!" Atrum yelled.

Atrum was taught never to underestimate the enemy, but the prospect that he would have to be cautious with a single warrior infuriated him. Atrum foolishly departed his teachings and engaged Oraien without fully analyzing his opponent. Atrum was agile, and he caught Oraien off guard with a violent blow from his energy sledge to Oraien's chest. The blow sent Oraien sliding down the Quarton's side. However, such pain meant nothing to Oraien by now. All that went through his mind were the images of his lost friends and the destruction of all that he knew. Oraien continued sliding down until he used his hands and his feet to grip onto the Quarton. He soon regained his footing and rushed back towards Atrum. Oraien speedily approached Atrum and heard him yelling from a distance,

-"Warrior, you have chosen a dreadful day to interfere, so let me send you to the dark universe!" These words did not slow Oraien down, but when he reached a safe distance to communicate, he stopped.

-"I don't know what you're talking about, but if you are talking about death you should look no further than me because your time is up!" Oraien tightened his hands as he glared at his enemy,

- "Who are you? I can tell that you are the one in charge, otherwise you would not have been able to even touch me."

-"I am Commander Atrum; I don't normally speak to my prey, but since you seem to have *some* power, and withstood a blow from my Xodus, I though it only fitting that you know the name of your executioner." Atrum answered.

Oraien picked his hands up and gazed into them, "This power, I don't know what it is, but I know that I'm going to use it to stop you."

-"In the end, only the strong remain. No more chatting!" roared Atrum. He then charged towards Oraien ready to clash.

Running at each other with amazing speeds, the energy given off from the clashing of their weapons caused ripples in the air. Blinded by arrogance, Atrum began a series of assaults, recklessly swinging his sledge at Oraien. Now on the defensive, Oraien began dodging the deadly blows. With each stroke that missed him, the pounding of Atrum's weapon sent energy surging along the surface of the Quarton. With such a large weapon as Atrum's tool of combat, Oraien was shocked at the sheer speed and accuracy of each blow headed his way. However, he soon began to notice how sluggish Atrum's movements became the longer he evaded, and when Atrum took a brief moment to regain his strength, Oraien seized the opportunity to begin his own furious barrage of attacks.

The two began to violently exchange blows and guards. Using his weapons to the best of his abilities, Oraien managed to disarm Atrum by striking the handle of his sledge and sending it flying. Atrum was now without a weapon and was open for attack, giving Oraien the ability to cut through his armor. Atrum fell to his knees, now unable to move as Oraien walked to deliver the finishing blow. He saw Oraien approaching him, and for the first time, he felt fear, a fear of his inevitable death. However, a high-pitched noise broke Oraien's concentration; it was the sound of the Niphiliem ship's cannon being fired directly at him.

The highly concentrated beam hit Oraien with a massive force and sent him plummeting over a thousand feet back towards the surface. The impact caused a large crater in the ground, cracking the streets of the city. Another craft came to retrieve Atrum from the Quarton, and once he was safely on the mother ship, it began its ascension of retreat, leaving behind many other small vessels. Painfully recuperating from the blow he received, Oraien took notice of the full fledge retreat. Once again, he began jumping from ship to ship, taking advantage of the position of the fleet, and strategically climbing his way up the array of ships to the highest point he could. With the mother ship in sight, he focused all of his energy into jumping as hard and as fast as he could towards it.

The amount of energy he released crushed the small ship under his feet as he rocketed towards the massive ship. At that point, Oraien was uncontrollable, and he no longer worried for his own life. The speed at which he traveled caused the air around him to explode as he broke through the sound barrier and hit the ship. The heavily armored ship was no match for his armor's indestructible metal. Oraien traveled straight through to the other side of the ship, tearing through the ship's main engine.

The deafening sound of the explosion filled the sky as the entire vessel began a fiery decent down to Luna's central ocean. As Oraien fell in the middle of burning steel and falling debris, he felt the power of his suit fading. Once again, he could feel the soft breeze of air on his face, and he closed his eyes, completely devoid of energy. Awaiting his fate, he suddenly felt someone falling next to him, trying to save him and holding him tightly.

- "Gotcha."

Chapter 3

Purpose's Introduction

-"Caileb-how is he doing?"

-"I'm surprised he is still alive, sister. He recently stopped bleeding and should've died, but his body seems stronger somehow," said Caileb.

An atmosphere of concern filled a room in which stood a female, her brother, and an officer. The room had two white beds, one of which slept a totally bandaged individual. His body was trembling from pain and loss of blood. He had been in this condition for the past four days.

Two more days passed as the patient's physical condition improved, and inside of his mind, he felt peaceful from a mysterious aura that illuminated over him for several hours each day. The next day, his eyes opened to a bright room that reminded him of the hospitals of Luna, with the exception of the strange young man in the room.

-"Who-who are you..." his voice scraped. A strange young man in the room was at a desk. He was slouched back reading a rugged dark blue book. He placed his book down and leaned in to respond.

-"You're awake. I am Caileb, the commanding officer aboard this vessel, and your name is...?"

-"Oraien...my name is Oraien Zeal."

Caileb began to anticipate what Oraien would do next: ask more questions or go back to sleep. Caileb could not understand Oraien's character as a young man and a warrior, and while Caileb performed his initial opinion, Oraien thought back to Luna and the invasion. Blood covered his mind as he thought of the unimaginable destruction. He knew the lives he took were to protect but could not embrace the hard realization of his rage.

-*I did it to protect my people*, he said to himself holding his knees tightly. *I did it for that feeling I got when I looked into the Quarton...* Oraien's fear trailed off as the familiar comforting feeling once again entered his body. He felt as if it had come from inside of him.

Oraien slid his hand under his shirt and felt the warmth from near his heart. Whatever it was, the fear had left him and that is all he wanted. An innocent confusion, like that of a child, filled Oraien as he held his chest. Without the fear clouding his mind, he began to remember how he fought. He remembered his strength and his constitution. He remembered it all, until his mind reached for the last bits of the event.

He wondered how he survived the explosion of the Niphiliem mother ship. He remembered the wind as he was falling; he felt so close to death at that point. However, he then recalled something peaceful and comforting, a woman's voice,

-"Where is the girl that saved me?" The question took Caileb by surprise. He was wrong about his assumptions about Oraien. He thought Oraien would be completely disoriented and confused about what happened after the explosion, but he seemed to have grasped the situation, even as he was about to draw his last breath. Caileb lowered his head with a smile,

-"How you remember her, I do not know, but her name is Calea. She is my sister," he said. "I will tell you where you are, who I am, and answer any other questions you might have," said Caileb.

"As to where you are, you are in an Anekie cruiser. The ship is headed for Nekio, my home planet, and home to all Anekie," stated Caileb. Oraien sat himself upright in his bed and pulled himself up against the wall to support him so he could properly speak with Caileb.

"So you came to help Luna. Thank you, but by the time you arrived, it would have been too late," said Oraien.

"Would have? What do you mean?" asked Caileb.

"I don't remember getting any help from anyone while I fought out there. I was alone," Oraien stated. "And I told my professor that this would happen, but she, along with the rest of Luna, was too sure that our defenses were flawless." Oraien then looked at Caileb and said, "Do you know how many people died, Caileb?" He then looked away, "Too many because you were late. Too many because the Assembly was too stubborn," Caileb looked down to sympathize with him but immediately held his ground and began to speak,

Echoes of Tempore: Revival of Light

-"When you talk about the tides of war, yes, we were indeed late, Oraien. But you only saved that city. There were two other major cities still under fire, and you were not going to save them while falling through the sky with a destroyed war-ship. You would have surely died as well as much of your world would have been, had we not arrived. My sister saved you with the help of our crew, while the rest of the Anekie forces aided the other cities. It was amazing, watching my sister save you..."

-"How much longer until we can deploy?" Calea asked.

-"We have just received word that the other troops have been engaged into combat," an operator seated at a control module followed.

Looking through a large visual screen, the crew watched as a powerful metallic being climbed his way up the ranks of fleeing Niphiliem ships by jumping from one to another. The picture displayed the flickering lighting that emitted from the being, and how each ship he bound from exploded under the crushing pressure of his leap.

-"That must be him. There's no doubt about it," the commanding officer Caileb spoke, but his surprise turned into alert when he saw that the being jumped straight through the Niphiliem's engines. "Everyone brace yourselves!" Caileb knew that the ships generator would explode.

Instantly the explosion displaced all the air around the war-ship causing an immense shockwave that traveled through the immediate vicinity that shook the crew and the commander within their ship. The crew had come on a secret mission but did not hold back aid for Luna. Immediately a woman yelled out, "No more sitting around, we came for him!" she touched the screen pointing at the metallic individual. "His strength is outstanding, but it looks like he is inexperienced. He jumped clean through the ship's main reactor and engine causing that explosion. The force of the explosion pushed him further upward and…" Her words stopped as the powerful individuals armor disappeared, and the appearance of a young Eluesian emerged as the suit's owner.

-"Team, we can't wait to fully descend into a safer jump zone. I'm going for it. I'm using the high altitude suit to dive from here, it's now or never, we cannot afford to lose him," said Caileb. The young woman put her hand on Caileb's shoulder, "Yes, Calea?"

-"Brother, no questions asked. I'm ready to go, and we don't have time to wait!" Calea said with assertive urgency in her voice.

-"Well hurry, he has already started to fall."

    Calea entered the jump room located on the bottom of the ship and professionally executed her dive through the sky. She was fluent, unbound, perfect, and each turn she made while cutting through the sky was made to reach the falling warrior as soon as possible. She had to pass through the smoke cloud left behind from the ship and also be aware of anything left in the cloud that could harm her. Coming out from the bottom side of the smoke cloud she approached the large ship and began to turn her hands, feet, and her entire body to channel the air around her to steer around falling fragments of the Niphiliem war-ship. After a challenging obstacle and some time, she could finally see the young warrior. He was unconscious and peacefully falling, but after Calea got closer to him, she saw the blood soaked clothes he wore.

    Calea turned upside towards the sky and grabbed him so that he was facing her. Then she wrapped her arms around him to latch a security harness to his body. Smaller automated belts attached his arms and legs to her arms and legs. Calea activated the jet-pack she had equipped and curved back up towards her brother's ship that was steadily descending. When she reached the jump room she landed on her back with Oraien still attached to her. Calea looked at the sleeping warrior and felt remorse for his home, but she also felt relief knowing that he was still alive. The automated harnesses unlatched themselves and retracted back into Calea's suit. She gently lifted him up and placed him beside her. The ship's crew and Caileb came and congratulated Calea on a successful mission, and the medical crew immediately took him.

-"So that's what happened while I was unconscious. She must be a good sister," Oraien paused and then continued, "Caileb. It seems that the Niphiliem recognized the armor I wore. It was so powerful... but they called me Xextrum," Caileb's eyes slightly narrowed,

-"Are you familiar with that term, Xextrum?" Caileb asked.

-"No, I can't say I've ever heard that name before. I-I got the power just after a severe fight I had with two other Niphiliem soldiers that almost killed me," Oraien looked to the side and became troubled. Caileb saw his expression and recognized his struggle.

Being in war for so long, it only took Oraien's expression to tell Caileb of his plight. Caileb had his share of brutality in unforgiving situations. Just reminiscing of his own past horrors brought him goose-bumps. When Caileb raised his head to look at Oraien again, the emotion in his eyes screamed: why. It was that single word that described the look on Oraien's face, but that word with a perfect confusion in its mix; Caileb had to do something. Thinking fast, Caileb came up with a question hoping to start a new conversation,

-"Did you kill them?" Caileb asked.

-"Yes, I did, otherwise they would have.... killed me," Oraien's mind began to recapture the past experience he had of brutally killing two soldiers. Reality struck Oraien instantly. He killed someone, and the thought made him feel sick to his stomach. Oraien looked away towards the ground and fought the disgusting feeling within him. Caileb struggled not to show his shock at what he had just heard.

-*Two? How did he manage to kill two soldiers at once with no military experience or the power of his Xextrum? A well trained soldier of any planet has enough trouble killing one in hand- to-hand combat, so how is it that he could handle two and live to tell about it? Perhaps he was right to send us to retrieve him after all.* Caileb thought.

-"Well. Oraien, you are going to be ok now. Just rest, when we get to Nekio, everything will be explained," said Caileb.

-"Tell me one thing," Oraien said. "What is a Xextrum?" Caileb crossed his arms and leaned forward towards Oraien.

-"Well, to tell you the truth, I'm not the expert when it comes to that. However, I know the legend," he began to calm his voice.

"They call upon the light to shine Natura's protection;
They call upon the light to shine Stegeton's protection.
Loyalty lies in the hands of these two.
Darkness comes when darkness calls.
So the tune of hope is touched, and the Xextrum arise.
The guardians of the ten corners of our system,"

Caileb paused. "That is one of the poems of the ancients. It explains that the Xextrum are protectors of the universe. So I guess if you were chosen, then that makes you one of them. The Luna Quarton chose you to hold its Neo-Quarton; you have a very special power. I also remember that the Neo-Quarton is actually a part of you now, like an organ. But ok-ok. Retsum will tell you the rest when we get there, that's all you need to know for now. Just rest," Caileb concluded. As Oraien was pushing himself out of the bed, Caileb's sister entered the room.

    Oraien did not know anything about her other than her voice and her touch. The voice came first and then the touch came when she grabbed him and wrapped him in her safety harness to rescue him. She saved his life, and Oraien thought that she would be a wonderful woman to rightfully meet. Her appearance was so pristine just like all Anekie, and her short black hair complimented her physique. Her brown skin was as flawless as the lips she spoke with, but her eyes turned into an assertive gaze as she began to speak,

-"What are you doing?! You get back into that bed; you aren't ready to get up yet. As a matter of fact, you will not get up for the remainder of the trip," Calea demanded as she walked towards her brother. Feeling embarrassed, Oraien laid back down.

-"Thank you," said Oraien.

As Calea passed, she paused and took a glance at Oraien's eyes. All her life there had been only a few times when she had been thanked for her services, but it was Oraien's sincerity that made her feel appreciated. Although she was grateful of his gratitude, she immediately caught herself and replied, "Thank you for what? You needed my help, and I extended it. No thanks is necessary."

Oraien looked at her, confused. He concluded that she was probably only a year older than he, and on top of that, her response made him think she was snooty. Calea stood about five inches shorter than he, but it was her beauty combined with her attitude that made her strangely attractive to Oraien.

-"Hey, I'm not a little kid, so you don't have to talk to me like that, I'm nineteen, so thank you," Oraien responded with hard set eyes. Calea opened her mouth to object, but Caileb raised his hand and shook his head 'no'. She turned and exited the room without looking back.

-"We are arriving into Nekio. It will take about half an hour to get through the atmosphere due to its two- mile barrier of water. Oh and Oraien, never mind what my sister just went on about. Strangely enough, she seems to be little protective of you, but you are in much better shape than she knows. Your body seems to have a mysterious healing power. At the rate you have been recovering, your body will be fully restored, so feel free to explore the ship in the meantime," Caileb left the room waving good-bye. "See ya later."

-"Alright, see you later Caileb," he replied.

-*Caileb must be the older brother*, Oraien thought.

Shortly afterwards, Oraien left the room and came to an observation panel and gazed into something that he had never seen before. He was looking into the beautiful water atmosphere that enveloped Nekio, filled with life and mesmerizing colors of refracted light. Amazingly, being so many tetras away from Luna, gazing into the water atmosphere of Nekio made him feel a surprising new sense of home. As he stood watching their ship pass by life in the aquatic marvel, his eyes widened once again as they cleared the watery atmosphere revealing the Anekie nations a few miles below.

Chapter 4

Preparation of a Legend

Oraien stepped out of the ship and into a world of beautiful ingenuity, and he could not believe his eyes as he looked upon the massive city. Nothing could have braced Oraien for the striking metropolis of buildings that looked down upon him. Apart from the awe-inspiring edifices, something even more spectacular caught his eyes: the glistening aqua atmosphere that covered the planet. Rays of light from Antares stunningly made their way through the atmosphere to the surface of Nekio. The dazzling rays of light danced along the surface, covering its buildings, its forests, and even its people. Without delay, the elegant rays reminded Oraien of the beautiful sea floors of Luna's oceans. Caileb stood next to him and spoke,

-"This is Breccia, the magnificent capital of our planet," he said as he began looking around in the same manner as Oraien. "Not only is this our most precious city, it is also one of the most influential cities in the E.Q.O.D.A."

"E.Q.O.D.A?" Oraien said curiously.

-"Yes, the Emuli Quadrant of Defense Alliance, a treaty created to join the forces of any planet within the Emuli Quadrant of the Antares star system against the Niphiliem." Their concentration on the matter was broken as a group of soldiers approached them. One soldier in particular stood out from the rest, not only by the decorated metals hanging from his uniform but also from the fact that Caileb greeted him as his father.

-"Good work son, I trust everything went according to plan," he stated.

-"Yes, father and you would be proud to know that it was your daughter that rescued him," Caileb said as he turned his head to signal Calea's presence. With that said, Calea made her way off the ship and over to greet her father.

-"I hear you were quite the hero, Calea. I am very proud of you," he said in a loving tone.

-"Would you expect anything less from the general's daughter?" she questioned jokingly. Looking over Calea's shoulder, Kilm spotted Oraien, the very reason why their team was sent to Vicero in the first place. They were the best, and he knew he could trust them to carry out such a vital mission.

-"This is Oraien," Caileb said as his father walked towards him.

-"Greetings, young warrior, my name is Kilm. I am one of the generals leading our forces against the growing Niphiliem threat. You have already become acquainted with my children and the crew. Are you alright?" he asked with concern.

-"I'm still a bit tired, but it seems all of my injuries have healed."

-"No doubt, thanks to your Xextrum. I wish we could talk more but time is of the essence. I must take you to Retsum at once. He has been expecting you for quite some time and is with the Council awaiting your arrival."

-"I'm ready to go, thanks to your son," said Oraien.

- "But first things first, we cannot have you address the Council like that," Kilm said referring to the condition of Oraien's clothing. "Calea, take him to the market to dress him and meet us at the Council hall shortly after."

- "Father must *I* do it? Wouldn't Caileb be better suited to...."

- "Calea," Kilm said in a fatherly tone, "Just do it, besides I have matters to discuss with your brother."

- "Let's go," she said to Oraien in a demanding tone as she walked past him in the direction of town.

- "What am I going to do with her?" Kilm asked himself before walking in the opposite direction with Caileb and the other troops. After Calea and Oraien walked in silence for a while, Oraien decided to break the ice and asked her a question.

- "Calea, who is this Retsum?" he asked as they walked through the streets of Breccia.

- "Well, he is an important figure here on Nekio. He is an elder that serves on the Council, but he has also played a vital role in the preparation and training of our troops in defending our world from the Niphiliem. He even saved your life by sending us to Luna to rescue you in anticipation of your awakening, not to mention he is the Xextrum of our planet, O'navus, the Xextrum of Life," she quickly answered.

-"Whoa, how did he know that I was..." he was quickly cut off.

"Before you even begin to ask me this and that about the Xextrum or how he knew about you, save all of your questions for Retsum. He will tell all you need to know," she said with her eyes fixed on their destination.

-"Well aren't you Ms. Bossy," he stated sarcastically. Without responding, Calea cut a sharp death stare towards Oraien before walking into the clothing store. Upon entering, they were greeted by the shop owner,

- "Calea! You're back!" The shop owner hurried from behind the counter to greet Calea. She was a heavy-set elderly, dressed in a long-sleeve shirt, long skirt down to her ankles, and a silk scarf wrapped around her neck. "It's good to see you again," she said.

-"It's good to see you too, I missed you," Calea responded.

-"How long has it been, a few months? And you're still as beautiful as ever," the shop owner continued.

- "Yeah, right," Oraien whispered to himself, looking around the store.

-"And who might this be," the woman asked curiously.

-"*That's* the reason we are here. We need some clothing for this boy,"

-*Boy?!* Oraien thought, quickly looking at Calea with extreme offense over her choice of words. Making eye contact with Oraien, Calea corrected herself,

-"I mean… Rai," she continued as she struggled to remember Oraien's name. "I am truly sorry to rush, but please make it quick. We do not have much time."

-"Follow me," the woman said in a calm voice walking up the stairs of the shop.

-"My name is Oraien," he protested only to be ignored as he followed the shopkeeper upstairs. In the few minutes it took Oraien to change, Calea took a seat and let out a deep sigh of relief as she reflected to the time when she saved Oraien's life.

-*He was cuter when he was unconscious*, she thought while staring blankly at the cover of a booklet. She snapped out of her daze, and her attention shifted to the stairs once she heard Oraien and the shop owner approaching. Oraien stood before her and turned around in a circle with his arms extended, and Calea seemed to be in somewhat in a state of shock looking at his new appearance.

-"So how do I look?" Oraien said looking into her eyes.

-"You look fine," she replied blushing slightly and turned her head away to break their eye contact. Pushing Oraien out of the way, she spoke to the shopkeeper standing directly behind him. "Thank you for all your *hard* work," she said sarcastically.

-"Always a pleasure, Calea," Oraien remembered that he did not have any form of payment for the clothing and felt reduced and said, "I'm sorry but I don't have any money on me."

-"Don't worry Rai. It's taken care of. Let's go. I'm sure they're waiting on us as we speak," Calea said as she walked out of the door while Oraien just stood there looking at her.

Calea actually did look attractive to him, but Oraien mainly noticed her unyielding insensitivity towards him. He thought of himself as appearing like a child before her, and Oraien began to think of how to show her he was not as timid or helpless than she assumed. Calea walked towards Oraien impatiently and quickly grabbed his hand and pulled him out of the store.

-"Calea, thank you for saving me and all, but you don't have to drag me through the streets like a child," Oraien said.

-"Well maybe I wouldn't have to drag you like this if you left when I told you to," she replied.

-"Sorry to burst your little bubble of command, but I have news for you. I don't jump when you say jump," Oraien replied sharply. Calea was shocked at his unexpected assertiveness and loosened her grip, but neither one let go of the others hand. Oraien calmly spoke, "Let's start this again. I really would like to make a good first impression." Calea looked at Oraien and realized he was not as helpless as she thought, so she decided to give him a chance.

- "Sure, Rai. If you really care that much, then yes," Oraien smiled and grasped her hand comfortingly, but they immediately let go of each other as soon as they realized that they had been holding hands for quite some time.

-"And Rai, this does not mean you're out of the hot water yet, for all I know you probably like me, and you're trying get another chance," she said as she turned and walked down the street.

-"My name is Oraien," he replied loudly only to be ignored once again.

Oraien started forward quickly until he reached her side and continued to argue with Calea. The two did not stop disputing until they reached the Council Hall. The Council Hall was a large culmination of architectural wonders that were the headquarters of the different branches of Anekie society. Despite being different sizes and shapes, when looked at as a whole, it was as if it were one structure. It was a physical representation of Anekie strength and unity. Making their way through the massive corridors, they spotted the others and hurried towards them. They all entered the meeting after a short greeting. Listening to much debate between the branch leaders, one turned to ask Kilm, "General Kilm, What priority level was this mission that elder Retsum secretly assigned to you, and please give as much a description as possible."

     Kilm gave a detailed account of the mission according to all the ship records and first- hand reports from the operation participants. After he finished briefing the leaders about the mission, Kilm introduced Oraien before the Council, and in unison doubtful whispers could be heard throughout the room as they wondered why he was of such importance. Soon one of the Council members spoke on Oraien's regard, "Members of the Council, I am sure you are all wondering why I sent a special force team all the way to Luna to bring this young man back, and I will keep you in darkness no longer—he is the Fifth Xextrum." Suddenly the Council became slightly abuzz with chatter. "But unlike the others, he has virtually no knowledge of its power. He will need my guidance to learn quickly."

-"Go on, Retsum," said Nolus, the Nekio leader of cultivation.

-"Members of the Council, I ask you to spare me one month to develop his skills and teach him the way of the Xextrum in order to fight for the E.Q.O.D.A. and more importantly, his home world."

-"Retsum, we are sorry old friend, but in times like these, we cannot afford to have a member of the Council away for that amount of time," Grigori, the council leader of the Nekio defense division, replied. Taking a deep breath he spoke once more, "Two weeks, two weeks is all the time we can spare for his training in such dire situation. If this were a normal affair we would ask for a demonstration of his power, but seeing as how you sent this team there in anticipation of his powers awakening, I think it's safe to assume he cannot summon the suit by will just yet. Retsum, you are excused from the meeting to begin his training, but please leave now, because as you know, we don't have time to spare. The Niphiliem could strike one of our allies at any moment, so he must learn as much as possible during this incredibly small window of chance," said Nolus rising from his chair. Walking out from his position behind his desk, Retsum reappeared in front of the small group of soldiers emerging from a green cloud of mist. Oraien couldn't believe his eyes as he watched Retsum's movements.

-"Before you leave, O'navus," one hard spoken leader managed ~ one of the few that called him by his Xextrum name. "I as well, as all the other Council members here, am curious as to what his Xextrum's element is," he asked awaiting an answer. With the room becoming as silent as a dead planet, the entire Council as well as Kilm and Oraien turned to look at Retsum awaiting his response.

-"But of course," he said, turning his head only far enough to look Oraien in the eyes. "He is Ioxus, the Xextrum of Lightning," he said with a smirk as he continued to lead the small platoon out of the room.

After a brief departure, Retsum and Oraien took the advice of the Council and immediately headed off to the eastern forests of Nekio. On their way to the training grounds Retsum and Oraien got to know one another before their relationship shifted to teacher and student. Retsum asked Oraien many questions as to his life on Luna and Oraien did the same. Once they arrived, Oraien laid his eyes upon what seemed to be an ancient training ground. The stones that comprised the large structure in front of him were worn and faded by the elements, and the overgrown moss along the building's frame signaled that it had long been abandoned.

-"Where are we? Oraien asked turning to observe as much as he could.

-"We are deep within the eastern forests. This is the Sectora Temple. Long ago, this was a bustling training ground in which warriors from all over Nekio would come to train and become more in tune with nature. You see, the air here boosts one's concentration, and the herbs in the surrounding area are good for healing wounds," Retsum said, looking at the scenery with nostalgic smile.

Retsum's smile faded as he came back to reality. He, more than anyone knew fully that he needed to train Oraien as hard as possible in the two week time frame, but even then, he knew Oraien's power would not be complete and ready for the fight against Nibiru. Oraien would need more experience, and Retsum knew just where he would eventually have to go. Shortly after, Retsum climbed the stairs to clean up and settle down in the temple. While Oraien was making his bed in his new temporary room, he remembered the question he needed to ask Retsum. Oraien looked all over the temple and saw that Retsum had already prepared the kitchen and living area, but he did not find him in either place. After some time of searching, Oraien found Retsum filling up a massive spring tub in the bath house, so Oraien began to help him by cleaning up.

-"Retsum, ever since I arrived here, everyone made it seem as though you knew that I would be the one chosen to yield this power. You even sent a team after me. How could you have known that when we were worlds apart?"

-"You see," Retsum started, "Every Xextrum possesses what is known as a Neo-Ray, a special ability that can see and sense life. Sort of like a sensor that spreads out over relative distances to relay the movements of active atomic or energetic organisms. Seeing as how I am the Xextrum of Life, my Neo-ray is different; my sensor is able to span the distance of many thousands of tetras across different planets. One thing I will teach you is how to concentrate and utilize your Xextrum's Neo-ray."

-"But even if you could have sensed my life, how did you know that *I* would become a Xextrum?"

-"I found you by using my senses, but I also had help from someone I cannot mention right now," Retsum said aloud, he then thought to himself. *She told me not to tell him, I will not break the promise.* Even after the last question was asked, Oraien still remained baffled.

-"So after this training, who do I take orders from?" Oraien asked curiously.

Retsum was taken aback by Oraien's question. It had truly been a long time since he thought of the Xextrum's chain of command. He couldn't help but smile to himself nostalgically as he thought back to when he first learned the answer to that question. Retsum placed his hand on Oraien's shoulder and spoke,

-"Listen to me very carefully, Oraien. Before we go any further, I need for you to understand what the Xextrum are," Retsum spoke as Oraien took a seat on the ground in front of him, and like an attentive student, he gave his undivided attention. "We are the guardians of the universe, protectors of the weak and beacons of hope for the masses. You are your Xextrum, and your Xextrum is who you are. We often stand alone in the ranking of power, though that doesn't always mean that we are the strongest. As a Xextrum, you answer to no one, not any single person or planetary organization. Not even another Xextrum if you see fit. And although we do work with the Councils or Assemblies of our home worlds, be aware that it is out of free will and the love we have for our home worlds."

The longer Oraien listened, the more he felt a sense of belonging. He was now a member of the most elite group of warriors in the universe, and he could not help but feel a new sense of pride building within him.

Over the next two weeks Oraien was put through the most rigorous training that he could have ever imagined. Oraien had to train his mind and body for each to become one with his Xextrum. Retsum divided the first week into three sections; the first three days were dedicated to sharpen his mind, the next two days were dedicated to his body without the use of his Xextrum, and the last two days were a combination of both with the application of Ioxus.

-"Master Retsum, I have a question. You only set out a plan for one week, what will happen the second week?" Retsum turned to Oraien and said,

-"If you survive the first week then we can talk about the next week," Retsum then put his arm on Oraien's shoulder and continued, "I trained myself for ten years, and all the intensity from those years will not be held back from you during these two weeks. Sorry, Oraien, but these two weeks will be the longest and hardest of your life." Oraien took in a breath of fear and let it pass him. He then gripped reality and stood firm to begin his legendary preparation.

-"Okay, I'm ready." Oraien replied.

-"Well then, let us begin. First we must get you in tuned with your Xextrum and your environment. For the next three days you will do nothing but try to solve a riddle." Retsum smiled. "And this is how the riddle goes..."

Eyes take in life's light, ears listen to its melody. Touch senses the creations; the tongue tastes their aura

And Smell is taste in the ambience,
But for the Xextrum one remains.
To see what you cannot see,
And feel what you cannot touch.

Oraien did not understand the importance of the first three days, much less the riddle he was assigned to solve; Retsum required that Oraien sit on a branch of a tree with his eyes fixed on the bark for nine hours twice a day. The first day made Oraien impatient and irritated, but the second day he calmed himself down and concentrated on his goal.

-I have to see what I cannot see. That's what Retsum told me. Well, what the heck can't I see? He asked himself. *I can't see air or the wind that blows, or heat, the cold, or....,* and as he went down the list, he realized something that they all had in common. They were all forms of *energy. Retsum was talking about energy. I can't see the air but I can feel the wind, and same goes for heat, I can see fire, but not the heat it produces. Energy, I can't see it but I can feel it!* He thought as excitement overcame him. "But wait, that doesn't explain how I can see energy," he said to himself. As he sat back down, he thought back to what Retsum told him shortly after they arrived at the temple. *Every Xextrum possesses what is known as a Neo-Ray, a*

special ability that can see and sense life. Sitting strait up he realized what the true purpose of staring at the tree was, "If I can see life, then it must be the energy that is visible."

    Concentrating harder, Oraien reached down to touch the tree. The bark felt soft under his fingertips this time, but Oraien focused on every aspect of the tree. After one hour Oraien could feel warmth, he could see the tree slightly begin to glow. Oraien was infatuated by this ability, but he wanted to try something even more amazing. He shut his eyes and focused on the tree's energy. Out of the darkness came light and Oraien could faintly see the compressed particles from the tree as little stars put together in the shape of a tree. Maintaining his concentration, he looked on to see a forest of energy beautifully standing before him. Oraien stayed for the remainder of the day, in awe of the new world he could see. He quickly woke up the next morning to finish his last day of meditation. After the day concluded, Oraien returned to the temple, and Retsum stopped him before he entered the bathing room.

-"I noticed that you woke up earlier than usual this morning and also that you were quite enthusiastic as well. So that means you finally figured out the poem. If so then you should know how to use your Neo-ray." Oraien faced him and replied,

-"I discovered it in the forest of my thoughts, tapping into the infinite universe of energy that we live in. Thank you, master, for showing me how to use such a beautiful skill," Oraien said.

-"Rai, I did not show you how; you just brought it forth from within you. You should thank your planet's Quarton for the gift of your Xextrum. And it is not a skill; it is a part of you, just like your five senses."

When the brief but meaningful exchange of words was through, Oraien proceeded to the bathhouse. After Oraien was finished training for the day, he went to his room and closed his eyes to rest for the next day of training. The next morning, Oraien woke up a few hours early and walked out to the temple deck. The sun had not risen yet, but its reflections could already be seen in the water atmosphere, illuminating the morning as if it was day. Oraien looked into the sky, and his memories began to come to life, and his mind took him back to the plain and peaceful days of Luna.

-Just a few weeks ago, I only worried about my studies. Now I am worrying about saving people of all sorts from these... Niphiliem... who have no meaning for destruction other than just senseless slaughter. But it's amazing how my life just went from that on Luna, to being a guardian, this Xextrum. It's just so overwhelming. A noise brought Oraien back to the serene deck of the temple; it was Retsum.

-"Are you ready for the next phase of your training?" he asked.

-"Yes," Oraien responded.

The two of them left the temple and walked out into the middle of the training grounds to begin the next phase in Oraien's training. Retsum needed something heavy for Oraien to work with and began to examine a very large tree, "Master, I can't work out with a whole tree.

"That's suicidal," Oraien said with concern. "But maybe if you let me use Ioxus."

-"No, you must train your body as well. What is the use of having such power if your body cannot handle its true strengths? Make no mistake, Oraien, there are enemies much stronger than the commander you overpowered on Luna with little more than blind rage. You were fortunate to have faced such a low level commander during your awakening, but the intensity from your upcoming battles will push your body and mind to the limit as you begin to draw out the full power of your Xextrum," Retsum said as he turned his attention back to the tree.

Retsum then walked up to a tree and placed his palm on it. He closed his eyes and concentrated his Xextrum's energy through the tree. Miraculously, the largest branches of the tree fell to the ground. They hit the ground with such a thud that the animals in the surrounding forest fled in fear. The last branch that fell landed upright in the ground and provided Oraien with a post to strengthen his attacks.

-"How did you do that without transforming?" Oraien asked in awe.

-"That skill comes after you have totally learned to be one with your Xextrum. It is not as effective as transforming, but when strategizing, it comes in handy. You learn how to call the minor powers of your element without transforming. Each Xextrum can achieve this through vigorous training, and after a while it simply becomes a casual ability. "

-"Understood." Oraien remembered something from his old training on Luna, "Master, in my mandatory combat training on Luna, the most important thing they taught us was to know our own weaknesses."

-"I see what you're getting at." Retsum sat upon one of the fallen tree branches and Oraien did the same on another. "The Xextrum are powerful beings, and they get stronger with experience and intense training. First, I will tell you what the suit can do, and then I will tell you what the weaknesses are. When you call upon the Xextrum, the Neo-Quarton from within your body takes atoms from your surroundings and converts them into the strongest materials of the universe. The first part of your suit is the inner lining which is a metallic fabric that is air tight and morphable. It even allows you to survive in space as long as you have energy that can be converted to air. The fabric can change according to your brain waves and body energy.

The second part is the armor, which is the exact same metal that Quartons are made of and is the strongest metal ever discovered. The armor's exterior is designed for protection, but its interior is fixed with a complex series of energy channels and ancient circuits that interact with the interior lining and your own body. Together the two parts act as an extension of your body. The suit also has three storage units for energy and one for quartiio energy. The Neo-Quarton is the main storage unit for energy, and the other three preside on your Xextrum. So as long as you have energy you will be able to operate your Xextrum. Ioxus utilizes atomic energy, which counts for the Xextrum's strength, however, Ioxus only has a limited amount of atomic energy, so to charge at any time, one must stop to do a Neo-boost, but the Key word in that is stop. In battle, one requires time to utilize the atoms around them to complete a Neo-boost. On the other hand, quartiio energy can only be used once and charged only by Quartons, but as long as the energy is there, it can be used to execute devastating abilities.

Retsum took a breath and continued, "The Xextrum's weaknesses are us, our bodies inside them. Even though the suit is very powerful, it cannot protect us from enormous forces. The particles of your body are changed slightly so that you body can keep up with the powers of the suit, but if you are crushed or smashed your bones can and will break. Also, the inner lining is left open for flexibility and maneuverability, but leaves little parts of your armor open for sharp object to pierce through it. The key thing you want to remember is that Neo-Ray uses massive amounts of energy the longer you use it, so be frugal in how you use it."

-"Let's continue. Oraien, I want you to attack that post with everything you have," Retsum commanded. Oraien took a deep breath. He balled up his fist and punched the tree limb. The large branch did not budge at all, and Oraien stood looking at his fist.

-"Close your eyes and concentrate. Feel the flow of energy around you, now attack again," Retsum said firmly.

Closing his eyes, Oraien allowed himself to become one with his surroundings, feeling the calm breeze flow over him. Slowly, the particles of energy started to form out of the darkness; he could see the energy of the tree forming in his mind exactly like it did during his mental training. So Oraien drew his arm back and let out a yell as he struck the limb. He hit the log with his new perception of it- energy. The force of the punch was so great that it sent a dense tremor traveling through the ground.

-"Well done!" Retsum said with enthusiasm. "Oraien, you possess much more power than you realize," he continued as Oraien stood in awe of what he had done on his own.

-*Incredible,* Retsum thought to himself, *he's able to draw forth that much energy, only days after he learned how to visualize it, he may very well surpass us all indeed.*

The next two days were a combination of extreme workouts that made Oraien wish that he had never been born. Retsum made Oraien lift many heavy loads of logs and rocks for extended amounts of time causing every muscle fiber in his body to rip. Retsum continuously healed Oraien while he trained so that he was able to continue his rigorous workout non-stop for an entire day. After nearly two days of treacherous training, every thread of his being ached and he no longer had the strength to walk, regardless of Retsum's assistance. He fell unconscious and Retsum put him on a hammock and dragged him back to the temple. Retsum then used the power of his Xextrum to speed up the process of healing Oraien's injuries so that Oraien would sleep without the fear of waking up stiff and sore as he normally would after such training. When Oraien awoke, he was surprised to see Retsum by his side.

-"You must rest your body, Oraien," Retsum spoke stopping Oraien from rising from his bed too quickly.

-"How long have I been out?" Oraien questioned.

-"Only a few hours but you need to rest a lot longer than that." Retsum replied.

-"But we don't have time for that, shouldn't I be training? Why don't you just heal me so we can continue? Oraien asked.

-"Because there is no substitute for natural rest. Your body needs it and it is actually more beneficial for you to recuperate this way. Don't worry, we have time." Retsum said as Oraien went back to sleep.

When Oraien awoke again, it was the next day and he could feel a drastic change in his body. He felt stronger and was surprisingly able to get out bed without a problem. He sat on the edge of the bed and examined his arms and looked up to see Retsum entering in the room.

-"Thanks for healing me," Oraien said,

-"I only healed you enough so that you would be able to sleep peacefully. A normal person wouldn't be able to do anything for two weeks if they had received the same treatment. So you can thank your Neo-Quarton for the speedy recovery," Retsum said with a smile.

The thought of working his body as hard as he did for the last two days slightly frightened him; he never wanted to feel muscle pain that way ever again. Oraien did realize that his body had become stronger since his training, and soon the real motivation came back to him. So Oraien got out of bed and prepared his mind for a day that would involve a mixture of mind and body to be applied to his Xextrum as one.

-"The last time you used your Xextrum it was done out of anger, panic, and the desire to protect," Retsum stated. "Now you must learn to call upon its power at will, and the only way to do that was to complete the mental training and visualize the energy around you in order to manipulate it and fuel your transformation."

Oraien closed his eyes once again to tap into his energy senses. The images were forming much faster than before, and the air around him began to react to his growing energy. Oraien stood still as the energy around his body illuminated the entire outline of his figure. Retsum stood in awe as he witnessed a Xextrum release in slow motion, forcing him to place his staff in front of him to brace himself from the assault of wind and lightning being discharged in all directions. With his own will, Oraien finally transformed into Ioxus, and in a flash of light, Oraien followed Retsum's words and manipulated the energy of his surroundings. Rocks and logs, mud and grass, every object's energy began to succumb to Ioxus.

-"You see Oraien, each Xextrum has a Neo-Quarton. The Neo-Quarton is a fragment of the original Stegeton Quarton. Each Neo-Quarton needs atoms to power it, and it uses the matter in your area as fuel. See the rocks disappearing."

Oraien looked through the eyes of Ioxus at the area around him and saw particles of energy flowing towards him. Retsum continued to speak;

-"They are being absorbed into your Xextrum's Neo-Quarton. After the atoms are converted into energy, the energy is then used as your Xextrum's special attribute; yours being lightning." Oraien became enlightened looking at his hands and arms of his Xextrum as he finally figured out the energy of atoms of every object were the power source of every Xextrum.

Lifting his hands, the outline of Retsum's body began to glow, alerting Ioxus as the energy began to shift around the training grounds. Looking around, Ioxus noticed that the logs and rocks that he pushed aside were beginning to glow green, similar to the glow around Retsum. With incredible speed Retsum launched one of the logs towards Oraien, tapping into the powers of his Neo-Quarton. Standing his ground, Ioxus drew back his arm and struck the oncoming log with such a force that it shattered upon contact. Jumping out of the way immediately after the debris cleared, he watched as another rock came flying towards him a split second later. This time the projectile made violent contact with Oraien. The rock caused Oraien to flail off the branch, and he hit the ground with a large thud. Jumping back into the trees to dodge another oncoming object, he landed on the branch of a tree and had little time to rest as the remaining objects under Retsum's control came flying towards him. Ioxus began jumping from tree branch to tree branch dodging and punching many of what seem to be an endless supply of flying objects. Drawing the weapons of his Xextrum, Oraien took the offensive and began attacking the objects being thrown his way. Slicing away with his lightning blades, Ioxus found that he was back in the middle of the training grounds and had cut everything thrown at him to shreds.

The next two days were nonstop training as Retsum pushed Oraien far beyond his limits. He showed him no lenience as he bombarded Ioxus with objects that sometimes made contact, dealing considerable damage. At the end of the second day of Xextrum training, though his stamina had greatly improved, Oraien still fell out once Retsum ended the extended exercise. The next morning, Oraien expected Retsum to start the next week with more exercises; however, Retsum gave news that allowed Oraien to feel slightly at ease. Oraien was given permission to rest his body and let natural healing run its course for the first two days of the second week. Only after the two days of rest would Retsum given any news of the next phase in his training regimen.

Taking advantage of his down time, Oraien found a quiet place within the training grounds. Oraien would climb to the top of a tree that overlooked the entire temple and the surrounding forest. It was there that he could reflect upon his thoughts. He continued to train his mind to better understand the flow of energy that he was now part of, all the atoms of energy that make up every inch of matter in the universe. For hours he would close his eyes and envision the world around him anew. Occasionally he would find himself thinking of his home on Luna, wondering how his classmates as well as Ms. Emery were doing in the post- invasion Vicero. On the dawn of the third day, Retsum came to Oraien and explained the next step in his training.

-"Oraien, though your stamina as well as your skills in battle has improved, your journey is far from over. With your skills as they are now, you should be able to defend yourself against enemies stronger than the previous Niphiliem soldiers you have fought. The warm up is now complete, and the real training begins now," Retsum stated. "At the northern border of this temple is the entrance to Limaris, the path you must follow to reach the sacred city of Vella. Within its walls lies a great power, a Key to be exact. That is what you must search for, and I am sure that you can find it."

-"Beware Oraien; beyond these training grounds Limaris is treacherous. Many have gone in search of the power within the great city of Vella, none have ever succeeded. When you reach the people of the northern lands explain that I have sent you personally to aid the E.Q.O.D.A," he said before pointing Oraien in the direction in which he needed to go. "I have trained you well. You possess more power than you know. Believe in yourself and your Xextrum, and you cannot fail."

-"Thank you master. I will always appreciate this time and training you gave to me."

-"You are welcome, Rai. I will return to Breccia to finish a few assignments of my own. When you find the Key, come find me. Then we will finish your preparation. Now go, we have no time to waste," he said, and they both went their separate ways.

Oraien reached the colossal northern walls of the training grounds that lead to the forest. Before he could proceed, he thought it would be smart to change, and with a more controlled shockwave transformation, Ioxus was summoned. Oraien examined the gate and noticed that it created a border that continued in both directions for miles. Further inspecting the wall, he saw that it was comprised of five ledges, each being approximately forty feet high. When Oraien finished calculating how to get over the wall, he simply scaled the gate by jumping from one ledge to another. The last ledge allowed him to jump over the trees and witness a field of tree tops that almost seemed infinite. Gravity then pulled him back under to the orange leaves of the ground. Oraien braced himself and did not let fear slow him down, so he dashed into the unknown.

    After running through the forest for only a few minutes, the upper section of the treetops became so high and so dense that they did not let one ray of light touch the ground. Oraien concentrated his senses and opened his eyes under the Neo-ray sight of Ioxus. The forest beamed with life, every atom of every living being was visible in collective images: trees, critters, and even the larger unknown fiends in the distance. He looked to the treetops, and his Xextrum quickly calculated that the canopy reached over five hundred feet, but Oraien did not let the strange yet amazing forest overwhelm him. Oraien continued rushing through Limaris and found himself facing many diverse life forms from big hairy creatures to large lizard- like monsters. The massive trees were far apart from each other, and their branches and leaves blocked Antares' light. The dark and massive environment corresponded with the large animals.

Cautiously, Oraien pushed his way forward, trying not to stray too far from the path that lay before him though he occasionally found himself completely off track fending off the stronger beasts. Everything in the forest pushed his physical strength to survive while also pushing his mental abilities to the limit when maneuvering around obstacles. He could now understand the warnings of Retsum. Very soon Oraien came to truly appreciate the trainings he underwent that gave him the strengths necessary to make it through the forest of madness.

After a day of fighting in the vast and seemingly endless forest, he reached the edge of the darkness that opened up to beautiful green pastures, full of open space and light. Oraien never thought he would be so happy to see a simple glimpse of daylight. After entering the open green lands, Oraien stopped to survey his surroundings and spotted the small town that he was informed about and began to make his way in its direction.

The town's people stood completely in awe of his appearance once he arrived in the city. Oraien took fast notice that he was still in

Xextrum form, so he quickly and carefully reverted back trying not to harm anyone. Afterward, Oraien asked whom he could speak to in regard to the city of Vella, but their fear hindered them from speaking to him. Oraien touched the ground and gently lit the ground around him with small sparks of electricity. At the same time, he stared into one of the villager's eyes and spoke the exact message Retsum gave to him. The electricity carried his message to the villager and instantly the villager ran towards the center of the town. Oraien sat down on the corner of a street where he rested and for nearly an hour nobody came near him.

-"Wake up, Ioxus," said a young boy's voice grasping Oraien from his sleep. "Ioxus, the elder is ready for you." Slowly opening his eyes, he saws some of the village inhabitants crouched down in front of him.

-"Thank you," Oraien said. "Even though it took a while, I appreciate it because I had the chance to rest." The boy moved to the side and revealed three elder Anekie men. The leader in the middle spoke, "The message from our old friend Retsum has told us everything, for he has been here to inform us of your arrival. Please excuse the villagers for being afraid of you, for at times creatures spill out from the dark woods." The elder looked at his right hand man, "His name is Ujio. He will accompany you to Vella. I am aware that you need to report back to Retsum within the next day. Thank you for coming, Ioxus. Now that the citizens know who you are, their spirits have been lifted because we see hope for our world through the Xextrum." After he finished speaking, he turned and started towards the town center. Oraien only had one question due their extremely brief meeting,

-"What is your name, Anekie?" Oraien asked loud enough to be heard. The leader stopped to reply,

-"Rroleo," he shouted as he immediately continued pacing his way to the center of town with his associates.

    They began making preparations for the trip that they would embark on momentarily. Only a few minutes later, a small platform-ship descended to pick up the traveling crew and Oraien. When they all boarded the ship and climbed into the sky, Oraien looked down at the treetops of the Nekio forests, noticing Limaris, the dark forest.

Ironic, he thought. *From up here it's one of the most beautiful places I have ever seen, yet I will never forget of its deception. Under those lush canopies lie treacherous grounds.*

Traveling for a short while in the speeding aircraft, they came to a stop hovering over a vast marshland. The pilot of the craft announced they had arrived, and Oraien began to look around in confusion,

- "If we're here, then where is the city?"

-"Look up, young master," a guide said with a proud smile on his face. To his amazement, he saw an enormous figure floating in the water-atmosphere of the planet.

-"Is that Vella?" Oraien asked with much amazement in his voice.

-"Yes," Ujio said walking across the deck towards Oraien.

-"Legend has it that Vella wasn't always up there though. Myth as well as geological evidence proves that at one time it actually sat right beneath us in this marshland," he said pointing to the surrounding landscape. "The city is only visible for about a day or so once every four years. Once that window of time has passed, it will disappear, becoming completely invisible and one hundred percent undetectable by any civilization's technology, even our own," Ujio concluded.

-"Incredible. Fate had me here right on time," Oraien said looking up at the dark figure.

-"Yes, either that or Retsum planned this from the start." Ujio replied.

Thanking Ujio for all he had done for him, Oraien bid them farewell and prepared to launch himself from the ship into the ocean above. He transformed into his Xextrum and put his feet into position to jump from the vessel, but Ujio stopped him to say one last word of advice,

-"Careful Ioxus, countless ships have been destroyed after encountering the city's intelligent defense system. You only have a few hours left to accomplish your mission. Once the cloaking mechanism is initiated, the city will flood its interior and seal off all exits, trapping you inside until it emerges again in four years," Ujio warned, looking Ioxus in the eyes.

-"Then that means I don't have time to waste," Oraien stated before he leaped into the watery atmosphere.

Swimming his way to the city, he noticed that the entire figure began to enlarge beyond all expectation. The structure was a complete sphere, and its outer extremities were shining with lights that surrounded its outer walls. About halfway to Vella, Oraien could see that the city had released many shiny objects that began to travel in his direction. As more and more of the objects became visible, he realized that he was anything but welcomed.

-*The city must be defending itself.*

Immediately, he started swimming faster to position himself to dodge the oncoming barrage of projectiles. With the speed of his Xextrum, Oraien managed to bring everything around him nearly to a standstill. He then grabbed one of the energy crystals and threw it into a group of many approaching crystals to his right. Quickly following his previous action, he grabbed another crystal and threw it towards a group to his left. As he slowed to his normal speed, the projectiles he threw exploded upon contact creating a chain reaction. Down below, Ujio and the crew watched the massive explosion as it spread across a portion of the Anekie sky. Oraien made it past the barrier and proceeded to what seemed to be an opening at the bottom of the floating city. When he arrived at the bottom, the water stopped, and there was air within the structure.

Oraien looked around the ancient city that was still wet from being submerged for the past four years. Further examining the area around him, Oraien found early symbols etched into a wall a few meters away from him. As he approached the wall, he noticed that he could partially read them. It was in Ms. Emery's ancient history class that he learned how to read and speak the ancient language of his home world.

-This is Demitian text, but why is it here? He wondered. Oraien turned his attention to the message, and it read,

Here these guardians sleep till called forth to protect that which lie behind these walls.

Oraien knew that his struggle to find what he came for was not finished and that something within the city would try and slow him down even further. Immediately after he finished his thought, Oraien hid himself under a high ledge because he heard a large mechanical being dashing towards him. Oraien breathed smoothly trying not to give his position away. The being was easily twenty feet tall and looked like nothing Oraien had ever seen. It was an ancient robot, which was comprised of stone tablets held together by a mysterious energy. With its sheer massive size, Oraien knew it would be much more challenging than any of the creatures he faced in Limaris. Oraien waited for the machine to continue walking away from him so that he would have a chance to search for the Key, something that he remembered during the trainings he went through with Retsum. Before the robot was completely out of sight, Oraien caught a glimpse of a symbol on its back that translated into *Tathios*, which meant guardian in the Demitian language.

Shortly after Oraien commenced his search, another Tathios Guardian stopped him, but this time Oraien chose to stand and fight. The guardian was slow but powerful. Oraien only needed to make sure he did not let himself take any direct hits. A few minutes into the fight, Oraien quickly disabled the guardian from his main power source by pulling out the receiver from its back. After much fighting and adapting to surroundings, he finally came upon what seemed to be the center of the city. He entered a room with a large statue of a creature that resembled a mantis, but Oraien was deceived by its looks because it was not a statue and the symbols on it translated into *Tathios Golem*.

Oraien jumped out of its range to avoid an attack from the giant golem. Oraien observed the giant Tathios as it approached him and realized that it was faster than the others. He made an attempt to find any energy receivers that he could disable but found none. Oraien underestimated the giant because of his speed, and when he placed too much attention on finding its weak point, Oraien was pummeled beneath its massive foot. Ioxus did not take much damage, but Oraien's body within the suit suffered. Although the Xextrum protected him, Oraien's body within the suite could undoubtedly be crushed if he was not cautious. Once again, the Tathios raised his foot to drop it down on Oraien, but this time Oraien caught his foot, lifted it, and threw it using his Xextrum's atomic energy. The golem crashed into the ground thus giving Oraien time to tune his senses back into the fight. Ioxus was low on energy due to the excess amount of atoms Oraien had been using during his journey. He thought that he had doomed himself, but Oraien almost forgot that Retsum taught him how to replenish his Xextrum with more energy.

Oraien concentrated his Xextrum and began to create a small barrier around him. He activated his Xextrum's ability to absorb the atoms from his surrounding, and like dust the atoms from the surrounding ground and air dematerialized and began to flow into the suit. The time Ioxus spent recharging gave the golem the opportunity to stand upright once again. Once it was balanced, it wasted no time in charging towards Ioxus. Oraien concentrated, and at the speed of lightning, Ioxus-Oraien jumped onto the golem's arms, over his head, and to the back of its skull. The weak spot was located here, and without stopping, Oraien kicked into the Tathios skull. Instead of falling though, the machine merely stood as it was before, a statue.

Once he disabled the guardian, Oraien proceeded into the central corridor. The room was a massive dome; beautiful in every way, but what really caught Oraien's eyes was what he saw in the center of the open space. Floating in midair was a rotating object drenched in a blinding light; it seemed as if it was waiting for someone worthy of its power to claim it. Walking toward the object, Ioxus came to a podium that gave a brief description of what he concluded to be the Key.

-This must be the Key I was looking for, but the important question is what was it used for?

Chapter 4.5

Ioxus vs. O'navus

He reached his hand into the light to claim his prize, and immediately, he was teleported to another location. Oraien was no longer inside Vella but was now in what seemed to be an underground chamber. He looked around and saw light seeping from a nearby opening. As he walked down the long ancient passage, he noticed that the light given off to illuminate the dark hall was the same energy given off by O'navus, Retsum's Xextrum. When he reached the end of the hall, his eyes shot open in amazement. Standing before him was the colossal Nekio-Quarton. It was only a section of the large structure as he noticed it continued through the ceiling and the floor.

Oraien started to advance further into the massive chamber, but extraordinarily, after walking a short distance, he noticed that he was walking in place. An invisible wall was preventing him from getting any closer to the Quarton. The barrier in front of him was protecting the

Quarton, and when touched, the invisible wall rippled, creating sounds similar to a sound of a water drop and distorting the image of the Quarton. Looking down at the Key in his possession, Oraien finally figured out its purpose and placed it on the barrier and released it from his hand. The Key stood floating, and when it was unified with the barrier, they both began to pulsate. Soon the Key disappeared, and in its place was an opening within the barrier, allowing in Oraien.

    Inside the barrier, Oraien felt weightless and soon began floating off the ground. He was hovering and looking at his arms and legs until he felt something gently grabbing hold of him. It was as if the Quarton was drawing him near, closer towards its metallic body. Once the two collided, there was a flash of light. When the light subsided enough for Oraien to be able to see, he realized that he was now in a different place. There was nothing but light. He did not move, and soon, he could see a figure focusing into form and color in the distance as it approached him. Oraien could feel a small amount of fear build inside him but continued to hold his stature. The figure was a man with white hair and skin that was tattooed with white markings; his clothes resembled a historical design. He held in his hands a broad sword and when he got close enough, he handed the sword to Oraien. Oraien reached out and grabbed the sword. Once again, light overwhelmed his sight, and he was back in the underground corridor by the entrance hall on his hands and knees.

-*Was that a dream?* He wondered. He felt uneasy at the sight of the evidence that was right before Oraien on the ground: the broad sword. He slowly lifted himself off the ground and took hold of the broad sword. He gazed into the details of the sword, reading the inscription written in Demitian text, *Exus, Sword of Ioxus.*

-"It's beautiful," Oraien said admiring its magnificence and detail.

In the center of the blade were three diamond- shaped openings. As he stood continuing to observe Exus, his concentration was broken by a voice in the distance, "You made it. I was beginning to wonder if you would even make it to Vella." Oraien looked up to see O'navus.

-"Master Retsum! I saw a man, he... this sword!? I don't understand!" Oraien yelled out.

-"You will not understand everything right away, Oraien. But through your journeys, you should trust Ioxus, and you will eventually find the answers you are looking for."

-"So what now? How did you even get here?"

-"As to how I arrived here, just remember that this Quarton gave me my power, and I have access to it at all times. Now," he said as his tone became more serious, "It's time for you to face your last opponent."

-"Last opponent?" Oraien replied curiously.

-"Me."

Retsum dashed towards Oraien and threw a powerful punch aiming for Oraien's chest. Although it was faint, Oraien caught a glimpse of O'navus before his punch connected. To defend himself, Ioxus used the sword, Exus, to block the attack by placing it in front of the punch to absorb the damage he would have taken. Using both of his hands to hold up the sword in front of him, he tried to stand his ground but slid back a few feet. It sent a loud echo throughout the chamber, and they came to a standstill with Retsum's arm still touching Exus.

- "Impressive," O'navus stated. "I used my full speed, giving you less than a second to react, and yet you only needed a fraction of that time to read my actions and position Exus in time to block my attack," he said. "Your skills have grown since the last time I saw you, but don't think that speed alone will determine the outcome of this or any other battle."

- "I know!' Oraien yelled out as he quickly pushed O'navus back and swung Exus towards him.

The strike missed, but that did not stop Ioxus from going on the attack. The two were quickly moving around the chamber using the speed of their Xextrum's. With every clash of their attacks, they both left remnants of their energy behind: a green misty cloud of smoke for O'navus and a zap of electricity for Ioxus. After every powerful stroke of Exus, the sword glowed, and small flickers of electricity was emitting from its outer blade. The reaction caught Oraien's attention, and he could feel the enormous buildup of energy stored within Exus. O'navus too became aware of the light the sword emitted and distanced himself from Ioxus to formulate a new strategy of offense. Oraien focused his thoughts on releasing the energy within Exus and struck his sword along the floor digging into the ancient grounds. The force Oraien put behind the swipe set free a large wave of electricity from Exus that traveled towards O'navus. It almost took him by surprise, and he barely parried the speedy attack. After Retsum cleared the wall of energy, he faced Oraien and spoke, "So you finally figured it out, have you?" he said with the sound of approval in his voice.

-"What do you mean?" Oraien responded, waiting for Retsum to continue.

-"Exus," Retsum began to explain as he now had Oraien's undivided attention. "The name of that sword derives from the Demitian word Eximetus, literally translating into 'Lightning Catcher.' Swinging the sword around activates its special ability. The openings in the sword serve as a net that can absorb the ambient energy and convert it into lighting."

Once again, Oraien stood in astonishment of the sword. He gripped it tightly as if he had accepted its power and faced Retsum with a newfound confidence. He raced towards Retsum and resumed his assault. Oraien used bursts of lightning speed to seemingly teleport around Retsum hoping to confuse his teacher. Retsum stood still with his eyes closed to assess the flow of energy around him. He summoned his staff by holding out his hands as it appeared out of green mist. Retsum sensed danger, and he quickly raised his staff with his left hand and blocked a devastating attack from Ioxus. Even though Retsum could not physically see Ioxus, he stood in one place, tuned into his surroundings and predicted each advance while Oraien remained perplexed. He could not understand how his master was able to block and dodge every one of his blows. Oraien slowed his movements to deliver his final strike, Retsum smiled in anticipation that Oraien would attempt to switch to power over speed. O'navus switched back into offense and used his concentration to step behind Ioxus to disarm him. Exus hit the ground creating a small crater underneath its blade. Oraien was stunned. He missed, and the battle was now over. O'navus stood next to Ioxus with the staff up to his neck and spoke,

-"Well done, Ioxus, for you to have only had this power for such a short time, you show great promise. My final piece of advice to you is to never underestimate your opponent. Though you are much faster than me, I won the battle. By using my Neo-Ray I was able to sense your energy although I couldn't see you. One of the greatest strengths you can have during a battle is patience, the patience to stand back and analyze your opponent and find a weakness. You would be wise to remember that in your upcoming battles," Retsum advised as he removed the staff from Oraien's neck and placed his hand on his shoulder.

-"I'll make sure to do that," Oraien said. Oraien loosened his grip on Exus, and it pulled away and automatically latched itself onto the center of his back. Oraien stood silent for a few seconds still in amazement of everything the sword did.

-"So what now?" he asked.

-"Now you run. From here, there is no way for you to exit. You must make your retreat from where you came, through the portal opened by the Key in the chamber down the corridor. I would suggest you use that speed of yours before you get trapped in Vella."

-"But you, how did you get here?" Oraien said in bewilderment.

-"As I said before, I have access to this planet's Quarton at all times, so in other words, who says I was here in the first place?" he said fading into a cloud of smoke as the Nekio-Quarton behind him illuminated the massive chamber before returning to normal.

-*Is everything a test with him?* Oraien wondered as he dashed towards the corridor.

Entering the first chamber, he jumped back through the closing portal and landed back within Vella. The entire city was shaking as it began its flooding sequence. Oraien knew his time was running out as he looked upon the city and could no longer see the city floor. His options were slim, and he decided to swim his way out of the soon- to- be water prison. Navigating his way back to the entrance was far more difficult since he was swimming against an overwhelming current. Swimming as hard and as fast as he could, Ioxus built up enough speed to propel himself out of the city, and that same speed sent him flying out of the atmosphere. He found himself falling through the sky and spotted Ujio and the crew below. He landed on the ship with a solid thud that shook the entire aircraft, and he stood there breathing heavily as he let his Xextrum disperse.

-"Just in time! You scared us halfway to death, you know," Ujio said in great relief as he pointed up towards Vella.

Above them was a terrifying maelstrom created by the city. It was sucking in all the surrounding water through its only entrance, located on the bottom of the sphere. Captivated by the site before him, Oraien was even more surprised by what happened next. As the cloaking mechanism began, the outer symbols on the city also began to glow a distinct red, and in the blink of an eye, the structure disappeared sending an echo that reverberated around the planet through the watery atmosphere.

-"I don't know how you made it out of there, but everyone will be glad you did," said Ujio. "Let me take you to Breccia. I'm sure Retsum and the Council are waiting for you."

Chapter 5

Hero's Beginning

Ujio dropped Oraien off at the eastern port of Breccia and bid him farewell as he departed back to his village. Oraien was tired and wanted to rest. However, he knew that he needed to report to Grigori as soon as he could. Meanwhile, Caileb was in an office a few stories high in Breccia's Inter Quadrant Treaty Tower dealing with issues of the Alliance. During the meeting Caileb caught an eye of Oraien below wondering the street as if he had no idea where he was headed. As soon as he was able, Caileb descended to the streets to find Oraien,

-"Hey, Rai!" Caileb yelled as he climbed down the steps of the massive building to get Oraien's attention. Oraien turned at the sound of the familiar voice and felt at ease since his journey to Vella.

The two of them spoke for a moment, allowing Caileb time to give an update of the whereabouts of his sister, informing Oraien that she had been sent on a mission to defend a foreign moon from Niphiliem attack.

-"So your father entrusted the mission to Calea?"

-"Yes, don't doubt her abilities. She can really lead, and she's much stronger than she appears. She saved your life." Caileb said. Laughing Oraien responded, "I never said she couldn't handle it. I simply wanted to know where she was off to."

-"The planet she is headed for is called Igni'ice. They require battle fleet forces because of an anticipated attack. Who knows, you may even help out." Oraien wanted to say he was ready to go and fight right then, but he trusted Retsum and Caileb, so he kept his patience.

After the brief greeting, Caileb told him that the Council was eagerly awaiting his return, and he led him to their location. When they reached the Council Hall, a guard stopped them from entering.

-"There is an important meeting taking place within the hall at this time. Unless you are scheduled to take part, leave now," the guard said firmly. Caileb smiled, as he knew the guard didn't recognize him,

-"Yes, my name is Caileb Loyl, and this is Oraien..." Caileb realized that he had forgotten Oraien's last name, but luckily Oraien got the hint and answered,

-"Oraien Zeal," Oraien quickly added. The guard's eyes widened with the mention of the names.

-"Senior Officer Loyl! Ioxus! I am sorry, please wait here, I will go inform the leaders of your arrival. Please forgive me." The soldier hurried into the meeting. Oraien looked at Caileb with confusion and immediately knew what it meant.

-"If you don't mind, I took the liberty of spreading rumors about the fearless Ioxus who single handedly thwarted the Niphiliem attack in Vicero. Just thought the people would want another beacon of hope in these dark times," Caileb said proudly.

-"Thank you," Oraien said smirking before his tone became a little more serious. "Caileb, last time we came here just about everyone spoke for me. Be there for me as a comrade, but let me use my voice this time," Caileb understood him perfectly and looked towards the room's doors. After only a few moments the guard returned.

-"They are ready, you may proceed," the guard said as he saluted the two of them. For the first time, Oraien felt how prominent he was or at least how legendary he had become since he and Ioxus became one. Caileb started forward, and Oraien stayed next to him. Once they entered the meeting room, Grigori spoke.

-"Welcome back Oraien, we trust your training went well. Oh, and hello Caileb, I also trust that the E.Q.O.D.A debates are keeping you busy. Now that you are here, what news do the two of you bring?" Oraien had to muster up the words to say because he had never spoken to such an important group before. However, he managed to grip his purpose and opened his mouth to say, "Well, Master Retsum fought with me himself and has personally tested my abilities and deemed me ready, not to mention that I traveled Vella to retrieve its Key and escaped from the Tathios guardians before the city's disappearance," Oraien spoke as he took a glimpse of the members' astonished countenance. Grigori responded, "No doubt that Luna chose well. You are truly worthy of Ioxus.

Do you think you are ready to join the Xextrum, young warrior?"

- "I made my choice long ago when my people were being killed without reason. And when I was granted this power, the power to fight back, not only for myself but for all of the people of my home world that couldn't, the answer was clear, yes. I am prepared to stand by my comrades to fight."

-"Good, because we have news of Luna," Grigori stated, catching Oraien's attention, "There is a group of Niphiliem soldiers who are still carrying out the missions of the invasion mounted on Luna nearly three weeks ago."

-"You're telling me that those monsters are still loose in Vicero, and no one is doing anything about it?" he asked with a resentful tone.

Grigori's tone changed before speaking again, "No, they escaped from our troops and have now set up a garrison in the ancient city of Sarren. Reconnaissance in the city tells us that they are led by an extremely powerful soldier that goes by the name of Vexus. They have taken the citizens that were trying to escape during the initial attack and have now made hostages out of them.

We have Anekie and Eluesian forces on site trying to put an end to this once and for all, but the confusing layout of the city makes it impossible." Taking a deep breath his frustration was apparent. "Making matters worse, among the hostages they intercepted was a very important leader of Luna, a guardian of light, Tarria, one of the last remaining Demitian ancestors."

-*There are still Demitian people alive!?* Oraien thought in astonishment.

-"As of now you are the last hope for the Demitian, and the other people of your world," Grigori said. Looking forward with a stern look on his face, Oraien replied, "I understand. Prepare a ship, and I will leave as soon as possible."

-"They depend on your strength, Ioxus. I trust you will get them out," Grigori whispered to himself as Oraien walked out towards the city ports. The guard that held him and Caileb at the entrance escorted Oraien to Nekio's fastest travel ship, informing the crew of their mission so that he could arrive in Luna within the day. On the ship, he prepared his mind the way Retsum had taught him but also incorporated his own elements; planning, practicing new techniques within his own mind and focusing on his will power.

    When they entered Luna's atmosphere, the crew's navigation specialist immediately set the coordinates for Sarren. Oraien ordered the ship's pilot to land near the outskirts of the city. The last thing he wanted to do was give away his position because alerting the Niphiliem leader would cause them to possibly begin a slaughtering of troops, hostages, and even the Demitian. A good advantage for them was that it was night time in Sarren when they approached their rendezvous point.

    Sarren was a beautiful city, and he had never seen it before. Against the night sky, Oraien could make out its layout perfectly. The city resembled a halo, and it beautifully encircled one of six Eluesian oceans. While they neared the eastern side of the city, the crew spotted a make shift base in the desert near a river that ran into the Sarren ocean. The city itself had four entrance gates; each entrance had a temporary base set up by either Luna or Nekio. Oraien had designated the commanding base that was operated by both peoples.

    When the ship landed, Oraien headed for the control center. As he walked through the camp, Oraien felt a burning sensation on the back of his conscience; it was the staring eyes of the soldiers of the encampment. For the first time Oraien could feel the subtlety of war slowly sink into him, like a new natural state of mind. He continued his pace while scanning the gloomy camp with his peripheral vision. Finally, Oraien heard strong voices debating plans and procedures of infiltration into Sarren and knew that he had found the site directors. Once he stepped into the tent, the military leaders within became alerted, but Oraien quickly reported who he was saying, "No need to worry, guys. I am an Eluesian just like you. I am here to help."

-"Ok. Who are you, and if you're Eluesian like us, then where is your uniform?" said a commander. Oraien focused his energy and transformed into his Xextrum, leaving the soldiers that stood before him in awe.

-"My name is Oraien Zeal, the Xextrum Ioxus. I am here to settle this matter. Do you need any more proof, soldier?" Oraien firmly asked.

-"Oh, sorry sir, we were informed of your departure but did not expect for you to arrive so soon."

-"It's ok. You were only doing your job. Now, fill me in on the details so we can create a plan."

-"We received word that the Niphiliem mission leader is a Xodus warrior. He specializes in long range attacks. Most of our troops went down right after entering the city because of him. Things do not look good sir," one said.

-*Xodus warrior?* Oraien thought.

-"Ok. Looks like I'm going to have to clear him out first. After I take care of the commander, I will signal you to enter the city to get rid of any remaining Nibiru soldiers. The signal will be a bolt of lightning reaching into the sky, so make sure you and your men are ready."

-"Beware and be mindful of your surroundings Ioxus, the city is riddled with secret passages that have cost both sides many troops. It is full of dangerous traps that may spring out at any given moment and floors that collapse into bottomless pits," said the soldier.

-"I'll keep my eyes open," replied Oraien. "Thanks for the info," Oraien said making his way to an entrance gate.

-"There is one more thing you should know about this city. Since we arrived here, the entire metropolis has rearranged itself in random sequences approximately every seven minutes. If I didn't know any better I'd say that this city was hiding something," The commanding soldier stated looking Ioxus in the eyes.

With that bit of information, he turned and made his way toward the city. Standing at one of the entrances, he could see and feel a deep rumbling. The many structures within the walls were moving and changing the entire layout of the town. He waited for the city to stop moving before he began his mission to save the hostages. Oraien wished to hide his presence while traveling through the city, but the few passages open to him through the streets exposed the above light of the bright Eluesian moon.

Oraien stopped and gazed into the far away moon. Sometimes he could feel his post persona surface at times when he felt most connected to the universe around him. Oraien felt as if he was letting his soul flow out of his eyes; reaching for the untouchable moon. Automatically, the eyes of the Xextrum shifted to Neo ray vision, and Oraien found himself gazing into a moon with calm flowing energy. It amazed him that everything around him, every atom, was all energy. Oraien's eyes left the moon and focused back on the streets in front of him.

-"Time to do this," Oraien said to himself with a profound conviction.

He made his way down a flight of stairs that undoubtedly lead him to the underground tunnels that he was previously warned about. Oraien reached the bottom in no time, and he found himself in awe of the massive corridors that seemed endless. Not wasting any time Ioxus began running through the dark and murky tunnels using his Neo-Ray for guidance. Oraien came across a wandering soldier who did not see him since Oraien was posted up above him. The soldier had fear in his face, and sat down in a corner. For the first time, Oraien saw that even the Niphiliem could display fear, but Oraien left the soldier when he remembered their intentions. His progress through the tunnels became especially difficult because of the traps and passages set in place long ago by the ancients.

Reaching a dead end with a flight of stairs off to the side, Oraien hoped they would lead him back to the surface. Observing his surroundings, he figured that he was now deep within the city. Moving out into the streets of the city, he could hear enemy soldiers scouring the landscape looking for him. Knowing that the city would shift again at anytime, he engaged the troops in combat. When the city began to reform once again, Oraien fought hoping that the shift would bring him closer to the Demitian and the others. As luck would have it, when all movement stopped, he found himself separated from the Niphiliem and now within the range of the sound of civilians.

-"Let go of me monster. I will never help you," a familiar voice declared in a firm tone.

-"Oh, but you will, whether you want to or not. We, Niphiliem, have our ways of persuasion. You will tell all that I need to know. And by the way, my name is Vexia, the last name you will hear before I kill you," the soldier said laughing as they disappeared around a corner leaving the other hostages alone in the room.

-*Vexia, I thought it was Vexus*, Oraien whispered to himself before rushing to aid the other captives. He silently approached the group and spoke,

-"I'm here from the Luna Military. Please be quiet and patient we will rescue all of you,"

Oraien then proceeded after them. Catching up to their location he could once again hear voices.

-*Why does her voice sound so familiar?* He thought to himself.

Oraien could only hear the Demitian's recognizable voice, and he looked at her shadow from each corner that he approached. Vexus was on the move with the captive, and Ioxus knew he needed to follow them wherever they went. He tracked them into a room with a long hall of doors and at the end a bright light. Moving closer and closer to their position, he could see a light glowing brighter with every step he took. Each door he passed through had a small room filled with ancient writing and magnificent art.

Moving into the final area, Ioxus began to adapt his eyes to the light. He found that he was in a large spherical room with a floor that was surging with energy. Oraien hesitated following them through the bright floor before stepping into it. Once his feet touched down, a noise similar to a shifting rock sounded. The light coming from the ground began pulsating, faster and faster until it became a steady white light. Off into the distance Ioxus could hear the rumbling of the buildings changing locations.

-*So that must be what's powering the city's movement,* Oraien thought. Looking around to see if he could find any trace of Vexus and the captive, Oraien saw a faint figure in the distance. *That must be them.* Oraien found them in the distant light. *Darn, but if I go into the light Vexus will see me.*

Instantly Oraien had a brilliant idea; he would charge the outside of his Xextrum with lightning. His plan was to blend in with the strong light off the floor. Once he charged his suit, he camouflaged himself in the light of the room. Vexus looked back to make sure that he was not being followed and saw nothing but blinding light, so he continued. Inside of the room and closer now to the hostage, Oraien looked down upon her face. Oraien could not believe his eyes; it was Ms. Emery. She was the guardian, one of the last remaining members of the ancient civilization. Some of the rocks on the ledge landed on the surface beneath the room. Oraien's presence was no longer concealed.

-"Who's there?" Vexus yelled in surprise.

Receiving no answer he looked up only to see the Xextrum Ioxus staring back. Vexus immediately dashed out of the room dragging

Echoes of Tempore: Revival of Light

Ms. Emery behind her and escaped into a chamber leading away from the pulsating light. Following suit, Ioxus reached the door they used to make their exit only to see the underground city. With neither Ms. Emery nor Vexus in sight, he slowly began his decent into the small cluster of buildings. Oraien hopped to the top of a nearby tower that he could use as a viewpoint to find Vexus, but because he was too concentrated on finding them, he was caught completely off guard. Ioxus was hit by a powerful beam from an energy-sniper rifle that sent him flying backwards crashing through the wall of a building.

Chapter 5.5

Ioxus vs. Vexus

Oraien needed to quickly come up with a plan so that he could get to Tarria. So he drew out his sword and quickly moved out from behind the building. Out in the open, Oraien was barely able to evade the oncoming shots due to Vexus's extreme precision. Using the buildings to his advantage, he flipped back and forth from wall to wall, jumping on to the roofs and back down onto the streets, all while using his swords to deflect the many shots being fired at him.

Oraien was finally able to locate the source of the attacks, a tall tower a short distance to his right. Ioxus deftly used his speed to move from rooftop to rooftop, avoiding the shots until he was in striking range of the building. Oraien jumped down to the street and took cover behind a building a few blocks away. His confidence was on the rise, and he knew he was going to reach them soon. Positioned on a ledge overlooking the entire underground city, Vexus lost track of his target and began moving his expanse-cannon, desperately trying to locate Oraien. Giving up on using his eyesight, he closed his eyes and allowed himself to feel the flow of energy around him. The images of the energy of the surroundings were forming before his eyes, and he could now spot his pursuer posted behind a building. With his mind clear, he focused the energy of his suit to power a spinning revolver on the cannon to fire a massive shot. The beam traveled through every building between him and his target to make a devastating connection. He fell to the ground and focused his mind on ignoring the pain. Nonetheless, Oraien yelled from within the suit due to the extreme sting of the shot. He then rose up from the ground and looked down to his arm to find that blood was dripping from his metallic fingertips. Using the energy stored within the sword, he continued to rapidly deflect the dangerous shots using one arm. Ioxus focused on releasing the electric discharge from Exus on the building itself, causing only enough damage to knock Vexia off the ledge so that he wouldn't harm Tarria.

    With his long-range weapon now useless due to close combat, Vexus readied himself for Ioxus. Vexus ran towards the room that he held the Demitian, but right when he entered the room Oraien violently kicked Vexus through the window. Vexus flew out the window, and Oraien quickly intercepted him and ultimately gripped him from behind in a choking lock.

-"Why are you Niphiliem so evil?! Why are you doing this? What have we ever done to Nibiru to deserve such harsh treatment?" Oraien tightened his grip on Vexus's neck, "I may never know the answer, but I will only show you the mercy you showed us: none." Just as Oraien was about to put all his strength into ending Vexus, he heard a snap, and the appearance of Vexus changed and he heard the struggling voice of a female.

-"Your-your people are safe," She struggled to get the words out because of Oraien's choke hold. Oraien was extremely surprised; he looked down her body and noticed her curves and female features. She was indeed, a female. Oraien then slowly loosened his grip.

-"I made sure that none of them were harmed once I began this operation. I told the soldiers to leave them for me to finish off and to go and fortify the city."

Oraien let go of the woman and jumped back a safe distance and waited for her to continue. She fell to the ground coughing, and slowly regained her breath. Oraien noticed that she was wearing a suit similar to that of the late Atrum. Examining her body more than necessary, Oraien could not believe how beautiful she appeared. After she stood up she removed her helmet, and her face perfectly matched what Oraien had seen from her thus far.

-"My name is Vexia, not Vexus. I understand that you needed to save those people, but is there any reason why you were so rough?" she asked.

-"Maybe because you tried to blow a hole in my chest and not to mention you kidnapped an innocent person. Oh and my arm! You... "

-"Okay first you gotta loosen up. I'm not going to fight back. Besides it's not like you couldn't take it, obviously, I mean look, you're already healing." Turning around to examine herself she continued, "Look, you even destroyed my voice and appearance amplifier. Now how am I suppo...."

-*She's,* he paused. *insane.* Oraien thought to himself. *One minute she's trying to kill me, the next she's talking to me as if nothing happened.*

-"Warrior, what is your name?" Vexia said as her tone became serious.

-"Oraien, You got my name and I have yours. So tell me why. Why are you doing these things?" he replied.

-"Oraien, huh. You're the first one to live after becoming my target and as a reward for your victory, I'll answer your question. I was sent under command of this operation by the leader of all Nibiru branches. I came in disguised as a male, Vexus, so that my subordinates would not hesitate to follow my orders." She looked at Ioxus with a serious yet flirtatious gaze, "When you were choking me and almost killed me, you broke my appearance and voice device. So that's why you did not see the real deal," Oraien slightly let down his defense and stood calm and spoke, "You don't look that different from me. You don't act like a barbarian. You're actually pretty cute," She blushed at his comment but kept her composure, she then calmed her face and looked directly into Oraien's eyes. "As far as my mission here is concerned, I was searching for The Scrolls of..."

-"IOXUS!" Tarria in a separate room yelled. He turned his head in the direction of the scream, and she was yelling for help from within the room. When Oraien turned back to face Vexia once again, she was gone, but he wasted no time and hurried to Tarria.

There were two Niphiliem soldiers in the room ready to harm Tarria, and Oraien dashed to intercept their advance. Oraien looked to the soldier closest to Ms. Emery, pulled out his sword, and plunged it through the soldier's body. Looking to the Niphiliem to his right, Oraien ripped the sword from the chest of the Niphiliem in front of him and kicked through the standing Niphiliem's body. The two soldiers were dead in less than a minute. Their fate was sealed once they decided to kill Tarria, and Oraien stood still in awe of his own power. Oraien turned to face Tarria and spoke, "Well, this was quite the surprise. Who would have ever thought that Ms. Emery would be of the ancient bloodline? But then again I guess that explains how you knew so much about the history of our world," he said through his armor.

-"I was your teacher? You are without a doubt Ioxus, the Xextrum of Lightning, but which of my students has become a Xextrum?" She asked while looking perplexed. Oraien focused his energy and made his helmet draw back so that she could see his face. Ms. Emery was uneasily shaken to see that it was Oraien who had inherited the powers of the Luna-Quarton. Under her exterior self-presentation, she held concern for Oraien.

So, she chose you to carry this burden?

-"Ms. Emery, or should I say Tarria, you would never have guessed it to be me. Oh, and I have a question; why didn't you ever tell me your first name?" Oraien asked.

-"Respect for teachers that's why, you should know that, my dear Rai." She let out a sigh and continued to speak, "Oraien, you were always outstanding in the class, not necessarily in a good way, but one thing I will never forget is that you never let your talent make you a shallow person. I am happy Luna chose you," her face suddenly looked concerned. "There is so much you and I have to catch up on, but that will have to wait for a more opportune time. Right now I must return to Vicero to convene with the Luna Assembly regarding the step for a counterstrike against Nibiru," she said with a tone of urgency in her voice.

-"Unless you know of another way out of here, that will be hard for us to accomplish with me fighting the rest of the Niphiliem soldiers while protecting you at the same time," Oraien said as he looked towards the chamber containing the pulsating light. He then pointed at the entrance from which he came.

-"Actually, I do," she said as she led Oraien into a building containing a flight of stairs which lead underground to a secret passage. Making their way through the darkness, Oraien asked her how she seemed to know exactly where she was going. She calmly replied with a smirk on her face, "Because I grew up here." Oraien's eyes shot open in the sudden realization of how old Ms. Emery truly was. "We have arrived," She said bringing Oraien out of his daze.

Entering a large room under the chamber of the pulsing light, he could now see the mechanism responsible for the light above. The source of all the cities energy came from a single Demitian ship, and it was unlike any spacecraft Oraien had ever seen before.

-"This is the great ship Ferra. It is one of the greatest achievements of the Demitians." Even after three thousand years of inactivity, it still powers the city's ever changing patterns, doing exactly what it was designed to do; keep outsiders from finding it and using it against Luna," she said with a sense of pride building within her as she looked at the ship.

Drawn to the ship in almost a trance like state, Oraien found himself wanting to reach out to make contact. With each step he took, the light began to pulse faster and faster until it became steady upon him making contact with it. Instead of hearing the rumbling of buildings in the distance like before, the city above the began to glow above the surface, illuminating ancient markings inscribed on the streets and buildings and also vaporizing all Niphiliem within the city.

With the resonating of Ioxus and Ferra, represented by the illumination of the matching symbols on both figures, the doors to the ship as well as the spherical dome structure above them slid open. Oraien almost forgot to give the outside bases the signal he promised them, and with the rise of his arm he sent a bolt of lightning rocketing upwards towards space. Oraien and Ms. Emery boarded the ship and rose into the morning sky. Almost as if the ship could read Oraien's mind, it set a course for the capital and blasted towards Vicero with speed unmatched by any ship in the star system.

Arriving on Vicero, Ms. Emery escorted Oraien to building with the emblem of Luna on the front of its edifice so that the two could discuss the matters at hand.

-"Hello, Jovan, it has been some time," said Ms. Emery.

-"Yes it has, Tarria. Please take a seat," Jovan said while looking at her through the steam of his coffee. "I am quite aware of the issue of the scroll. If they find the other scrolls then..."

-"That's why I am here. We must stop them, send the other scrolls to Nekio, Ioxus has been awakened," Jovan quickly put his cup down in shock.

-"Ioxus?! So the five guardians within the Emuli Quadrant are united again," Oraien listened to Jovan not knowing who he was, and simultaneously Jovan carefully observed Oraien wondering who he was as well.

-"Oraien," Ms. Emery said to get his attention. "Jovan and I have to talk a little further. Feel free to go through the city and find your old class mates."

-"But Ms. Emery..." Oraien stepped forward.

-"I do not mean to treat you like a child, Rai. You have grown. Believe me, I know, but I need to talk to him in private," Ms. Emery said in a motherly tone. Oraien gently nodded his head as a sign of acceptance and departed.

As Oraien explored the ruined city of Vicero looking to join a relief group, he was spotted by one of his former classmates who updated him on their situation.

-"Oraien, you Duro, where have you been?!" the young student said.

-"Believe it or not, I've been on Nekio all this time until I returned to Luna last night. What are you doing here? I would never have imagined that you would be helping out. Honestly, I really can't picture anyone from our class doing anything like this."

-"Well, a few weeks ago you might have been right about that. We were quite the selfish bunch and were all about our studies, but you should be happy to know that you helped to change all of that."

-"Me?" Oraien stated in confusion.

-"Yes you, don't you remember what you said? *Will we sit back and do nothing?* All of us heard you out in the hall. It rocked our foundations because we all received the message you sent us the night before, but yet and still we did nothing."

-"Wow, I had no idea that you guys could hear me," Oraien responded.

-"Yep, and ever since that fateful day, we have been helping to rebuild our planet as the newest recruits of the E.Q.O.D.A." She said with a smile.

-"Hey!" a Luna soldier yelled out, trying to get the attention of Oraien's classmate.

-"I guess that's my cue, so I'll have to catch up with you some other time Rai, take care, and thank you for your bravery," the petite young woman said rushing back to her duties.

-"Well it's good to know that they have joined the fight against those monsters," Oraien said to himself turning to continue walking through the city.

Oraien continued exploring the city as it was under construction. Talking to each familiar face he could find, Oraien heard that one of his classmates joined a volunteer group that was moving fragments of destroyed buildings to be reconditioned and reused. Oraien joined the group under temporary volunteer status hoping that he would spot more familiar faces.

Work was hard under the hot rays of Antares, and Oraien did all his share of work while also occasionally stopping to fully observe the devastation the city suffered. Even though the day went by without Oraien finding any more people he knew, he did not let it slow his aid for the group. One man did stand out to Oraien, though not by the fact that he recognized him, but because he felt as if he knew him. He also noticed that the young man that did not speak with anyone of the men of his group, nor did he even bother to work with anyone in his group. It was as if he was there to pay a debt. Later that day when Antares set, the stars dominated the night sky. Oraien decided to introduce himself to the silent co-worker. Approaching him Oraien spoke, "Hey, I noticed you haven't said a word to anyone of your group. So I'm taking the initiative to say hi. So...," Oraien said while flexing his face into a smile, but the guy just stared at him and looked up towards to sky with his arms crossed.

-"Thank you, but you should go on your way now," the stranger said while still looking up.

-"At least tell me your name. I'm Oraien." The fellow lowered his head as if he was stunned to hear his name. "What, you heard my name before?"

-"No. Sorry, you just look really ugly."

-"What? Hey, man, the ladies fall before me," Oraien said thinking of Calea. "Never mind. Come on man, you call me ugly. So you owe me your name."

-"I don't owe you anything, stranger... But my name, it's Xan."

The two worked together for the rest of the night and became strange buddies. Oraien actually enjoyed talking to him more than he did the others. Xan also felt a close connection with Oraien. He continued to look at Oraien in disbelief, as if he knew something about Oraien that even the young warrior did not know about himself. Xan continued to try to figure out what it was Oraien was hiding but couldn't put his finger on Oraien's secret, the secret of his Xextrum Ioxus. So both kept secrets from each other but never let them interfere with their moment in time together. The conversation between Tarria and Jovan continued elsewhere in Vicero.

-"So that was Oraien, as well as the Ioxus?" Jovan concluded sitting back in his office chair after hearing the long story from Ms. Emery. "Now that's interesting. His birth must have been out of our hands when…"

-"Yes. It was a long time ago, but obviously she chose him. I just wanted you to see him and how he's grown."

Chapter 6

Unexpected Counterstrike

At the start of the next day, Oraien returned to Ms. Emery to report for his next assignment. But before he could take off on his own into deep space, he needed to be instructed on how to operate Ferra. The more difficult aspect was that Ferra was no ordinary vessel; she was an ancient treasure yet far more advanced than any ships of the contemporary era. Oraien's high intelligence allowed him to learn fast, but the number one reason he was learning at such astonishing rate was solely due to his instructor, Tarria Emery, who he was very comfortable with.

She taught him everything about the ship, from how to operate the Information Directory System (I.D.S) of the ship, to in-depth hands on experience with Ferra's Jeno-ray and all her armaments, including unique cannon designed to propel Ioxus into space. Being taught by Ms. Emery again did make Oraien remember the things he liked about her. He felt as if she was a mother to him, but he knew that it was because he never felt the warm embrace of his real mother. He did not know anything about his family. He lived all alone his entire life and spent his early childhood living in an orphanage in lower part of Vicero. At times, it would weigh heavily on him, but his character allowed him to move on when he was entering his early teens.

-"Oraien, I always forget how fast you learn. You are so lucky to have that gift," she said touching his face. "Oraien, today you must rest. I have received news from Retsum regarding your next mission, but I won't tell you just yet. Allow yourself to absorb all that we went through today and prepare to leave tomorrow."

-"Ms. Emery, thank you."

-"Your room number is 36 and is located on floor H-756. I'll be waiting for you tomorrow morning at Luna Port 5L. Please be there before the seventh hour of the morning."

-"Yes ma'am," Oraien proceeded to his quarters and prepared himself for bed. He was back, and everything was ordinary once again, or at least for this night, he thought. He woke up the next morning and arrived at the docking station respectfully early by the sixth hour. He waited for her on a bench near the entrance of the foyer of docking station 5L. After about half an hour, Ms. Emery showed up and sat next to him.

-"Okay, here is your mission brief. I have not read it yet; it's not mine to read." she gave him an enclosed mission, a gift, and a hug, all with reluctance to let him go.

-"Oraien, please take care. Come back, okay? Just come back here safe," Oraien could not say any words so he just held her tightly, and afterwards he took everything and proceeded towards Ferra. Right before he could board the ship, Tarria yelled one last message from behind the port line, "Open it when you enter space, then input the information into Ferra's I.D.S, exactly the way I taught you.

     Space beautifully flew by as Oraien sat back in the pilot seat while Ferra sailed to their destination. As a child, he always dreamed of exploring space and touching the stars. Now Oraien could do just that, or so he thought. As peacefulness set in, he began to close his eyes. He felt serine for the first time since his studies on Luna before the brutal Niphiliem attack. A gentle smile grew across his face.

Before Oraien could completely dive into sleep, he opened his enclosed mission and read over it carefully. His mission was to travel to Igni'ice, a planet located approximately thirty tetras' towards the outer region, to aid them in their defense against oncoming Nibiru Forces. Examining the statement further, he located quadrant coordinates and realized that all he needed to do was input them into the I.D.S. and activate auto travel. He pulled the last page out and noticed that Retsum also left him a note,

Oraien, you have been a good student and friend to me. I trust your abilities and I will never doubt your potential. There is an old saying in the great ring; 'Even the most powerful stars can die.' Take those words to heart and you will never fail. In order for you to get stronger, you must call upon the powers of other Quarton. Once you reach Igni'ice, speak with the Calfieren elders about the Fire Core. They will know what to do after that. I will see you soon, and I can't wait to see how much you will grow.

Oraien sat the letter on his knee and sat back to absorb its contents. He had a great appreciation for his teacher but knew that it was his time to reach the respectability and power of all Xextrum. After he entered the coordinates into the ship, Ferra took control, and Oraien let his mind go once again as he gazed into the stars as he drifted away into sleep.

As he enjoyed his peace, a gentle beeping began to sound from the ship's systems. Oraien's eyes mildly opened and turned to view what the ship desired to show him. Oraien saw a screen that displayed his ship in the center and a large object traveling parallel to Ferra. Oraien's eyes concentrated on the figure while he pushed a button that allowed him to see the entity. The screen flashed and Oraien saw a large asteroid.

One very important lesson he learned from Retsum and Ms. Emery was that many ships have a special ray. *This ray not only detects life, but it can also detect activity. It is called the Jeno-ray,* he thought, recalling his teachings with Tarria.

-"Ferra, this asteroid looks strange. Please scan it with Jeno-ray," he said moving closer to the screen.

As the ship was searching the asteroid, it increased its magnification to penetrate the surface, and many areas with life and activity were found. Oraien inspected the targets on the screen and found them worthy of investigating. He also noticed that a Nekio defender ship laid in ruin near a large metal door in a depression.

Oraien hastened to the back of the ship and called forth his Xextrum. With a burst of energy, the suit materialized onto his body, and Ioxus was summoned.

-"Ferra, stay hidden while I examine this further, activate Celestial Stealth." When he gave the command, Ferra changed the composition of its shell into a mirror, reflecting space within itself to give the illusion of invisibility. Ferra also was able to hide her energy from enemy radar detection. "Propel me towards the comet using the trajectory cannon."

With that said, a floor panel opened, and Oraien slid down into the cannon. The ship calculated the best point of intersection through space to catapult him, and once he was jettisoned, Oraien glided through space towards the massive asteroid. Observing the asteroid, Oraien noticed a Nekio Defense Cruiser on the surface. Although most of the ship was intact, much of it was littered across the exterior of the asteroid.

-"Maybe there are survivors. I'm sure they will need to keep at least one crew member alive to interrogate."

Oraien's momentum gave him a firm landing; making contact with the floating body like a small explosion had gone off, creating a small crater sending dust into open space. He stood up and looked around with the eyes of his Xextrum that helped him see in the darkness. He jumped into the brightest crater and floated down silently while keeping himself close to the walls.

Slowly, the light became brighter as the rocks turned to smooth solid walls. At a distance, he could see windows and large hangers made for ships. Oraien pushed himself off the wall with his legs and traveled towards one of the gates. Afraid of blowing his cover, he knocked with three hard punches against the metallic doors. A few minutes later the door opened, and ten Niphiliem soldiers poured out of the gate in space suits to look around. Oraien had already made his way into the base using his lightning speed, and all the Niphiliem could see was a flicker of electricity.

-"There must be an electric shortage in the door. Get someone to fix this before I have to!" yelled a soldier.

The soldier that commanded was in a strange suit that reminded Oraien of Atrum and

Vexia from his past battles on Luna. Oraien hid until all the soldiers left his view. Afterwards, Oraien jumped onto the floor of the dome. He looked around until he saw a hallway. Oraien approached the entrance of the corridor and made sure no soldiers were in sight, so he used his power to get to the end of the hall within the second. Not aware of his surroundings, Oraien was spotted by two Niphiliem soldiers. One soldier immediately fled to set an alarm while the other ran to subdue him. The soldier pulled out a gun and shot at Oraien. Oraien swiftly ducked under the shot and dashed towards the soldier with great agility. Oraien grabbed his arm and plunged the soldier into the ground causing a string of sharp cracks. Oraien then threw the lifeless soldier towards the runaway Niphiliem attempting to alarm the base. The soldier was knocked unconscious by the force of impact. However, the bodies of both soldiers hit the alarm switch, and the base suddenly began to cry.

  Oraien dashed to switch it off, and the base was once again silent. The base only sounded the alarm for five seconds, and Oraien sighed in relief. But soon after, the alarms broke out once again. Oraien stood up and focused on where he could find the passengers of the Nekio Cruiser with his Neo-ray; he found one survivor. Making his way through the base, he ran into many Niphiliem that he quietly fought on his way through the labyrinth.

As Oraien finally approached the room containing the survivor he could hear screams of torture, he felt a powerful being approaching. Oraien forced his way into the door and found Calea unconscious. His mind almost lost its place when he saw her on the floor lifeless, but his training prepared him to stay focused. The room was large that extended upward. At the very top was a skylight window that displayed the stars of the universe.

-*That's my exi*...before Oraien could finish his thought, he was blasted from behind with massive force. Oraien flew to the other end of the room crashing into the wall causing the pillars to collapse.

Chapter 6.5

Ioxus vs. Sendo

The blow was delivered from the Niphiliem commander presiding over the base. He used his large gun to make sure Oraien was down permanently by blasting the fallen debris that covered him. He then proceeded to pick up Calea to finish her off as well.

-"It's a shame we could not get the interrogation underway," he said holding Calea by the neck as her feet dangled in the air. "Is this what you are here for Xextrum? She is ours," he said as he prepared to kill her. Calea was still unconscious, but she soon awoke to hazard coughing, and as soon as she was able, she looked around to see what was going on. She brought her hands up to the Niphiliem's hand to try to release the pressure.

-"No!" yelled Calea.

Like all things in existence, Calea knew death was inevitable, but she wanted to die in battle or of old age, not by the hands of her captor. Nothing ever really made her want anything else, but she always wanted a little more than her confined military life. Sendo roared as he dropped Calea and violently kicked her into the air toward the skylight. The kick severely injured Calea's side, and she tried to hold on to the last bit of life she had. Calea closed her eyes as if she was ready to fall into eternal sleep. Sendo then lifted his massive gun and aimed to shoot. Within Calea's mind she said one word, *Good-bye.*

An explosion assured Sendo that Calea had died, but as the smoke subsided a figure holding Calea appeared. Oraien was still alive, but at the limits of his suit. He had little energy left. He looked into Calea's crying eyes, and she did not realize that Oraien had saved her life. Calea slowly looked into Ioxus' eyes and saw Oraien.

"Rai?" she whispered.

Oraien never realized how beautiful Calea appeared to him mainly because of the way she treated him, but this was the real Calea without the facade. This was the Calea who saved him. His protective instinct naturally initiated itself over her. He placed Calea on a ledge.

-"Stay here, I promise I will protect you so don't cry anymore. You are safe as long as I am here," Oraien said with a tender voice.

-"Xextrum! You live? Then no more underestimations, come!" cried the commander.

-"Who are you?" Oraien asked.

-"Sendo, captain of Niphiliem Base N2, the last name you will hear before you die!" he said dashing towards Ioxus.

-"That's not the first time I have heard one of you say that," Oraien said bracing himself.

They met fist-to-fist and knee-to-knee. Due to Oraien's lack of energy he had to move slower allowing Sendo to match his movements. In any regular case Oraien could outpace him, but the unexpected energy blast Oraien was hit with coupled with Calea situation, putting the odds overwhelmingly in Sendo's favor. Sendo lifted his large gun over his head and caught Oraien on the head. He brought it down with such force that Oraien smashed into the ground with a loud howl. Sendo stood back to prepare his gun to fire, and with that Oraien emerged from the hole, alive, but severely injured. Sendo knew he could not shoot Oraien otherwise he would evade it, so Sendo dashed towards him instead.

  With the electricity in the massive room cut due to the damage Oraien and Sendo caused, the only source of light was from the sky window above. The two of them used their surroundings to propel them towards each other with greater speed. Out of the darkness the only thing that could be seen were their weapons clashing, occasionally connecting in the illumination of the skylight. The only sound to be heard was the clanking of metallic weapons and the occasional blast from Sendo's cannon. Realizing that he could never hit Oraien with a direct shot head on, he turned his attention to Calea who was lying on a ledge, battered in the corner of the room. Sendo fired the blast in Calea's direction hoping to kill two birds with one blast, but to his amazement, Ioxus deflected the blast with Exus. Oraien sent the blast into a wall on the other side of the chamber, blowing a massive hole in its structure. As the ruble from the blast settled, Oraien could hear the alarm sounding, and the footsteps of soldiers quickly approaching.

Oraien was pressed to conserve energy if he desired to make it back to Ferra in one piece, so he deflected Sendo's body towards the skylight. Oraien then called forth his sword, Exus. Sendo made a 180 turn and aimed his gun and shot, but that time allowed Oraien to emerge directly in front of Sendo. In one fluid motion, Oraien sliced through Sendo's gun and turned his body around to kick Sendo upwards towards the window. Oraien let out a procession of sword attacks upon Sendo causing him to gain speed towards the glass. The skylight shattered as Sendo's body traveled through it, causing the safety shield to cover the opening. The cuts in Sendo's armor from Exus caused the vacuum of space to kill him.

-*That wasn't so bad*, Oraien sarcastically thought to himself falling to his knees. *Why do I feel so heavy? There's hardly any gravity here.* He pushed himself to stand and began to charge Ioxus with energy and quickly tended to Calea once he had what he needed.

-"How can I get you to my ship?" he asked her, but he did not expect her to answer. Oraien began to think of ways he could on his own. Oraien carefully placed Calea into an empty Niphiliem space suit and once again, Oraien could sense a powerful presence heading towards them.

-"Sendo? Damn! I don't have time to figure this out, we better get out of here because I'm not ready for another fight."

Oraien could feel the presence approaching from the outside of the shattered window. Calea was in dire need of attention, so Oraien fled back into the Niphiliem base. While Oraien made his way through the base, he felt another strong presence of a familiar energy. It reminded him of the energy of the Nekio-Quarton when he received Exus. He made a quick detour carrying Calea on his back.

The room he found was surging with energy and in the center was a glass generator. The source of the power was something that Oraien could feel. It wanted to tell him something, and the message was that of distress. Oraien broke the glass and reached for the fragment. When he touched it, he felt as if he touched a Quarton. The only exception was that this time instead of being blinded by an overwhelming light, he entered an unforgiving darkness. Out of the darkness, seemingly random images began to flood Oraien's eyesight. He stood silent, trying to comprehend the barely visible ensemble of names, dates, planets and items passing by in front of him. Oraien managed to piece together a few images and made out a name: The Scrolls of Anteeo. When he let go of the fragment, he became sad realizing what he was holding. It was a broken portion of a Neo-Quarton, and he knew that the other pieces were out there somewhere. It was as if he could feel its pain of the planet from being separated and misused. When he looked down at his hands, he noticed that the cryptic markings on his suit were illuminated, and he knew exactly what it meant. Energy surged through Ioxus, and the Xextrum had received a new ability. Oraien could feel it within him; it was a new type of energy.

-"This must be the quartiio energy Retsum told me I would receive," said Oraien as he remembered Retsum's teachings;

Ioxus utilizes atomic energy, which counts for the Xextrum's strength, however, Ioxus only has a limited amount of atomic energy, so to charge at any time one must stop to do a Neo-boost, but the key word in that is stop. In battle, one requires time to utilize the atoms around them to complete a Neo-boost. On the other hand, quartiio energy can only be used once and charged only by Quartons, but as long as the energy is there, it can be used to execute devastating abilities

After Oraien obtained his new power, he purposefully overheated the generators causing the base to explode while he escaped with Calea. He called Ferra when Oraien was a safe distance away from the chaos caused by the explosion. She picked them both up and fled from the oncoming explosion.

Chapter 7

Journey

Calea was running, not knowing why. She had her eyes closed, running for her life. She heard a very familiar voice, so she opened her eyes and stopped. She was in a dark plane, so she could not see anything, not even her own hands in front of her. After looking around in fear, she could see a large bright figure in the distance running towards her. No more than a minute later, she screamed.

-"Sendo! No, you're dead! I won't let you hurt me again!" she said with doubt deep in her heart. A name flickered within her mind, *Oraien. He– he saved me last time, but where is he!?* she thought. *No, I don't need him, I am a soldier.* She then focused an offense on Sendo.

Sendo stopped at a distance and aimed his cannon at her. Calea began to run towards him in the attempt to reach him before he open fired, however even with her agility, she could not stop him. The cannon exploded, and Calea was in the center of its course. Calea jumped to the side to evade the shot, but her left arm suffered a massive blow.

-"Oraien! You said you would protect me!" Calea yelled out as her eyes opened to reality.

-"Calea, calm down. You're having a nightmare. I'm here. I told you I would protect you, and I have," Oraien said softly. Calea was lying in Ferra's bed. She looked into Oraien's eyes but could not recognize him. *He's changed. He's more mature. He's...* She began to feel strange. She could not stand to look into his eyes any further. A warm feeling was building within her, and she was embarrassed.

-"Where are we?" she said looking at her surroundings.

-"Ferra," Oraien stated proudly. "A ship created by the ancient Demitians of Luna."

-"Demitians?" She said in disbelief.

-"Yeah, it's a long story," Oraien stated.

-"Well... stop looking at me," Calea said gently.

-*That's the Calea I remember*, thought Oraien to himself. They had been on the ship for two days. Calea had several broken ribs and bruises all over her body on the first day, but Oraien remembered Ms. Emery explaining that Ferra had a special ability to heal wounds and severe injuries at a rapid rate if the person was placed in her bed.

-"Ferra healed you, Calea," Oraien said as he walked to the small section of the ship that had food to hand her some water. "When I first brought you in this ship you were severely injured. I didn't know what to do so I put you in Ferra's bed. I asked her to help me. One of the coolest things happened next, Ferra sealed you in a small force field, and immediately your wounds started to get better. The process took a whole day, but I thank her for it." Calea looked around at the ship as if Ferra was alive. Calea still could not look at Oraien without feeling strangely comforted, protected. She felt satisfied to be in the warm ship with him at the time.

-"Soooo, you haven't said anything about......"

-"Thank you," Calea said trying to sit up in the bed, pulling the sheets to keep her chest covered.

Oraien paused when he heard Calea's last comment. Immediately he thought back to their very first encounter back on the Nekio Cruiser after Calea had saved his life. He tried to thank her for what she did, but her unexpected response left him speechless. He began to walk closer to her and smiled,

-"Thank you for what? You needed my help and I extended it, no thanks is necessary. But I'll accept the offer." Oraien had quoted her exact words, and Calea could not help but to blush and smile. Her eyes soon fell calm again, not only because of how he made her feel, but of how true he was being. She knew that before when they met she had acted above herself: snobbish.

-"How are you feeling?" he said as he approached her, reaching out his hand as if to check her temperature.

-"Don't... don't come any closer," She said turning her head away. She was too shy to let Oraien touch her. She feared that if Oraien touched her face, the feeling would overwhelm her, a strange yet warm and comforting feeling.

-*Do I like him?* she asked herself. Oraien was extremely confused at this moment, but the tension was broken between them as the screen on the ship began to show activity. It showed a communication call that Oraien went to answer. As soon as he was connected, Kilm was displayed on the screen.

-"Father!" Calea yelled out.

-"It's good to see you're awake darling. You have no idea how worried we were over here," he said in a caring tone.

-"I know, we lost all communications when we were blindsided by a strange asteroid. They came out of nowhere. Papa, I thought... I thought I was going to..."She had to grip her composer so she would not start to cry.

-"My darling...be strong," he paused, and then continued, "The asteroid you spoke of was the Niphiliem N2 base, Oraien explained everything to us while you were sleeping."

-"I tried to fight back...I fought with everything I had, but I wasn't strong enough," Calea said as she hung her head, and tears began to form in her eyes.

Oraien too hung his head in remorse as he empathized with how Calea was feeling. He thought back to that very same feeling he had back on Luna during the invasion of his world and knew all too well how deeply she was hurting. He wanted to comfort her. At the same time though, he respected her request for him to keep his distance.

-"I know better than anyone that you fought back, and I am most proud of you. But you not being strong enough is partly my own fault," Kilm responded.

-"Your own fault? What do you mean, Father?" she said as she looked up in confusion.

-"I can't go into much detail now, but it would seem that fate has given me a chance to right this wrong. I want you to travel to the fractured moon Cratera, a research facility located thirteen tetras from your current location. There you will find a Dr. Larenis, tell her who you are, and she will know what to do," Kilm stated looking around to see if anyone was watching or listening in on his conversation. "I'm sending you the coordinates now, hurry, no one must know of your visit there. I will be contacting you both shortly." Kilm then disappeared off the screen.

Oraien and Calea looked at each other and began to scramble and organize themselves to head out to their destination. Oraien ran to the pilot seat and inserted the coordinates of Cratera while Calea dressed herself and made her way to the front of the ship to sit in the co-pilot seat next to Oraien. Once Ferra calculated the coordinates, they blasted off from their stationary position towards Cratera.

-"I wonder what this is all about," Oraien stated trying to break the silence between them.

-"I have no idea, but I have never seen my father so secretive. It must be pretty important."

With the incredible speed at which Ferra traveled, they reached the moon in a little over an hour. Cratera had no atmosphere and was full of craters from collisions with various heavenly bodies over the course of many eons. They arrived on the light side of the moon and looked on eagerly trying to find any sign of life. Both Calea and Oraien were beginning to wonder if they were in the right place until they came upon the true purpose in which the moon got its name. On the other side of the moon in the center of its surface was a large rip as if it had been split open from the impact of an immense collision. It was there within the unbelievably gigantic trench that they found the research facility Kilm told them about. The metropolis was spread out from one end of the rugged deep channel to the other. The city like structure illuminated the darkness on the small moon, and Oraien and Calea found themselves slowly floating above the darkness, peering deep into the moon's interior as they tried to see just how deep the lights went. A communication request appeared on Ferra's display screen, and Oraien connected to it.

-"Identify yourself!" said a voice over the Ferra's intercom.

-"Oraien Zeal, ship name Ferra," he replied.

-"How did you come across this location?" the voice continued.

-"We were given the coordinates by General Kilm of the Anekie Forces. His daughter, Calea Loyl, accompanies me; we are here to find Dr. Larenis." After a long pause the operator returned,

-"Dock in port C7, I will inform Dr. Larenis of your arrival." When they reached the port and had exited the ship they preceded to the inner section of the facility where a beautiful woman wearing a long white lab coat greeted them.

-"My my, you look so much like your mother," a scientist said approaching Calea.

-"Thank you. So you knew my mother?" Calea asked.

-"Very well actually, but I'm more surprised to see that you're finally here. I have been waiting a long time for you," the scientist replied.

"And who might this be?" she said turning to Oraien.

"Oraien Zeal," he said extending his arm to shake her hand.

-"What do you mean, waiting a long time?" asked Calea.

-"Come, I'll show you," she said as she began walking down the wall. "I don't get many visitors, it's nice to see someone so young and handsome here for a change," She said as she turned and winked at Oraien.

    Oraien smiled at the gesture, and Calea threw him a death stare out the corner of her eye which made him look away with a half smirk across his face. The three of them walked further into the massive complex, hearing various screams and laughs along the way to Dr. Larenis's lab.

-"Don't mind those old fools, if they aren't blowing themselves up, they're laughing all diabolically because they think that they have made some sort of break through," she said giggling to herself. "They are all quite harmless, I can assure you, here we go," she said stopping in front of a large wall with the outline of a door etched into it. She placed her hand on the door, rubbed her hands downward and walked through the structure. Calea and Oraien looked in awe and slowly and fearfully took a few steps back in unison until she walked back through a few moments and instructed them both to do the same. When they placed their hands on the door it read their heartbeat, fingerprints, and molecular makeup before they were allowed into the lab.

-"Well, that's something you don't do every day," said Oraien. "Why did we just walk through a wall and more importantly, how?" Calea jumped and covered his mouth, "Sorry, Oraien tends to ask a lot of questions."

-"It's ok. To put it simply, it is a hallway filled with electric titanium. People can pass through the metal if the security computer allows you to. So when you placed your hand on the wall, the system read your DNA makeup and allowed you two to pass behind me as guests. Otherwise, you would not have been allowed safe passage. Understand?" the scientist informed.

-"Um... yeah" Calea said confused. She did not understand a single word the scientist had just said, but Oraien nodded his head, simply amazed at the technology.

- "Believe it or not, you just traveled through thirty feet of that stuff. It's one of my favorite inventions," she said.

-"Inventions? Wait, *you're* Dr. Larenis?" Oraien said in great confusion.

-"Yes, I am," she replied. Calea thought that she would look older, but she was honestly wrong.

-"You look very young to be a friend of my mother."

-"Thank you," She laughed, "It must be the air around here."

Once inside, they gazed at the many gadgets and technologic wonders created by the scientists. In the corner of the room was an elastic material stretched out into the form of a woman. That entire section of the lab was dedicated to this mysterious material and all its accessories. Calea walked closer to it and reached out her hand to feel it. When she made contact with it, a purple aura of light spread out over the suit before fading back to normal.

-"This is what your father sent you here for," said Dr. Larenis, "This is the ELX 10-22, a bimolecular material made especially for you, Calea. Why don't you try it on?

-"Wait, that little stretchy stuff over in the corner is what we came here for?" Oraien said in disbelief.

-"Yes, Oraien. Besides, everyone knows that good things come in small packages," the scientist said.

"Oraien, could you please wait in the other room," Dr. Larenis said pointing towards the living quarters. "You can't just stand there while she gets changed." Oraien blushed and then walked into the other room.

After Oraien left Calea looked towards Ms. Larenis, "What is this, and why are you asking me to put it on? My father told me to come here with no explanations. I just met you and you're asking me to put these clothes on? I don't know what going on, I have so many questions, and no one has time explain everything!"

-"Trust me; your father is just about the only one who could have told you about this place. We both know he wouldn't do anything to put you in harm's way, so please put it on and I will explain everything once I get you situated."

Calea reluctantly began to change, slowly pulling up the pants up her legs and then proceeding to pull in the sleeves as she put on the shirt. She needed to discard of all of her previous clothes so that the suit would lie directly on her skin. When the two pieces of the material were on, they fused together becoming a single garb.

Inside the living quarters, Oraien found himself tinkering with gadgets that the scientist had lying around. He took notice to the many V.D.'s Dr. Larenis had set up throughout the room. On the left side of the room was the bed and restroom area as the right was the kitchen and eating area.

-It's much more spacious than my place back on Luna, Oraien thought. Further looking around the scientist's technical abode, a metallic block on the floor caught his eye. When he reached down to pick it up, he was surprised to see the writing etched into its metal form. Once he made contact with it, the dark etchings in the block began to light up, prompting him to read the contents.

-Demitian text? Oraien thought to himself. Examining the artifact further he was able to translate a few of the symbols, "The Millennium War," Oraien said, "I wonder what that means," he continued until he heard his name called by Dr. Larenis from the other room.

When he came back in the lab area, he could not help but ogle at Calea. The ELX revealed all of her curves, curves that were hidden under her Anekie uniform. Dr. Larenis was standing next to her with her arms folded in a proud manner as she watched her greatest feat finally in the hands of the person she designed them for.

-The doc was right, good things do come in small packages, Oraien thought.

Dr. Larenis proceeded to hand Calea hip and shoulder harnesses that attached themselves to the material. All the former garments of her uniform were then thrown away. Calea's new look made Oraien notice that she really was not just beautiful but striking. She stood before him wearing the ELX, which now had become a dark purple color. Her short black hair framed her face and matched the black long-sleeved short jacket provided by the scientist. Calea's new look was completed with a pair of stylish black mid-ankle boots. Next, Dr. Larenis handed her two handheld guns that were to be worn on her hips and a small jacket shirt covering her chest strap. Calea was totally suited up, and it made her feel stronger.

-"So how do I look?" Calea asked with a smirk remembering Oraien's words to her on Nekio.

Oraien chuckled knowing exactly what game she was playing.

-"You look fine," he replied. Dr. Larenis smiled as she observed the chemistry between her guests before she continued.

-"Vito and Vita, unlike the typical weapons of today, will never run out of ammo, and the six revolving barrels will provide you with continuous fire. Here are two more guns. These two are called Gld-01 and Krd-02. Those are their model names on the account of me not having gotten around to naming them yet. The Gld-01 will provide you with laser missile fire, and the Krd-02 will be your heavy energy shooter. Calea... you can thank your mom for the guns, it was her study of the Demitians that allowed for the technology put into them." Calea hesitated to ask but her curiosity overpowered, and she began to ask questions.

-"My mother... how did she, how did she die?" The flare in Dr. Larenis's eyes faded, and her head turned away from Calea. Calea instantly knew that she did not want to force it upon her, "It's okay, doctor. I will find out some day," Calea said approaching her and affirming her that they could continue with the mission. Dr.

Larenis turned back to Calea with eyes of hope and handed the last of the guns over to her. "Amazing," Calea said as she griped one of her revolvers. When she held it to aim, the barrels began spinning rapidly.

-"Now, to answer your questions since I'm sure you don't have much time," Dr. Larenis started, "As I said before, the ELX is the reason you were sent here. Your father's reason for not explaining the situation then is because according to Anekie society, your mother and I died seventeen years ago." Both Oraien and Calea's faces dropped.

-"Back then we worked on the prototype ELX, and when I presented it before the Council, it had a few problems. They deemed it as an immoral experiment and cut the funding," She paused for a moment looking at Oraien then continued. "The rest of the story, I promised your father I would not tell. But the material was finished. The reason it did not respond to me in the presentation was because it would only respond to your mother's DNA. When we made it, we revived a part of Demitian technology that only allows the first person that touches it to wear it until it is destroyed. Kind of like babies, you know, the first thing they see they think it's their mother. Anyway, now the suit will only work for you because you have her DNA, and that is the reason the Nekio council found it to be immoral; anyone other than your mother who put it on was killed by the suit."

-"Immoral? My mother?" Calea finally understood how Oraien felt. He had so many things happen to him so fast, it changed his world in a matter of days. Now the same thing was happening to her, and it was hard even for her to hear such secrets about her parents. She let all the many questions stay at bay and asked a less depth probing question, "So what can it do?"

-"The suit works on an atomic level. Each atom of the suit in constructed to work together like a... like one organ or, you could go as far to say, mechanical organism. I constructed each atom and have come to call them egotoms. They work only when they touch a certain type of DNA makeup. Calea, in this case, the ELX will only work for you. When they start to work they have extraordinary abilities. They line your feet to make you jump higher when you're in the process of jumping because it detects your brain waves. The material would also allow you to climb walls on occasion as well. It multiplies your strength when needed, and it can even sustain you in space as a space suit. Your dad wanted you to have them for protection. Oh, and I still haven't discovered all the secrets of the ELX myself. You will be the only one able to bring out the true potential of the ELX, Calea."

-*I see, so this... material is what my father meant by giving me a second chance. I guess he thinks this will make me stronger.* Calea realized. Oraien turned around and looked at the display area the outfit was held. He was confused and curious as always.

-"I know I ask a lot of questions, but, what is this place, and how has it been hidden from everyone for so long? Why do you look so young?" After Oraien finished his barrage of questions, Calea looked at him wondering why he always has to ask so many questions. She also felt that she could slap him for the last question as she thought it to be rude.

-"It's quite alright Calea. I like his inquisitive mind," Dr. Larenis said as she began walking towards the door. "Cratera is a research facility first established two hundred years ago, by a persecuted group of scientists from the planet Xegus. You see, they were just like the rest of us here who have been used or tricked by the government they worked for. Fearing that they would be used to create unimaginable weapons, the founders built a safe haven here, mainly because the deep crevice we reside in hides a great deal of the energy the city gives off. After they settled on a location, they spread the coordinates throughout the Great Ring to scientists of all worlds in the form of a code. Anyone able to decipher the code would then have access to the coordinates and granted safe passage into Cratera,"

-"Wow, that's a lot of security just for coordinates," Oraien spoke.

-"Yeah," Calea said in agreement.

-"Well, the coordinates as I said before, allow the person seeking refuge safe passage. They send out a signal through the traveler's vessel that allows them to pass through the energy field. There's nothing worse than being blown up by an invisible barrier."

-"Invisible barrier?" said Calea.

-"Yes, it's set up around this facility. I'm sure the guards were startled to see your ship, creeping above the city." She paused turning around to face Oraien and Calea with a serious expression. "Major planetary governments to this day have never had access to the whereabouts of Cratera. You see, the second and most important line of defense the 'founders' took into accountability was the scientists themselves. This place only survives as long as the scientists who want a home away from home ensures and maintains its secrecy."

-"You have nothing to worry about, Ms. Larenis. We won't tell anyone of this place." Calea said anticipating that was what the scientist's last statement was regarding. Oraien nodded his head to signify that he too would keep Cratera a secret.

-"Wow, so all of these scientists are from different planets?" Oraien asked.

-"Yes," Dr. Larenis said pointing to the open lab rooms as they passed through the halls. "Miru, over there is from the planet Ardesco," looking to her right she continued, "Calba, the woman inside that room there is from the planet Calabim, and down the hall there, that's He'gin, from the planet Ckushon."

The conversation was interesting, and at the end of it all, they ended up at port C7. Neither Oraien nor Calea realized they were subconsciously following the scientist as she explained everything to them while simultaneously leading them back to their ship. They understood this was a secret haven for people that needed to go into hiding.

Dr. Larenis continued, "Your father is a good man; you tell him if there is anything else he needs for me to do, to just let me know."

-"I will, thank you. I will make sure to try to clear your name," Calea replied, "Oh! I should have asked before, but, what should I do when I want to wear short sleeve clothing?" Calea asked right before the ship's door sealed shut.

-"It will read your brain waves." Dr. Larenis said loud enough for Calea to hear it over their distance. "When you want it to turn to short sleeves—it will morph itself as you desire. Bye Calea, you two take care of yourselves." Calea looked at Oraien, and then proceeded into the ship with him.

Oraien and Calea took off into space once again together. An hour into the flight, Calea noticed that Oraien was very tired. She approached him but held herself back because she began to feel warm again. This time Calea wanted to comfort Oraien the same way that he comforted her. Oraien was sitting in the pilot seat examining a holographic map of the quadrant. Calea came from behind the seat and placed her hands gently on his shoulders. She expected him to jump, and even her own stomach jumped from touching him. However, Oraien did not even feel her contact. Calea began to massage Oraien, and it was then that Oraien jumped, he slightly turned his head and then put his focus back onto the map.

-*My life... my life... can it possibly change anymore? Can anything else happen to me that will turn my world inside out?* He looked out the left window into space and sighed. *Funny thing is, I have not had the time to sit and absorb it all yet. I have not been able to talk to anyone about it either.*

-"Oraien," Calea said gently, breaking his train of thought. "I know you want to stay up and make sure we arrive safely, especially because I'm onboard, but," she continued to caress his shoulders. "You can't kill yourself, you have to sleep." Oraien dropped his focus of the map and shivered slightly.

-"Oraien, just do me this favor. Get in bed; Ferra will make it easy for you to have a good rest. If you still want to talk we will have plenty of time. Oh and don't even try to get around it. I'm sure I can handle this ship for a few hours on my own. Go." Oraien touched her hands, and it sent surges of butterflies through Calea.

-"Thanks, Calea," Oraien did not have a problem falling asleep. He did it rather quickly. Once he was asleep Calea began to slightly hum to herself and the hours passed peacefully. The soothing ambiance of Ferra took its toll on her as well, and she too fell asleep.

Calea woke first. She went to the back of the ship to see if Oraien had yet woken up, but he was still peacefully sleeping. At that moment, her feelings were not so hard to fight off since Oraien was asleep. She got closer to his face and said,

-"Wake up you lazy bum!" Oraien impulsively grabbed Calea in a subduing position, as if she was an enemy. The closeness made Calea blush like never before. She pushed him off and fell to the ground in front of him and began to laugh.

-"Why did you scare me like that!? You're the one that told me to sleep in the first place!" He proclaimed. Calea was laughing so hard she could not hold it back any longer. "What is so funny?"

"You're such a scaredy pants, to think you saved me all by yourself. Yeah you've grown, but still," she said while she giggled. While Calea was laughing, Oraien just sat and watched. This was the first time he had seen her laugh so hard. He was looking at her with a smirk across his face, happy to see that she was happy and waited until she finished shedding tears of laughter.

"I did it all alone, and I did it for you," he said moving closer to her. His comment surprised Calea. Her first response would have been to tackle Oraien and begin wrestling him till she had his arm at breaking point, but she just opened her eyes and allowed her feelings for him to flow freely.

Oraien at that point noticed that her eyes shot open, and there they were. Calea was sitting on the floor, and Oraien was sitting in front of her. Calea wanted Oraien to say something; her feelings were getting stronger and stronger. Her face slowly flushed, and the more they looked at each other, the harder it was for her to look at him. Oraien could feel himself moving closer to her. He wanted to talk to the Calea that saved him and the Calea that he saved, and this was her; but she would not say a word. He looked at her and began to blush at the beauty her false attitude covered. Ferra began to give off a soft beeping that called Oraien for his attention.

-"You should go check that," Calea said sitting still. Oraien reluctantly pulled away and examined the screen.

-"Ferra, you're killing me with all the beeping," Oraien whispered to himself.

Chapter 8

Ones Impact

In the distance, they were quickly approaching the majestic planet of Igni'ice. It was a planet unlike any other in the great star system. The eastern hemisphere was known for its volcanic eruptions, hot surface, and fiery atmosphere; the western hemisphere was completely frozen, covered by mountain chains easily visible from space, seemingly dead from the outside looking in. Down the center of the planet, there was a massive ring of energy that was apparently separating the two extremes from one another, bringing balance to the planet. Over the intercom they could hear orders to identify themselves from the Igni'ice defense force. Oraien notified them of his orders from Retsum to travel to the planet to aid their troops. After being granted permission to enter into the planet, they traveled to the fireside of Igni'ice to backup the ground army and drive the invading Niphiliem out.

As they made their way through the atmosphere, they could see the ferocious battle being fought on the surface. The surface was an ocean of magma with many islands of rock. It was there in the open spaces that the battle was taking place between the Alliance, and the monsters bent on domination. They landed along with many other alliance battle ships and prepared themselves for battle, as Oraien wasted no time transforming into Ioxus.

-"I'll make those monsters pay for what they did to me," yelled an angry Calea. As her heartbeat rose, coupled with her continuous thoughts about entering into battle, the ELX began to slowly expand up to her neck and proceeded to cover her face. The motion of her new suit took her by surprise, but she calmed down once she realized that everything was ok. She noticed that her vision through the ELX was no longer normal but more like a mechanical sensor. She looked at Ioxus and was stunned by what she saw.

-"Rai, you're glowing. It's like you're radiating power."

-"You're one to talk. I wish you could see the kind of energy the ELX is giving off right now,"

Oraien responded as he focused once more. "Stay close to me," Oraien said as he opened the spacecraft's doors. "And yes, they will pay!" He said with a smirk on his face reassuring Calea. Turning his attention back to the matter at hand, he focused his energy and covered his face by completing his transformation. Once they landed on the surface of the planet they could hear the ferocious battle waging in the distance. One Igni'ice troop roared to the others,

-"We must defend Evalesco!"

    Both he and Calea ran towards the center of action. Oraien fought as he always fought, without holding back and without mercy. Calea used Oraien's protection to make her way through the roaring masses of Niphiliem. She and Ioxus fought with their backs to one another continuously rotating. Oraien used Exus to slash through the oncoming enemies while Calea used her two revolvers: Vita and Vito. With the help of the ELX, Calea manage to keep up with the regular pace of Ioxus. The ELX heightened her senses, and the speed at which the two were rotating, allowed her to see the battle just as Ioxus saw it; slightly slowed down. When Oraien would slice through an enemy, she followed by shooting through the spraying blood of his victim to take out the unsuspecting soldier behind. The shots emitted from her guns were so powerful that the energy bullets passed not only through the armor of the Niphiliem she was aiming for but through the soldier directly behind, many times killing three soldiers at once. The scene of the battle quickly became a blur of slashes, bullets and falling bodies as blood was splashing everywhere.

As the two warriors paused to coordinate their next attack, across the field they heard the cries of a small regiment of Igni'ice forces being overrun with no sign of back up coming their way. Oraien nodded to Calea, signaling her to go and help them while he handled things in his area. Not wanting to let the Niphiliem know of their plans to aid their allies, they continued to cover each other's backs until Calea quickly broke formation. Ioxus lowered his body and held his position for a few seconds to allow Calea to jump off of his back and into the open field. Once she was airborne, she opened fire on the Niphiliem from above, severely reducing the troops surrounding Ioxus. Once Calea began her descent, she used her downward momentum to enter into a succession of front flips. By placing her hands in front and behind her body while holding the triggers on her new weapons, Calea was able to shoot enemies in both directions to clear the path in front of her. Looking up to see if Calea was ok, Oraien was amazed to find her tucked in a ball whirling through the air, continuing to cause heavy damage.

As Calea hit the ground, she continued running in one fluid motion. She placed her guns back in their harness and pulled out the Gld-01 and shot a highflying curving energy missile towards a group of Niphiliem trying to advance in the distance to her right; causing a large explosion on impact. The explosion alerted the Niphiliem in front of Calea, and they redirected their attention towards her. The oncoming enemies fired their weapons at her, but it was to no avail. Calea was running fast enough to dodge them and kept moving forward. In an acrobatic display of agility, Calea ran into the Niphiliem troops, charging towards them across the searing surface of Evalesco. She did a backwards summersault and dove into the ranks of the Niphiliem that were overrunning the small battalion of Igni'ice forces. As she was upside down in the middle of her flip, she quickly pulled out her two revolvers and fired into the faces of two Niphiliem at point blank range, killing them along with a couple of soldiers that were directly behind them. She hit the ground and went on to do a few handsprings before jumping into a full back flip in the open space provided by the fearful soldiers who were backing away.

As one tried to decapitate her with a energy axe while she was upside down, she place her left hand on the Niphiliem's swinging arm and used it as leverage to push her body upward to complete the flip. On her way down, she fired to her right and twisted her body at the same time to fire upon the Niphiliem in a complete circle. The force of which she pushed off of the now fallen Niphiliem soldier allowed her to land next to the Igni'ice troops who were in the center of the invaders.

-"Down!" she said in a commanding tone.

As soon as the allied troops hit the ground, she unleashed a furious barrage of attacks on the Invading Niphiliem. Holding her arms out in front her, she used Vito to fire infinitely and the Gld-01 to provide missile fire. Any of the Niphiliem that somehow managed to escape the Gld-01's large explosive range undoubtedly moved into the path of Vito's fire. She decimated their numbers with the combination of weapons. The Niphiliem troops were being blasted around and shot at with no mercy until none were left standing in the immediate vicinity. In the heat of battle, Calea did not realize that a single Niphiliem soldier ducked when she told the allied forces to do the same. With her left hand, she calmly reached for the Krd-02 and placed Vito back in its harness. The wounded Niphiliem stumbled to his feet and immediately began running towards the Calea. Standing firm, Calea stretched out her arm and took aim at the charging soldier.

-"You purple Duro, look at what you've done! I'll kill you!" the soldier screamed out as he increased his speed and jumped into the air.

Once the Niphiliem soldier was in range to strike her with his weapon, she opened fire with the Krd-02. The shot blasted through the soldier, and his body disintegrated into the purple energy he was hit with. The allied forces couldn't believe their eyes after watching Calea single handedly wiped out hundreds of Niphiliem in such a short amount of time.

-"She is on our side right?" one soldier said to another.

After making sure the soldiers were ok, she turned and began to scan the field in search of Oraien. From a distance away, Ioxus was seen as an unstoppable force. In his wake laid many bodies whose spilled blood was bubbling on the hot surface, and in the path in front of him, he flung dozens of soldiers into the hot magma and using hand to hand combat to kill them with each blow and swing. Anywhere Ioxus was, there were soldiers flying left and right, but in the distance something caught Oraien's eye. Not far from his location a similar sight could be seen, the Niphiliem were being slung around effortlessly, and once a few bodies fell to the ground, it was all too clear who was doing the damage.

    Now there was not only one center of devastation but two, and the other causing Nibiru massive losses was a figure covered in similar armor as Ioxus. Although they were different, he too, had markings on his armor that lead Oraien to one conclusion; that he too, was a Xextrum. Being preoccupied with fighting many of the enemy forces at once, the mystery Xextrum failed to see one of the fighter aircrafts ready to strike him from behind. Using Exus, Oraien threw the sword like a spear towards the ship. The sword pierced straight through the craft causing it to explode before it landed the attack on the unsuspecting Xextrum. Ioxus proceeded to extend his hand outward to his side to call his sword using charged particles in the palm of his hand as a powerful magnet. Exus flew through the air in a large parabolic course back into his hand leaving behind many more destroyed ships. Turning around in the aftermath of the commotion caused by Ioxus, the unknown Xextrum made his way over to him to communicate.

-"I don't remember asking for your help just now!" he said as he ungratefully pushed past Ioxus. "I don't know who you are, but let's get one thing straight, I, Ferverous, the Xextrum of Fire do not need the help of some Xextrum wannabe with no skill." He stated as he returned to battle.

-"The name is Ioxus hothead, and if I'm not mistaken, I just saved your life. It looks to me that you're the one with no skill," he said as anger began to build within him.

Ferverous stopped in his tracks as he turned his head slightly, revealing smoke that he blew from his nostrils. Unapologetic for his words, Ioxus returned the glare with lightning being emitted from the eyes of his Xextrum. Feeling that things were about to get out of hand, Calea stood between them declaring that this was not the time or place. Maintaining eye contact with Oraien and her position between the two Xextrum, Calea pulled out the Gld-01 and shot a laser missile into a group of advancing Niphiliem, creating a large explosion. Calea's demonstration that the fight was not over prompted them to redirect their focus into defeating the last of the now retreating Niphiliem forces. Leaving the few remaining fleeing troops to the airships above them, both Ioxus and Ferverous stood with their weapons still drawn staring at each other from opposite ends of the battlefield.

-"Rai, let's go," Calea said as Oraien and the mysterious Xextrum reverted back to normal. "The Igni'ice forces have invited us to meet with their leaders," she pulled Oraien by the arm towards the rest of the Allied troops.

-"This way," another group of soldiers yelled out.

They led Oraien, Calea, and the Anekie soldiers to the base of the nearest volcano. Oraien looked back to see if he could catch one last look at Ferverous, but by the time he looked back, the warrior had already left the battle field and had regrouped with his comrades who were loosely following the group towards the volcano. All that remained were the corpses of fallen Nibiru warriors, their bodies now subject to the harsh environment of Evalesco, the eastern hemisphere of Igni'ice.

-"What about the bodies that are still on the field?" Calea asked one of the Igni'ice soldier.

-"Do not worry about them. None of them will be there in a few hours. That may seem cold since we have to leave our dead behind as well, but to become one with Evalesco is something that we Calfieren are proud of. Any of us would gladly make that sacrifice if needed," the soldier said.

-"Then what about all the ships?" Calea followed. "Rai, what about Ferra?" she continued.

-"Don't worry about Ferra. I sent her to orbit the planet in stealth mode once we exited for battle. Right now, I'm the only person that knows where she is," Oraien answered.

The troops led them across a bridge of dirt and rock towards a gigantic volcano. They walked side by side as the two of them gazed at their surroundings while continuous volcanic eruptions occurred in the distance.

-"It's actually quite beautiful to look at," Calea said as she continued looking at the many minor eruptions. The setting of their star, Antares, made it all the more beautiful.

The leading soldier continued on a path that allowed them to approach the mountain from behind while the lava it spewed flowed along its southern side. As the group was nearing the targeted volcano, Calea became frightened at the sight of an eruption very close to them. She began to subconsciously move closer to Oraien;

-"I thought it was beautiful," he said alerting Calea of their closeness.

-"From a distance, yeah, it is," she said as she blushed and folded her arms in a pouting like manner.

-"You have nothing to worry about," a soldier said. "We have been using this entrance for ages."

At the base of the unstable mountain, they continued to walk into the darkness of a nearby cave. They walked along the wall to make sure they were following each other and to prevent from getting lost. After some time, a small light could be seen at the end of the cave. It was bright red, and it reminded Oraien of Antares. Reaching the light, they noticed that their bodies felt different somehow, as if they were no longer bound to the gravity of the surface. Even though their feet touched the ground when they walked, they felt as if they were walking on air instead. The two of them stood by as they watched the troops by the masses jump down a tunnel and disappear from sight.

-"As I told you before, we have been using this entrance for ages. Now hurry, the elders are waiting for you," said Jinla, the soldier that guided the two.

With reassurance from the guide, Oraien leapt into the tunnel with Calea following suit. They allowed their bodies to float downward towards the other side head first, following the actions of the Igni'ice forces. Ferverous jumped in a few groups behind Oraien and Calea and looked down to see Oraien uneasy about his new experience and smiled. Oraien then looked up to see Ferverous following with his hands in his pockets, completely calm as if he had made the trip a million times before.

After eye contact was made between the two, they each turned away. The bright tunnel continued to lead the group deep into the planet, and at the end of the freefall journey, gravity at the end of the passageway began to push against each person, slowing the speed of their decent. Once they were nearing the exit of the massive shaft, an underground air current carried their bodies forward out of the hole and the new gravity took full effect on their bodies. One after another the soldiers emerged from a large hole in the ground. Around the opening, the ground was decorated with arrows that pointed outwards, signifying that the shaft they jumped through was an entrance. Oraien and Calea both realized that although they were upside down according to how they entered into the tunnel, they were now standing right side up. Immediately everyone began to proceed forward, and when they walked to the edge of a large stairwell, they finally saw what Jinla was referring to the tunnel as an entrance to; an underground city that lay against the insole of the planet. While they looked around in awe, the soldiers walked normally. Neither Oraien nor Calea could bring themselves to say a word to describe what was before them: the fire city of Evalesco, Novalis.

Chapter 9

Calfieren Capital

-"How is this possible?" Oraien asked himself. Calea looked at him as he took the words right out of her mouth.

The sky of Novalis was a clear red, but Oraien could not bring himself to think of it as a sky because they were in reality, underground. It felt bizarre to Oraien, but the sheer size of the massive city made it bearable. Calea was not bothered at all at the sight of the underground world; because it actually excited her to know that such a place could exist. Looking around, Oraien could see many flying creatures and many land animals as well. While Oraien was looking skyward, he noticed a figure that looked like a small Antares, but the more looked at it, the more he realized that he could sense its power; it was the Novalis-Quarton. The group continued forward as more and more of the landscape became visible. Mountains, lakes, and many grass valleys, all upside down underground. After walking down the stairwell, they entered Novalis, and Jinla began to speak.

-"Long ago, the ancients manipulated the energy of our Quarton to provide a suitable environment for us since the surface proved to be too hostile," Jinla said. "The Quarton hollowed out the ground under the surface to create a massive area the size of a small moon.

-"But why don't we...." Oraien started.

-"Yes, why don't we fall towards the Quarton, right?" Jinla interrupted with a smile. "The gravity from the surface is, as you would put, naturally generated by the planet itself."

-"So wouldn't the surface fall into this concave area?" Oraien asked.

-"Well, that's what makes Novalis so special. The Quarton here generates particles that travel along the interior walls of the planet's crust to cancel out the natural gravitational pull of the surface. So in other words, our Quarton creates an artificial gravity that binds us to the city even though we are upside down. That's why we sped thought the tunnel entrance when we jumped from the surface, but slowed down once we neared the exit towards Novalis." Jinla looked back to Ferverous and signaled him to come up to their group. After Ferverous made his way to their position, he continued to walk at Jinla's side. "The elders request an immediate audience with you Ferverous as well as the guests sent here by the Anekie Council. Please lead them there."

-"Yeah, yeah, I know," Ferverous reluctantly replied. He immediately started in the direction of a very large building not too far away from their current position. About half way to the building Oraien asked,

-"So I know your Xextrum's name is Ferverous, but can I ask what your real name is?" The warrior looked at Oraien and looked away towards their destination without breaking stride..

Making their way to the large edifice, the tension was still in the air as Oraien, Calea and the unnamed warrior walked in silence. Coming upon the building they noticed two massive doors. The doors began to open automatically when Ferverous touched the right door. Inside of the temple-like structure were very large dim lit halls that seemed to go on without end. Undoubtedly, any outsider would get lost without the help of someone leading them to their destination. After walking for a short while, they came to an open room with dark figures surrounding them sitting in front of flames that lined the wall in the background.

-"Greetings comrades, we appreciate all that you have done to aid us with the Niphiliem," one man spoke. "I see that you have already met Azrun, the Xextrum of Fire," he said with high esteem. "What are your names young warriors?"

-"My name is Oraien Zeal, but the allied forces know me better as Ioxus, the Xextrum of Lightning," Oraien stated.

-"Ioxus, the fifth Xextrum has finally emerged? Now the E.Q.O.D.A. once again has the five guardians," the leader stated as he turned to Calea awaiting her response.

-"I am Calea Loyl, daughter of General Kilm Loyl of the Anekie offensive division," she followed.

-"I don't mean to be too forward, but time is a luxury none of us can afford since we never know when the Niphiliem will strike again. When I received a mission briefing from

Retsum telling me to come here, he mentioned something about a Fire Core that could aid my abilities. Do you know what it is that he spoke of?" Oraien asked with the utmost of respect. The room fell silent as the other elders began to look at their counter parts, even Azrun looked at Oraien with a puzzled look on his face.

-"Elder, you can't seriously be considering just letting him go there?" Azrun yelled out in anger and confusion. "It took me many years to be deemed worthy, and I am the *Xextrum of Fire*!"

-"Yes, Azrun but desperate times call for desperate measures. We simply don't have the time to conduct the long ceremonial process."

-"What about our traditions? Whatever happened to earning the right to stand before our Quarton?" Azrun protested.

-"Then we must strike a balance," one other figure proclaimed. "Because we do not have that kind of time, and his power like yours is a valuable asset to the EQODA," he said as he searched for a solution. "Maltoris, you should have a solution to this matter," he said looking towards his left,

-"Yes, and it should please Azrun and perhaps Oraien as well," Maltoris, the head member of the Novalis Conflagration. "Instead of us making this decision, why not let the young ones decide through a challenge of our choice? Let us allow Azrun to challenge Oraien to decide if he may go or not." Soon the others began to nod in approval of the suggestion. Oraien smiled at the prospect of challenging Azrun, remembering their short conversation back on the surface.

-"Now that sounds like a plan to me!" Azrun stated with excitement. "What kind of challenge did you have in mind, Elder?" he said eagerly awaiting his response.

-"Combat, of course," Maltoris said smiling. "Held at the surface training grounds at dawn tomorrow. How does that fair with you Oraien?" he asked.

-"Fine by me," Oraien stated as he and Azrun looked each other, both fully satisfied with the outcome of the situation.

-"This should prove to be very interesting. It's not every day that you see two Xextrum dueling," Maltoris said as he sat back in his seat folding his arms. Azrun then walked out of the meeting room and disappeared into the city. Oraien and Calea then proceeded to the court entrance. "Make sure to alert the rest of the Alliance of the battle." Maltoris spoke.

-"So," Oraien looked at Calea in confusion. "What now?" Calea looked at him with her hands holding her hair in the wind,

-"My brother has sent two guides. They should be here by now." Calea was fixing her hair. Even though it was short, she managed to have a hair clip in her hair.

-"How do you know that there are people coming to meet us?"

-"My brother gave me this mobile I.D.C. so he could keep in contact with me, but it only works in cruisers and planets due to the need of a relay tower. When we arrived at this planet, I received endless messages from countless people because they all expected me sooner. And thanks to you, I made it here. So to answer your question, he sent me a message that two of my peers are on their way." She removed the pin from her hair to fix it due to the wind blowing it into chaos. "Can you hold my hair clip?" she said as she handed him the clip.

-"So it was your brother, Caileb, that gave it to you?"

-"Yes, Caileb, do I have any other brothers?" She then looked away from him.

-"I'm not stupid; I know he's your brother. It's just that I haven't seen him in a while. I swear you have a smart answer for everything." Oraien said.

-"Calea!" a person down the long stretching stairway yelled. "Hey! Over here!"

-"There they are Rai. Let's go." Approaching the two guides, Calea's heart skipped a beat when she fully saw the male leader. When they met, the female guide bowed her head as a sign of welcome, whereas the male guide who barely slowed down from running towards her proceeded to wrap her in his arms. The sudden display of affection caught Oraien off guard as he stood in silence unsure of what to do or say.

-"Lok, I'm ok," Calea said softly trying to push away from him, afraid of the look on Oraien's face. When they finally separated, Calea was unsure of what to do and could only look down as she stood between Oraien and Lok.

-"I am so happy you are ok, Calea. I missed you so much. You have no idea how worried I was when I found out that your ship went down. What happened? How did you end up here?" Lok said. Oraien watched as Lok talked to her staring into her eyes warmly. Lok was completely focused on Calea and did not even notice Oraien.

-"Our ship was destroyed by a Niphiliem base, but I'm ok now," Calea said.

-"No, you're not. Look at this bruise you have on your forearm." he gently grabbed her arm and examined the bruise. "Oh see. We have to hurry and get you to a place so you can rest."

-"Hey Lok. I'm ok, seriously."

-"It's good to see you again," the female soldier interrupted.

Oraien examined the two and saw that the female guide was a little on the heavy side. She had a cute face and appeared to be very healthy. She had a comforting smile and her aura almost made her Oraien's friend at first sight. Lok however, was very intimidating to Oraien; mostly over the fact that he held Calea for so long, but his height was also a factor. Lok was easily four or five inches taller than Oraien, and he appeared much more muscular. He wore fitted clothing and wore his metals on his shoulder to broadcast them to everyone.

-"Look at you Kisca, you look great," Calea replied.

-"Hey Calea, who is this gentleman with you?" Kisca asked. Calea's heart skipped another beat as she noticed that Oraien was still standing there.

-"Oh, him?" Those words acknowledged that Calea had forgotten about Oraien, and he received a murderous blow to his pride. Oraien slightly let his head down but tried not to let it affect him too much. "This is Oraien."

-"Oh wait, I remember you. You were the injured guy from Luna right?

-"Yeah, I remember him too," Lok added. "Sorry man. I didn't even see you standing there." He continued. Lok proceeded to walk up to Oraien in an intimidating fashion and extended his hand for Oraien to shake. The two shook hands, and Lok formally introduced himself.

-"Hi, I'm Lok, Anekie Military squadron C."

-"Oh, so you guys know each from Nekio since you were both soldiers," Oraien said hoping that was the only way they knew each other.

-"Yeah, that and the fact that I'm Calea's boyfriend," he said slightly jerking his head towards Calea as if to confirm his statement. At that moment Calea's eyes met Oraien's, and the two looked at each other. Although they only made eye contact for a split second, her silence confirmed Lok's statement, and Calea knew the damage had been done.

Oraien tried his hardest not to let his face show his shock, so he introduced himself the best he could,

-"Oraien," he said clearing his throat. "Zeal, Oraien Zeal, Xextrum of Lightning" he finished, fighting off his dying pride and growing anger. "So umm... how long have you two been together?

-"About five months now," Lok responded backing away and lowering his intimidating demeanor.

-"Five months, huh?" Oraien said looking at Calea with a faint smile on his face as he tried to calmly play off the situation. Calea could hardly look Oraien in the eyes knowing the full gravity of the situation.

-"Are you two here together?" Kisca asked.

-"No, what would make you think that?"

-"You two are standing pretty close to each other, and he has your hair clip, the one you never let anyone touch," Kisca added. The mention of her hairpin made her realize that Oraien was still holding it so she took the hairpin from Oraien and put her hair up.

-"Actually, it was Oraien that saved me from the Niphiliem base and brought me here, that's all," Calea said with an uneasy look on her face walking away from Oraien and towards Kisca and Lok. Kisca stood silently as she observed Calea's body language and knew that the situation was bothering her.

-"O...k," Kisca replied eyeing Calea suspiciously as she began walking past her and over to Oraien.

-"Oraien, I have this for you. It's from Caileb. Use it at any inn, and you can sleep for the night. Tomorrow morning, Caileb will arrive here in Novalis," Kisca said.

-"Thanks, well I'm going to go ahead and get ready for tomorrow, see you later," Oraien said leaving the group standing there. Calea couldn't bring herself to say anything to Oraien as he walked in the opposite direction.

-*Wow, I never saw that one coming*, Oraien thought to himself, staring down at one of the many staircases that led into the city. Calea looked back only to see Oraien's figure disappear as he descended down the staircase. She wanted to tell him goodbye and thank you but missed her chance. Soon, she found herself caught up in yet another conversation with Lok as they continued walking.

Oraien took off into the city alone, soon forgetting the unexpected encounter with Lok. The diverse city in front of him helped him forget, so he marveled at the construction of the city; each building flowed into the grown like mountains and hills. The taller sky-reaching buildings also had the same pattern and reminded Oraien of stalagmites of the Eluesian caves, only they were made of rock and metal and were massive in comparison. Oraien walked through the city for hours until he finally decided to find a place to rest. Walking a little further, he found a flower inn, and its name spoke for itself. The buildings were massive trees positioned in a triangle to support its tenants. The base held lobbies and elevators and the tips of each tree's branches were connecting the trees together, creating tiers of triangular open spaces that reached the top floor. Along each of the non-connected branches were the residential rooms, and each room was a giant flower blossom native to the jungles of Novalis. Inside was a flower bed and everything he needed for a nights stay. The Quarton's light drenched Oraien's room as if it was the Antares star.

    Once inside the magnificent room, he took advantage of the room's natural hot tub and allowed himself to wind down and relax. The hours passed, and a cool breeze woke him. He walked over to the window to peer at the Novalis Quarton because his room, like the rest of the city, was hardly lit. When he looked up, he saw that only the cryptic markings on the Quarton were glowing red now, giving the illusion of nighttime underground.

-*Now, that is pretty cool,* Oraien said to himself.

His mind wandered. He tried his best to mentally prepare himself for his battle the following morning, but he could not stop thinking about Calea. Even though he found out that she had a boyfriend; he thought of the real kind-hearted side of her. That night after Oraien went to bed once more, he noticed that he actually grew to like Calea. Thinking of her made him feel better and being with her made his new life bearable. Time slipped away, and sleep took Oraien away as the night went by with him wondering, *where is she?*

"-Ok, now that Lok has finally left, tell me what that was all about earlier," Kisca said sitting down on the foot of Calea's bed.

-"What do you mean, what happened earlier?" Calea replied leaning back on her pillow, tucking her legs up under her and folding her arms.

"Don't play dumb, you know exactly what I mean. I saw you. What was with your whole demeanor while Lok was talking to Oraien?" Kisca squinted her eyes devilishly at Calea as she continued to interrogate, "What exactly happened between you two on the way here?"

"Nothing," she said placing her hair behind her ear.

"Well it didn't look like 'nothing'," Kisca said backing off the question. "Something seems to be bothering you," Kisca added.

-"It's just that...." She paused and took a deep breath.

- "Calea," Kisca said moving a little bit closer to her, "You can talk to me."

-"It's just that I don't want Oraien to be mad at me," Calea said with a sad look on her face. Fearing that Calea would draw back into her shell, Kisca didn't ask the most obvious question of what Oraien could be mad at her about. Instead she decided to choose another route.

-"Lok gets mad at you all the time, and it doesn't even seem like you care, ever." Kisca responded.

-"It's different with Rai, even though I say crazy things to him all the time. I know he never really gets mad because he's too busy thinking about how to get me back," Calea said.

-"So why do you care when it's Oraien that is mad at you, but you don't when it's Lok and he's your boyfriend. I mean, how do you feel about Oraien?

-"I don't know how I feel. It's hard to explain, but Rai makes me feel different. Don't get me wrong. Lok is wonderful and caring. He has his good points, but it's just not the same with Rai. I don't have to pretend or put up this false persona..." Calea's words were interrupted by a beep. It was from Kisca's MICE informing her she had a message. She paused and read the message.

-"It looks like the commander wants to see me. Before I leave though, I want you to think about what you just said. You seem content to be with Lok and all, but you definitely don't seem happy knowing that Oraien could be mad at you. There is a big difference between the two."

With that last bit of advice, Kisca left the room letting Calea wander in her thoughts. Once the door closed, Calea collapsed into her pillow, burying her face into the soft material, completely unsure of her feelings for Oraien or what she should do.

Chapter 9.5

Blue Light vs. Red Fire

The previous day, Calea was separated from Oraien when Kisca and Lok escorted her to a room on a top floor of a lofty inn building. She woke up in a hotel room reserved for her by her brother, Caileb. Caileb was far away on the Moon Base orbiting Igni'ice. He was making preparations to travel to Evalesco as fast as possible to see his sister, and in the process, he heard of the fight that would begin in the morning between Ioxus and Ferverous. Word of the epic battle had spread throughout the quadrant all the way back to Nekio, and Oraien's home planet, Luna, where after suddenly being thrown into the harshness of war, he was now championed by the Eluesian's as a symbol of hope, much like the other Xextrum were for their people. The entire Alliance would be tuned in eagerly awaiting to see the abilities of the two young Xextrum.

Oraien woke up early that morning, and he sat up and then crossed his legs and prepared his mind. Being the Xextrum way, he remembered to prepare himself for all possibilities, and like Oraien, Azrun was in his room doing the same. Both nourished themselves and came to the surface to meet one another before the showdown.

Though it was early, Novalis was alive with a bustling energy that shocked Calea as well as Kisca and Lok who had met up with her that morning outside of the inn where she had previously spent the night. The three stood in place looking at all the Calfieren rushing through the streets. Luckily, Kisca knew the layout of the city and knew the perfect place to catch some early morning food and to watch the fight on the Visual Display unit it had inside the café.

"How exactly are we watching the fight? Calea asked curiously.

"S.A.N.D. Surveillance and Networking Display. They are microscopic cameras so light that they actually float. Thousands if not millions of them are released at a time hence the name, and together they put together one collective image from every possible angle." Kisca replied pointing to the V.D.

When they arrived, they were happy to see it was not crowded yet, but one group of men at the other side of the café carried a conversation that caught Calea's ear,

-"It's to his advantage; the surface is covered in fire, lava and volcanoes. I'm telling you, with all those things in Ferverous' favor, Ioxus does not stand a chance. So just let it go, Jingoa!" one man yelled.

-"But look," he pointed at the screen. "That boy is Ioxus, and his speed is unmatched by anything but lightning itself! I'm standing firm with the Eluesian. You three can stay believing that Azrun is going to win, but you only think that because you know him," one of the three men standing together spoke.

-"You're on your own, Jingoa. You have never been known for choosing the winning side," he looked at the other two with a smile of satisfaction in his eyes. "Let's place bets!" Jingoa was the only one of the four friends that stayed on Oraien's side, and Calea smiled in her heart for Oraien,

-*You already got a fan, Rai. It's good that this planet's people can have some fun for a change.* She looked into the V.D and saw Oraien sitting on a rock looking into space.

Oraien was looking into space at a distant object that appeared to him as a small star, Luna. The look on his face was pure and calm, but he could not hold it for long. The fourth hour of the day approached, and Antares rose from the south pole of the planet. Azrun stood to his feet as Oraien followed; they both knew the time had come, and they could almost feel the strength of the spectator's cheers through the hot ground of the planet.

Oraien and Azrun found themselves transforming into their Xextrum's against the vibrant sunrise of the fiery surface. All eyes were on them as the elders along with the rest of the allied forces watched the soon to be battlefield with great anticipation. Ferverous took a battle stance and held his right arm in front of him. Suddenly his hand began to glow fire red, and metallic chains of fire emerged from his hand. Ferverous then swiped the ground with the chain, and the fire of the chains began to burn the rock now attached to it. Slowly, as the fire spread it changed the composition of the stone into the very metal of his Xextrum, becoming a large fiery mace. Following suit, Ioxus called upon the great sword, Exus that ejected from his back and traveled to his hand before emitting its intimidating electric discharges.

Staring each other down for a short while, they lunged at each other with all might. Ferverous began swinging his Fire Mace with great accuracy forcing Ioxus to take the defensive; dodging and parrying all of the oncoming blows. Oraien realized that a direct hit from his powerful weapon would undoubtedly wound him. Finding an opening, Ioxus took the offensive creating a series of attacks that cause Ferverous to be mindful of the distance between them. Dodging attacks from one another, they began running parallel to each other with great speed, leaving the safety of the training grounds and into the hostile environment full of active volcanoes.

The cameras on the battlefield had trouble keeping up even though they traveled through the air. The battle that they captured riled the audience and excited the masses. Back at the cafe Calea, Kisca, and Lok watched with great trepidation. Lok anxiously hoped for Azrun's victory while Calea secretly wanted Oraien to come out victoriously. Kisca, on the other hand, was too excited to be on any side. Suddenly on the V.D, everyone saw Oraien deal a massive kick to Azrun's side that threw him hundreds of yards away into a volcanic slope.

-"Ah! See!" Jingoa roared. "Did I not tell you Ioxus' speed would come out on top!" the other three paid no attention to Jingoa because Azrun had emerged from the magma unscratched.

-"You were saying?" said one of the other men. "If you bet on Ioxus, then you're going to lose your money."

-"I'll take that bet!" The four men, Calea, Kisca, and Lok looked towards the person who had just entered the lobby with the announcement, Caileb. "Put my money on Ioxus, guys," Calea ran over to Caileb and hugged him for the first time since her kidnapping. "I knew Oraien would return the favor one day," he said looking at his sister.

-"Yeah, he did," she said blushing, letting go of him before Lok and Kisca saluted him. The four men roared with enthusiasm as Azrun unleashed a furious combo upon Oraien. The exhilarating atmosphere was contagious and soon, Calea,

Caileb, Kisca, and Lok found themselves cheering and yelling just like the four guys.

Swinging his mace overhead, Ferverous began to use it to build a ring of fire. In response, Ioxus began to charge his sword preparing to release the stored up energy. Azrun brought the mace out of the circle down to the ground and sent the ring rocketing towards Oraien. Ioxus then dashed towards the left and noticed that the ring followed him, so while he was dashing, he discharged the lightning stored within Exus toward the oncoming ring of fire. In a dazzling display of power, the techniques canceled each other out as the two Xextrum's began leaping in the air, exchanging blows every time their paths intersected.

-"Why do you think you are good enough to be a Xextrum? Hopefully Luna's not blind because I cannot see any real power in you." Azrun yelled over the distance. Oraien did not know what to say but eventually figured that he should prove himself.

-"I don't know why Luna chose me either. I didn't ask for this, but I know that I will use this power to figure out the reasons," Oraien replied then shot towards Ferverous, reengaging in the battle.

-If the Council can't determine his true motives, I will! No one gets close to my home without my consent, Azrun thought to himself.

Ferverous gained the upper hand by using smoke to hinder Ioxus' sight, and he used his upward momentum from the jump to attack Oraien at full power. Ioxus was caught flinching after each heavy hit, hindering him from defending himself. Every hit made Oraien more and more disoriented, but he knew that he had to gain control of himself and the situation. So, he let the pain of each hit fade away mentally and concentrated.

Oraien had a flash of energy overwhelm him once he tapped into the atom energy around him, much of which came from Ferverous himself. He allowed just a little amount of energy to flow freely. The power briefly allowed Oraien to stiffen his body to such a degree that all of Ferverous attacks landed as if they were making contact with the Luna Quarton itself. Ioxus stood unmoved as he absorbed the brutal onslaught, alerting Azrun that he should distance himself from Oraien as he jumped high into the air. Without any warning, a bolt of lightning pierced the sky and hit Azrun simultaneously with Ioxus' devastating blow. Both forces together sent Azrun plunging through the air like a comet into an ocean of magma. Oraien landed on a small ledge that protruded from the lava not far from the collision. Ioxus gazed into the lake and saw the magma finally settle behind the downward wake caused by Azrun's impact. Oraien stood silently for a few minutes carefully observing the fiery lake. He began to drop his guard thinking that he may have won until he saw a slight wake in the lava. Something began to emerge from a beach of the red ocean, walking calmly, glowing red hot, while evenly brushing the lava off his shoulders—Ferverous.

-"Oraien, Oraien," Ferverous said turned and looked at Ioxus with eyes as red as the surface. "Surely you didn't think that would finish me, the Xextrum of Fire, don't you know I come here to cool off?" Azrun dashed towards him not giving him any chances to regroup and called upon his mace to strike him. Ioxus managed to block the attack with his sword creating a large shockwave around them. The force of Azrun's blow caused Exus to ricochet from Ioxus' hands and into the distance. Splitting apart into two segments, Exus became two swords that pierced the ground, landing not too far from each other. -*Two swords?* Oraien thought to himself. Looking at the swords, Ferverous too was thrown off by the splitting of the swords, but knew not to give Ioxus the chance to retrieve his weapons, so he quickly recommenced his attack.

Oraien needed to find a way to Exus which was now in two pieces. He came up with a plan that surprised the audience but mostly Azrun. Oraien was blocking attack after attack awaiting the right chance, and once he saw one of Ferverous' stronger attacks, Oraien allowed himself to be hit. Azrun knew that Ioxus let the hit through his defense, and Oraien suffered injury to his abdomen. Using the momentum from the attack, Oraien let out a succession of back-flips along the ground and one massive back-flip in the air towards the swords. In one fluent movement, Oraien landed pulling both swords from the ground while allowing the angle at which he hit the surface to propel him forward. Under the immense pressure of his take off, the ground crumbled. Dashing towards Azrun with two swords crossed, Oraien took notice to a slight difference in Exus,

"The flow of energy is completely different now," he said while rushing through the air.

Oraien lifted the sword in his right hand, while keeping the sword in his left hand by his side for defense. Ferverous quickly formed his fire mace and prepared for a fast paced battle. Oraien swung hard while Ferverous sidestepped to dodge and counter strike. With the sword in his left hand, Oraien blocked the attack as well as keeping the pace of the mace rotation. Again, Ioxus swung with his right, only to have Ferverous side flip above the swing and land with his counterstrike already in motion towards Oraien. Flipping while blocking the attack with the left sword, he sped up the speed of his counter to Azrun's counter. The two warriors constantly flipped and rotated while holding their ground while the only thing visible to the spectators was the sparks being emitted by their clashing weapons. The coordination of their attacks tested the very limits of their agility and reflexes.

The more Oraien used the swords separately, the more comfortable he became using both weapons simultaneously. Oraien jumped in the air and tried to strike Azrun from above. However, the fire Xextrum already anticipated such a move. Azrun swung his mace upwards with all his might in an attempt to stop the force of Oraien's downward momentum. When the two weapons made contact, it was Ferverous that sent Oraien flying backwards. Oraien's body spun sideways due to the angle at which Azrun swung. Trying to take advantage of Oraien's position in the air, Azrun swiped the ground numerous times and sent a large wave of fire projectiles headed directly for Oraien. Reacting quickly, Oraien spun his body sideways while placing the glowing swords perpendicular to his body. As he spun through the air, he used his lightning speed to slow things down and released the energy stored within both swords. As he spun, he released small but powerful bursts of lightning toward each of the oncoming projectiles. Azrun couldn't believe his eyes; Oraien perfectly timed each of his releases while spinning to cancel out his attacks before landing firmly on the ground. Before he landed, Oraien sent an extra release hurling towards Azrun to return the favor. Azrun stood unmoved and deflected the attack with his mace, sending it flying to the left. The lighting energy hit the ground and created a large explosion. The wind from the surface of Evalesco blew the debris across the field between the two Xextrum, but once the wind subsided, the two rushed toward each other again.

-"Did you see that!" roared Jingoa to the crowd as they watched the fight. Caileb stood to second the motion and back Jingoa up while they rooted for Oraien.

-"I told you, Ioxus is powerful and fast. Look at how he countered Azrun's fire missiles. You can't tell me that wasn't the coolest thing you have seen," Jingoa continued.

-"I admit that was cool, but the way Azrun sent his missiles towards Ioxus was also cool, not to mention the way he swatted down Ioxus last lightning technique as if he was swatting an annoying fly," Jingoa's friend countered.

Calea watched Oraien on the V.D. in complete awe of his fighting skills. Just watching him on the screen made her feel more secure knowing that he had protected her with the same tenacity he was now displaying before the Alliance throughout the quadrant. She was standing next to Lok and Kisca who were also drawn into the fight, but Kisca occasionally glanced over at Calea to see how she would look at Oraien on the screen. Kisca smiled when she saw how Calea was staring at the V.D. Calea's eyes were soft and she had a fixated smile across her face, completely entranced by Oraien's movements.

-I wish she could see the look on her face right now, Kisca thought to herself. *She really can't see that she's falling for him.*

    As the battle waged on, both Xextrum began to feel fatigued due to their excessive use of energy. Deciding that he had to do something quick before he completely drained his energy, Oraien waited until Feverous thought he had gained the upper hand. Combining his two swords to form the more familiar Broadsword, he released a massive discharge by slamming his sword into the ground, sending the energy surging along the surface of the planet and into Ferverous. Standing in place nearly drained of all his energy, he had to plant his sword in the ground and use it as a crutch just to remain standing. When he saw Ferverous rise off the ground, he knew that he was in serious trouble. Running full speed towards Ioxus, Ferverous balled up his fists and drew his arm back with all his might preparing to strike. Stopping just short of landing a direct hit, he spoke.

-"You may be a Xextrum wannabe, but I got to admit, you got some serious skill," Azrun said jokingly. "Permission to travel to the Fire Core, granted."

Back in the city, the elders shook their heads in agreement. Calea looked at the image of Ioxus and smiled with adoration. Jingoa and his friends roared with satisfaction as the fight had ended so perfectly.

-"Technically he did not lose, Azrun stopped the fight, see!" Jingoa said hoping that he would not have to pay his end.

-"I agree!" Caileb quickly added seeing as how he also had his money on Oraien. The five men began debating on the subject, and Calea laughed at her brother's helplessness.

-"So you like that move I pulled in the end, huh," Oraien chuckled.

"Let's head back to the city before I change my mind," Azrun laughed. "But yeah, it was pretty cool," he added as the two battered warriors began making their way back to Novalis.

Chapter 10

Journey to the Fire Core

-"Hey Azrun, you know everyone is probably going to be waiting for us in the city, and that's going to slow us down," Oraien said as he sat on a high cylindrical rock.

-"Yea, if Nibiru strikes now we're done for. Hmmm. Where can we go to avoid the crowds and recuperate?" Azrun added.

-"I have the perfect place in mind," Oraien smiled within the armor of Ioxus. He remembered that Ferra was close, orbiting the planet near their location.

- "Let's rest now," he placed Exus on the center of his back, and it locked into place like metal wings. "My ship is on her way," Oraien held his right arm up and let out a lightning bolt as Ferra's signal to his location. She landed next to the two and opened her doors to Ioxus. "Ferra, I have a guest, so be nice."

-"What do you mean be nice?" Azrun said while not moving one step. Oraien laughed and added.

-"I'm just kidding with you. Come on in," Oraien entered the ship, and Azrun slowly began to approach the doorway. Once the two entered the ship, Ferra closed the door and began to ascend into the higher atmosphere.

-"Hey! Wh-wh-what is the ship doing?!" Azrun asked panicking.

-"Cool down, Azrun," Oraien looked at him confused. "I thought you were all big and bad. Guess looks can be deceiving."

-"What's that supposed to mean?!"

-"Hey man. I didn't bring you here for no reason. My ship has a cool ability, and that's to heal people quickly," Oraien walked towards the living area on the ship and began to dial a few keys on a nearby wall display screen. Once he was finished, he stood in place and dismissed Ioxus, and with a gust of energy particles Oraien stood partially bruised and beaten. "I'm pretty positive that under Ferverous you're pretty banged up too. You have to admit that I'm not bad for a beginner."

-"I don't have to admit anything," Azrun said while dismissing Ferverous. He too had many scars and wounds from their previous battle.

-"See this bunk," Oraien pointed at the ships bed. "When you're injured and you lie down to rest, Ferra begins to produce life energy, which is the same energy that the Xextrum O'navus utilizes, to mend each wound within a matter of minutes. So, are you going to get in or what?" Both Oraien and Azrun had not rested since the highly anticipated battle, but they both knew that they needed to hurry and recover.

-"I don't think so, Rai. This thing looks cool, but it looks like it hasn't been used in centuries, literally," said Azrun. Oraien pushed Azrun into the bed and the healing process began. After the restoration was finished Azrun rose out from the shining bed. "Wow. I feel great. But Oraien," Azrun said. He connected a fist to Oraien's jaw while saying, "Don't ever push me into something I think is strange." Oraien fell to the side and he immediately got back up and began to fight with Azrun. After Oraien healed himself he piloted Ferra to the nearest entranceway and docked so they could speak before the Council.

The two troops soon returned to the center of Novalis. Shortly after arriving, they met up with Calea and Caileb who were accompanied by Lock, Kisca, and two troops from the moon base. Calea wanted to run to Oraien and hug him, but knew she couldn't as she thought back on how he had found out her relationship with Lok. Oraien approached Caileb and shook his hand firmly, and Azrun followed.

-"That was quite the battle," Caileb said as his statement was reinforced by the sudden outburst of the roaring crowd behind them. "You've grown tremendously in such a short amount of time Oraien," he said smiling. Azrun had a question that stayed in his mind from the very first time he met Oraien, and the desire to ask it became stronger and stronger each time someone would comment on Oraien's rapid progress,

- "Just how long have you been a Xextrum?" Azrun asked Oraien out of curiosity.

-"For about a little over a month," Oraien said as his attention was turned to a small Calfieren child who saw him battle neck to neck with Ferverous, so he knelt down to talk with the child face to face.

-*A month?* Azrun thought in disbelief as he watched Oraien play. *I knew he was a noob, but how is it possible for him to use such techniques effortlessly after virtually just becoming a Xextrum? Trained by Retsum or not, there is definitely something different about him.* His concentration was broken as he heard his name being called,

-"Azrun, how long have *you* been a Xextrum?" Caleb asked as Calea and the others turned their attention to him.

-"Four years," he started. "I have been fighting those monsters every since they attacked Evalesco in an attempt to access our Quarton. They were monsters then, and they are monsters now. So I make sure to repay them for everything they did to us and continue to do. Only this time I had some help," he stated looking at Oraien and Calea.

-"That's right," Calea said with pride. "I was able to test out the ELX as well as my new weapons, although Oraien accounted for more of the major damage."

-"Well don't give Oraien all the credit. I was down here destroying seventy percent of all their invading forces while the planet could only suffice for the other thirty before you guys arrived. Why do I always get the short end of the appreciation stick?" Azrun said in grief.

-"What is an ELX?" Caileb asked Calea curiously.

-"It's this purple material I'm wearing right now. It's DNA-based, so that means you can't have one!" Calea said jokingly as Caileb started chasing her to take a good look at it.

"Wow, so cool," Kisca said watching the two siblings play.

"That's not fair, how come I don't have one?" Caileb said obstinately. Turning back to Oraien, he spoke,

-"Oraien, you're making a name for yourself. The battle between the two of you was broadcasted throughout the E.Q.O.D.A, and the people of your home world were rooting for you as well." He paused before remembering to say one more thing to Oraien. "Thank you for saving my sister, by the way I have not had the chance to tell you," he said turning to face her. "Calea, when you're ready we are going to the RE2 Nekio moon base." Caileb then looked at Oraien and Azrun and continued, "Well, you two, when I got here, the Calfieren at the bar explained the reason behind the fight, so don't do anything crazy, and be safe on your journey to the Novalis-Quarton."

-"Actually, Caileb, the real name of the fire Quarton is Fuegus, the Fuegus-Quarton," corrected Azrun. "But before we head out, we need to speak to the Elders," he finished.

Caileb, Calea, and the others began their journey to the ship port to enter space and head to the nearby moon orbiting Igni'ice. The moon base was one of five E.Q.O.D.A. central hubs, and was large enough to be visible from the surface of Evalesco. Oraien and Azrun turned the opposite direction and strolled down the streets of Novalis in the direction Council Temple.

-"That was a hearty battle, young warriors," Maltoris spoke while the other Elders nodded in agreement. "If I'm not mistaken, I, along with the rest of this council, heard you give Ioxus permission to travel to the Fuegus-Quarton, correct?" he continued.

-"Yeah, as much as I don't want to admit it, he does have some skill, at least enough to possibly survive," Azrun answered.

-"Good. Then Oraien," Maltoris said raising his head, "You have the blessing of this Council on your journey to the Quarton. Of course he will need your guidance to get there, Azrun." At that very moment, Oraien felt a deep pounding feeling in his chest. The sensation took him by surprised and he had no idea what it meant or where it came from. He placed his hand on his chest and kept it there, listening silently to the Elders until the feeling subsided.

-"Two steps ahead of you," Azrun replied turning around to leave. "Let's go," Azrun stated placing his hand on Oraien's shoulder. "I have a feeling that we need to do this quickly. I'm sure you felt it, too," he said looking Oraien in the eyes. Oraien nodded his head in a confusing manner, confirming Azrun's statement. Turning quickly, Oraien bowed his head to the Council and vowed that he would make it back ok.

-"What are we going to do with that boy?" another Elder spoke in regard to Azrun's repetitive behavior whenever he was addressing the Council.

-"Leave him be," Maltoris responded. "He took the death of his parents pretty hard. He is a loner and does not interact much with his peers. He has become a rebel, but it's just his way of protecting himself. Brethren, he is a Xextrum who has been fighting for us rigorously, but let us not forget that he is still young. Yes, he is more mature than the other nineteen year olds, but we need to allow him some time so that he can mature into an adult."

-"Hey, let me ask you something," Oraien said as he boarded Ferra.

-"No," Azrun said with a smirk.

-"Why is this Quarton called the Fuegus-Quarton instead of the Evalesco or Novalis Quarton?

-"Oh, you'll find out when we get there," Azrun had a habit of leaving people empty handed, but the real goal was to make Oraien anxious.

-"Soo, can this ship really sustain the heat of our planet because we need to travel very far under the surface to reach Fuegus," asked Azrun with a concerned tone. Being the Xextrum of Fire, Ferverous could withstand any high temperature, and he knew that Oraien would perish under Igni'ice's heat. "Your Xextrum can't handle the heat, that's why I'm asking if this ship can."

-"Ferra, please display the total amount of heat you can sustain, and if it is necessary, you may include our Xextrum's energy to support your heat shield into your calculations," requested Oraien.

Ferra was silent for a few seconds. Her main screen displayed numbers and figures racing each other. Finally, Ferra came up with two calculations, one displayed the maximum heat she could endure without the Xextrum's aid, and the other displayed the calculation including their extra energy.

-"So, Azrun. Which one would be best?" Oraien asked arrogantly.

-"Whaa! She can stand that much without us! AND THAT MUCH WITH!" Azrun said with his eyes glazed and focused on the first figure. He settled down and said, "The first one is fine. We probably would only ever use the second one to enter Antares itself anyways."

So the ship took off rising above the molten plane of Igni'ice. Azrun pointed to a volcano that would be the entrance to the core. The ship took off slowly while approaching the mouth of the volcano, and then the ship dove into the magma with little turbulence. Ferra turned on her heat shield and began to use the heat from the magma to fuel the journey.

-"Man, I love this ship. I wonder what else it can do?" asked Oraien.

-"Don't touch anything Rai! Get to know her when you're not swimming in a pool of death!" said Azrun as he held Oraien's arm from pushing a button.

-"You're too tense, Azrun. Just relax. I think if you lie down in that bed, Ferra can even loosen up your muscles," said Oraien. As the two talked to one another, the ship took the corridors that lead to the core. After a few hours, Ferra finally arrived at a cave deep within Igni'ice.

-"This is it. We will have to travel on foot from here," said Azrun.

Echoes of Tempore: Revival of Light

Once they landed the ship, Oraien signaled Azrun to distance himself so that they could summon their Xextrum. They both called the Xextrum simultaneously, and in an instant stood two Xextrum side by side. Ferverous exited the ship first. Ferra closed her door, and they found themselves in complete darkness once they were both on the solid rock of the cave floor.

-"I'm not sure why, but I was expecting some light down here," Oraien said.

-"You thought the light from Antares would be all the way down here?" Azrun questioned.

-"No, not from Antares but from the lava or something," Oraien continued.

-"Well, believe it not, there are places that not even light can reach. You do know how to use your Neo-ray, right?" Azrun asked.

-"Yeah," Oraien responded.

The two Xextrum stood there and prepared to use their Neo-ray. Absorbing their surrounding into their suits, the cryptic markings on their bodies lit up. The marking on Ioxus lit up a bright blue while Ferverous markings were a dark fire red. Once the energy surge subsided, they both looked around the fully visible cave. Oraien looked on in amazement of all the life he could see along the dark and murky walls, and Azrun looked on in a nostalgic manner.

-"It's been a while since I've been here," Azrun paused. "You feel that, right?"

-"Yeah," Oraien replied. "That's the Quarton I'm sensing, right?

-"Right, so there is no time for sightseeing Rai, let's go," Azrun said dashing off.

Immediately, both of them dashed off in the direction of the Quarton. While running and jumping though countless obstacles and passages, Oraien broke the silence and asked Azrun about the Quarton again.

-"Something is telling me that I should know why it's called the Fuegus-Quarton," Oraien yelled out.

-"Good," Azrun yelled back. "You should trust that feeling. It may save your life one day, but to answer the question, there's a guardian down here. Its name is Fuegus. It is said to be a Tathios Guardian left here by the Demitians to protect the Quarton from unwanted guests," Azrun said keeping his eyes straightforward. "Turn left up ahead," he continued.

They approached a large open area. This section of the cave was almost as large as the city of Novalis but totally empty. At the far end of the massive opening was the Quarton. It radiated beautifully in the magma bed in which it resided. Oraien began to walk slowly across the underground dome, but Azrun stayed behind.

-"Aren't you coming?" asked Oraien.

-"Nope, the rest is up to you. I just came to see the show," replied Azrun.

-"The show? What are you talking about..."

An explosion on the left side of the dome shook Oraien and interrupted his speech. Oraien faced the blast and stood in a defensive stance. The explosion caused magma to flow into the cave and towards Oraien and Azrun. Remembering what Azrun said about him not being able to sustain the heat for a prolonged period of time, he jumped to the ceiling.

-"Oraien, don't run. Stand your ground," Azrun said as he jumped to a ledge near the entrance.

The magma began to slow down and drew backwards towards the Quarton, then it began to mold into the shape of a massive creature. The outer layer of magma cooled and became an exoskeleton for the fire creature that began to crack and revealed the flowing lava underneath with each movement. The joints of the creature were what appeared to be large marquise diamonds the size of an average man. Oraien let go of the roof and dropped to the floor. It took him a few seconds to reach the bottom due to its great height. He looked up and saw a large creature roar. After the creature was stable, it began its pursuit.

-"This is it!" Oraien ran toward the large monster in preparation of battle. "I guess this is him—Fuegus!" As Oraien approached Fuegus, the creature unleashed fire from his mouth towards the young warrior, and the battle began.

Oraien leaped out of the path of fire toward Fuegus and began to dash up his arm. Oraien pulled out his swords and performed a three hundred and sixty degree back flip allowing him the chance to sever Fuegus' left arm. The arm crashed into the ground, and Fuegus bellowed in pain. However, the lava within the arm melted into his feet, and Fuegus grew the arm once again.

    Oraien continued to fight Fuegus to no avail. Soon, Oraien began to think he was indestructible, so Fuegus began to close off with numerous attacks. Oraien jumped off Fuegus to a distance that allowed him to look at Fuegus, and he observed diamonds at his joints and on his forehead. Oraien combined his two swords as he did with when he fought Azrun, and leaped into battle with more determination.

    Azrun observed that Oraien had combined his swords and smiled. He was actually surprised to see that Oraien had such a determined mindset while fighting a creature of Fuegus size and strength. He enjoyed watching the intense battle but also wanted to join in. He found himself wanting to blurt out hints and often throwing his hands up out of frustration from Oraien's mistakes. While holding his head down in disappointment, a ground-shaking blow to Oraien caught his attention. By the time he looked up, the only thing he could see was Fuegus' arm extended and Oraien who was speedily crashing along the ground, bouncing along the surface like a rock against a body of water. With a thunderous cry, Ioxus slammed into a wall on the other side of the cave, causing major damage to its structure.

-"Ouch! That had to hurt," Azrun said. After a few minutes went by, there was no sign of Oraien. The only thing interrupting the silence between Azrun and the pile of settled rocks on top of Oraien was the howls coming from Fuegus that filled the cave. Azrun paused, refusing to believe that such a thing could keep a Xextrum down. He raised his head and folded his arms in a manner that silently demanded Oraien to rise. The rocks shifted, and Azrun slightly relaxed.

-"Hmph," Azrun said watching Oraien emerge from tons of rubble, his eyes more determined than ever. Oraien broke through the rest of the fallen debris by jumping as hard as he could and ran towards Fuegus. The sight of Oraien prompted Fuegus to once again go on the offensive. Fuegus lifted his right leg and dropped it, causing a fire shockwave to erupt from the ground. Oraien ran through the fire and took a magnitude of the damage, although surprisingly to his advantage. He leapt towards Fuegus' right leg and swung blindly. He accidentally struck the diamond that served as a kneecap, causing Fuegus to go crashing down into the ground. Oraien had found his weakness at last. Oraien quickly disabled the other diamonds on Fuegus until he reached the final one. Oraien put his broadsword away and grabbed the crystal and pulled it out of Fuegus forehead. Fuegus disappeared into the air, and so did the diamond in Oraien's hand.

  Azrun stayed seated on the rocky ledge, amazed and proud of his new partner and friend. Oraien gazed into a hidden opening that Fuegus protected and began to approach the Quarton. The closer he got, the more he could feel it touching him; the power was reaching out towards him. Oraien observed the markings on the Quarton and was in awe of their beauty. Oraien extended his hand out to touch the Quarton and felt his body and Exus transformed with a new ability. As if Exus was being controlled by the Fuegus-Quarton, it began to hover in front of Oraien. Oraien reached out to touch it and as soon as he did, an unexpected surge of electricity from his body traveled through the sword. Instantly, Exus split in two. To Oraien's amazement, the two swords connected at the bottom of each handle producing a double-ended sword. Looking at the markings on the sword, he noticed that they changed.

-"Exus Clavus," he read out loud. *Lightning staff?* Oraien thought to himself curiously. Once the two blades were connected, it fell with one of the ends planted into the rock. The ground of the cave within a thirty-foot radius was surging with deadly lightning, and immediately after the Quarton's display of the new ability, the sword was raised out of the ground and into Oraien's reach. When Oraien touched the sword again, the double-ended blades of Exus began to shift. Both of the ends slanted towards Oraien slightly, and in the middle of the two handles, was a ball of lightning. Examining the sword again, the markings on the sword were once again different.

-"Exus Arcus," he read, "Lightning Bow." Holding the sword steady with his left hand extended, he reached into the ball of lightning with his right hand and pulled backwards.
    Oraien let it go of the energy towards a wall a few hundred yards away causing an explosion of electrical particles. A cloud of dust arose from the rubble, and Ferverous stood motionless and impressed by Oraien's display of power.

-"I have to admit, that's pretty cool," Azrun said to himself as the two of them began to make their way back to Novalis with good news to tell the council.

While Oraien and Azrun reported to the leaders of Novalis, they heard the city's alarm sound, alerting everyone in the room that something was happening. Danger had arrived in the form of a Xodus that blasted his way through the outer defenses of the E.Q.O.D.A. He arrived at the battlegrounds where Oraien first met Azrun, and he soon made way towards the Novalis port. Once he arrived, he began to destroy every ship he could, and he blasted his way through the port and straight into the city. The meeting instantly ended when news of the invader's arrival was reported to the officials, and Oraien and Azrun rushed to the scene. It was there that the Xodus stood, and it was there that the two Xextrum defended the city.

Chapter 11

Terrus Revenge

-"Who are you?" Azrun asked.

-"I am Terrus, one of the four generals of Nibiru's higher forces. Now...which one of you is Ioxus?" Terrus calmly demanded.

-"Oraien, be careful. This guy is Xodus," Azrun said.

-"Xodus?" Oraien said in response.

-"The Xodus are chosen Niphiliem generals that harness the power of Nibiru's Neo-Quarton, but unlike our Neo-Quartons, theirs was purposely broken into many fragments which they dubbed the Xodus-Quarton," Azrun paused, "But unlike us they don't have elements. How low do you have to be to destroy something that's natural? They used some of the pieces to imitate the Xextrum, while they use other pieces as massive power sources; some of which are used to sustain their bases.

-"Well when you put it like that, I've had two encounters with a Xodus. The first was a crazy woman named Vexia, and the second was on the base I destroyed while saving Calea, but I never imagined that something like this could happen to a Neo-Quarton." Oraien looked at Azrun and then looked at Terrus to see if he could determine how strong their opponent could be.

-"One more thing Rai, we need to get him out of the city somehow, and we need to do it quickly before his reinforcements arrive. If the fight takes place in here, the damage will be beyond repair."

-"Gotcha," Oraien replied. "Let's do this," he finished.

Terrus was getting tired of hearing them whisper to each other and began to move closer to them, alerting Oraien and Azrun. "I'm only going to ask one more time. Which one of you is Ioxus?"

-"I am," Oraien spoke. With no warning, Ioxus blasted off from his position with Ferverous following suit. Oraien swung his sword with deadly force, forcing Terrus to counter.

Oraien swung low, his sword breaking the ground underneath until he brought it upwards. Once the two weapons made contact, Terrus was sent flying backwards through the very entrance he had just made. His body was sent into the large port of Novalis with the Xextrum following closely. As Terrus struggled to regain control of his momentum, Azrun noticed many Niphiliem soldiers entering the port through the massive hole created by Terrus. The two parties were on a collision course and would soon meet in the middle of the port where gravity was neutralized.

-"Rai, we can't let them enter the city!" Azrun yelled out.

-"I know!" Oraien yelled out.

The oncoming Niphiliem were piloting one-manned vehicles and immediately set their sights on destroying the Xextrum to aid their General. They opened a small path for the General to travel through but tried to close the gap in their ranks and engage the Xextrum. Ferverous quickly released two chains that began to glow red as his energy poured into them.

So he had two chains? Oraien thought. *I guess he was taking it easy on me the same way O'navus did.*

Returning his focus onto the quickly advancing Niphiliem, he and Feverous began their onslaught. They moved around each other with ease despite the fact that they weren't bound by gravity. The Niphiliem fired from their vehicles but to no avail. Ioxus split Exus into twin swords and decimated all who came in contact with him while Ferverous used his red hot chain whips to quickly slice though many vehicles at a time. The Niphiliem couldn't keep up with the fast moving speed of the Xextrum, and their numbers began to rapidly diminish. Attaching Exus into its Arcus form, Oraien fired heavily upon the uninvited soldiers.

He took aim at every soldier that he could, often firing in Azrun's direction. Azrun continuously dodged Oraien's incoming fire, allowing it to kill the unsuspecting soldier in front of him. He whipped his chains behind Oraien to kill any soldiers that attempted to harm Ioxus. The two Xextrum plowed the low ranked Niphiliem until none were left and the only thing left to show off their existence were their lifeless bodies and the destroyed aircrafts left to float in the heavily damaged Port. After watching all of his troops get destroyed, Terrus finally regained control of his body, but it was too late. Azrun's and Oraien's quick plan worked, and all three warriors were now outside of the port and back on the surface. They all landed firmly with the Xextrum couching down to reduce the force of impact, and Terrus hitting ground creating a small crater. Both Xextrum noticed that Terrus did not bend his knees at all from the heavy impact and was completely unaffected. Turning his head from one side to the other slowly and as hard as he could to get the crooks out of his neck, Terrus spoke, "You will pay dearly for that,"

-"I'm sure, but first tell me this," Oraien responded, "What are The Scrolls of Anteeo." Azrun looked at Oraien through the eyes of his Xextrum looking baffled.

-"See to it that the women and children get to the evacuation chambers and barricade the damaged port to prevent any more intrusions!" Maltoris commanded.

-"Yes, sir," a Calfieren troop responded.

-"You there," Maltoris continued, "Quickly, release the S.A.N.D. to give us a visual of what is happening on the surface. Make sure you transmit this to the RE2 moon base, for I fear there are more reinforcements on the way."

-"How do you know of the Scrolls, Ioxus?" Terrus asked.

-"When I released the Xodus-Quarton within Sendo's base it gave me two things: the ability to use quartiio energy and some knowledge of what the bases mission was which included the search for the scrolls of Anteeo. So tell me."

-"They say the scrolls can lead to eternal darkness and power, but there is no need for you to fret over such matters. You'll soon be dead anyway, young Ioxus." He then looked at Azrun, "You too, and this entire planet," said Terrus. "I am sure that you remember sensing my energy coming into Sendo's base from the sky-light. Well, let's just say that I'm here for revenge." Pausing he began to lift his hand, "You see, there are a number of things you did to piss me off and cause you inevitable death, Ioxus."

Azrun turned to Oraien, who looked back and shrugged his shoulders in an extremely confused manner.

-"The first," Terrus said slightly disturbing the energy around him, "you killed Sendo who was my brother. The second," he continued as he balled up his hand and a purple aura of energy engulfed his body, creating a small circular barrier around him, "you shattered the Quarton Fragment onboard the ship. And third," he spoke as he crouched down and released his energy further, lifting small rocks on the surface of the planet, "you blew up that very same ship with me still in it!"

Immediately both Xextrum began releasing their energy in a similar manner as Terrus. Oraien released sparks of lightning and Ferverous released searing heat waves from his body that slightly distorted his image.

"Allow me to pay you back ten-fold by showing you how strong we Xodus really are," Terrus yelled.

-"Then you have to fight me first!" Azrun yelled in response.

Ferverous dashed towards Terrus and side-flipped into a devastating roundhouse kick that he aimed at Terrus's energy barrier. The kick warped the barrier but did not pierce it, and when Azrun landed on the ground, he noticed that there was a small amount of fire left where he connected his kick. Terrus violently intensified his charging and it was then that Ferverous executed his technique. Azrun jumped over Terrus, drew his weapon and whipped the chain to the precise point on the barrier with fire and latched onto it. With his chain still connected, Azrun then pulled Terrus from his spot and flung him overhead into a magma bed nearby.

Terrus plunged into the lava and Azrun jumped in after him. Oraien wanted to follow them but remained alert on the sidelines knowing that his Xextrum couldn't withstand being fully submerged for an extended period of time. Under the melted rock Azrun and Terrus fought destructively. Terrus attacked and defended simultaneously, which would have caught Azrun off guard off guard, had he not specialized in hand-to-hand combat. With each attack, parry, and block there was so much magma displaced that it looked like an under-molten eruption. Terrus became impatient with the repetitious combat that they had come to, so he broke the pattern and activated an explosion,

-"This is my true power!" He yelled as the explosion pushed Azrun out of the lava and high into the sky overhead. Azrun knew that Terrus next move would be dangerous, but he had no idea what it could be. Soon a large creature emerged from the magma; Terrus converted all the surrounding lava to become part of his Xodus, thus being able to control it as if it were an extension of his body. One massive arm made of lava reached into the sky to grab Azrun as Terrus used his other giant arm to pull himself from the melted depths. Afraid that Azrun was in trouble, Oraien surged his energy though Exus to transform it once again into its Arcus form. Without hesitation, Oraien opened fire on the lava arm holding Azrun. Many of the shots passed straight through the arm, and he could hear them hitting ground behind, creating small explosions. Out of desperation, Oraien slowed his pace and started shooting more powerful shots, each one causing more damage than the last. As the lightning bolts pierced the lava, Ioxus could see an opening forming the more he shot in the same spot. On the final shot, Oraien was able to pour more energy into it by holding it at firing point longer than normal. Once the energy made contact with the arm, it completely disconnected, separating the hand from the rest of the arm. The separation allowed Azrun to fall to the ground and regain his composure.

Once Terrus had pulled his entire new form onto solid ground, he stood twice as tall and twice as massive as the Tathios Guardian Fuegus. Not wasting anytime, Terrus showed that his large size did not come at the expense of speed. He could almost match Azrun's speed, but only because Ferverous had already blown away much of his energy.

After being pummeled around and injured, Ferverous came to a realization; he did not want to accept the fact that he needed Oraien's aid to defeat Terrus, but by that time Azrun was short of energy and needed time to recharge. He underestimated the power of Terrus' Xodus, and it had cost him dearly. Azrun was very frustrated that he allowed pride to put himself at a disadvantage, and the only other solution Azrun could think of was to separate Terrus from his outer form and allow Oraien a chance to strike his center.

-"Oraien," Azrun yelled running towards him, dodging one of Terrus's assaults. "Get ready to shoot, aim for his chest and take the first direct shot you get," Azrun finished as he ran past Oraien and back into battle.

Without hesitation, Oraien readied Exus by charging a single shot and held it in firing position awaiting his opportunity. Azrun broke past Terrus defense and got close enough to disperse all the lava surrounding his body.

-"Firestorm blast," Azrun yelled out. The massive explosion separated Terrus from his large exoskeleton body, and Azrun fell to the ground motionless. The shockwave was strong enough to force Oraien to brace his body against the wind while he struggled to retain his position holding the charged shot. Once the debris from the explosion subsided, Oraien was able to make out a large figure through the smoke. The person was trying to stand but fell down soon afterward. As the person stood again, he clumsily made his way through the smoke, revealing his identity. It was Terrus with his guard completely down, and by the time he looked up to see Ioxus, it was too late.

-*That's my signal!* Oraien thought to himself as he let the bolt pierce Terrus chest.

Echoes of Tempore: Revival of Light

Inside of the RE2 moon base, the alarm was sounding. It was the highest level of alert the soldiers could be on, and everyone inside was scrambling to get to their posts. While the base was in a panic, many V.D.s popped up, allowing all the people inside a visual of the battle between The Xextrum and Terrus. Calea was frozen in her tracks as she saw Oraien on the display while Kisca stood next to her as she noticed the intensely worried look on her face.

-"You want to help him, don't you?" Kisca asked.

-"Yeah, but even with the ELX, right now, I would only get in the way. Besides, we have strict orders to stop the oncoming Niphiliem forces," Calea responded.

-"Then how about we protect him by stopping the reinforcements?" suggested Kisca.

-"They'll wish they never came back," Calea said firmly.

Oraien proceeded to jump in Terrus's direction to make sure the hit finished Terrus, but when Oraien could not see him, he used his senses to find his opponent. Quickly Oraien drew his sword and raised it above his head to block one of Terrus massive attacks. Oraien's knees buckled at the pressure of the blow, even though he successfully blocked the attack.

-"How did you survive that?" Oraien asked, his voice clearly showing the strain his body was under from blocking the attack.

-"That was quite the feat, catching me when my guard was completely down," Terrus stated, "But luckily my Xodus is different. You see, I have more than one Xodus fragment, and all of them are embedded in my armor. Fool, how else do you think I could survive after being completely submerged in lava?" Terrus erupted into laughter. "I am stronger than him," Terrus continued looking at Azrun's body. "And faster than you! Now die!" He said raising his sword to strike Oraien again.

-"Faster than me? We'll see about that!" Oraien yelled as the marking on his suit began to glow.

Oraien used his special ability to move at the speed of lightning which gave the effect of time slowing down, allowing him to counter Terrus. Magma from erupting volcanoes rained slowly in this state as the two traveled around the surrounding landscape. Ioxus continuously flipped around Terrus who was far less agile to gain the upper hand. To his amazement, every time he tried to attack from above and below simultaneously, his opponent had already seen through the maneuver and was able to disregard one of the attacks and focus on the more perilous of the two. Finally regaining consciousness, Azrun managed to stand. He tried his best to see the battle between Ioxus and Terrus, but failed due to his disoriented senses. All around him he could hear the clashing of weapons between the two, but stood in place not wanting to mistakenly walk into the line of fire.

Terrus and Oraien both noticed that Ferverous was back on his feet, and Terrus decided to take the rare opportunity to kill the unguarded Xextrum. Terrus diverted his attention from Oraien and sped towards Azrun, alerting Oraien of his plan. Azrun stood unsuspecting while Terrus sped towards him with his sword raised. Azrun's eyes shot open as Terrus' sword came to a stop directly in front of him. Terrus' blade was just a few inches from his neck shaking up and down as Ioxus stood firmly holding it at bay.

-"Wake up!" Oraien yelled, "Hurry and do a Neo-boost while I hold him off." With that, Oraien pushed Terrus back, and the two disappeared into battle again. Azrun wasted no time as he began to charge his Neo-Quarton.

The upper atmosphere of Evalesco was chaotic at its best as the Alliance was fending off the many Niphiliem reinforcements. Caileb was in charge of the operation and during the air battle, he sent orders to everyone involved in the battle.

-"Directly below us, the Xextrum are fighting for the well being of this planet. And it is our duty to make sure that they achieve an uninterrupted victory by cutting off the general from his troops up here. Besides, we can't let them get all the credit!" Caileb finished. A horde of battle cries could be heard over the intercom as the soldiers agreed with Caileb's every word. Calea had a determined smile across her face as she was doing everything within her power to do just what her brother said and keep the Niphiliem from reaching the surface of Evalesco.

As the battle waged on, both Oraien and Terrus slowed their pace due to the massive amount of energy moving that quickly required. Oraien kept his word and held Terrus back long enough to allow Azrun to recharge. They were now fighting at a pace that Azrun could match, and he immediately jumped into the battle so that they could attack concurrently to finish Terrus. Azrun landed many devastating punches to Terrus, who was more concerned with blocking Exus. Eventually, he realized that even though Azrun was not using a weapon that could slice through him, his punches were causing terrible internal damage as he began to cough up blood. Azrun was punching as hard as he could, and when the blows made contact, they made a heart-wrenching thud that slightly trembled the ground underneath. Fearing that his armor would not last against much more punishment, Terrus leaped out of harm's way toward Oraien and held Oraien in the path of Azrun's attack. Immediately after, Terrus round house kicked Azrun across the field. Terrus began to mercilessly beat Oraien as he held him in the air by his neck and continually punched him with his right hand. Azrun ran at full speed to reach Oraien and clutched Terrus throwing him as hard as he could towards space.

-"Oraien? Wake up! You can't die by this punk. Get up!" yelled Azrun. "Damn! Looks like I got no other choice."

Azrun took Oraien's hand and held it up to his Neo-Quarton. Oraien was injured more than he had ever been before, but Azrun did not give up. Ioxus drew from the power of Ferverous, revamping his Xextrum enough to use one final attack. Azrun fell to his knees from fatigue as he had given most of his remaining energy to Oraien. As Ioxus powered up to attack, the markings on his suit began to glow, but something was different this time. The markings on his right arm slowly began to change colors from lightning blue to a very rich gold. The change started at his fist and traveled all the way up his arm to stop at his shoulder. He drew energy of Ioxus from the quartiio energy stored by the Xodus fragment on NB2 and readied himself to use it to the best of his knowledge. Infused with the new energy, he let out a deadly scream that shook the ground.

-"Lighting!" yelled Oraien as he jumped upwards towards Terrus.

When Oraien jumped into the air towards Terrus, he initiated the attack. Ioxus first traveled faster than the speed of light, causing space itself to fold in his wake. The distance between Oraien and Terrus was about two feet, which also gave Ioxus the ability to punch twice in one second causing his fist to travel one second back in time. When the punch connected to Terrus, his Xodus immediately shattered and Terrus body folded and ripped with space itself. His body then disintegrated and the speed of sound finally caught up with the punch. All the way from the moon to the surface of Evalesco, a loud thunderclap of victory could be heard.

Chapter 12

Remedy

While the last of the Niphiliem were being destroyed by the Alliance, Oraien found himself falling from the upper atmosphere. After enduring such a strenuous battle, he let his body fall freely back towards the surface. As he fell with his back to the surface of Evalesco, he could see many air ships rushing towards him. The ships proceeded to match his speed of descent, and one of the pilots gave Oraien the thumbs up signal, pointing his finger upwards and downwards in an asking manner, referring to his battle with Terrus. Oraien nodded his head yes and gave the soldier a thumbs up. A large smile grew across the soldier's face while throwing his arm in the air in celebration. Oraien then put his hand up towards the pilot's ship to signal him to move away since they were descending too fast for the ships to land safely. Immediately, they all pulled upwards into the atmosphere to descend again slowly. Ioxus turned his body around to face the surface and spread all of his limbs outward to slightly slow his rate of descent. As he fell closer to the surface, he entered into a succession of back flips to further reduce his speed. Ioxus slammed into the ground creating a large crater with dust and debris flying across his immediate area. Oraien managed to fall within walking distance of Azrun and made his way over to see how he was holding up.

    The deafening sound of the airships filled the air as the vessels landed not too far from where the two Xextrum were located. Ioxus helped Ferverous to his feet and they watched as a group of soldiers approached their location. Among the soldiers at the front was Calea who looked more troubled than both battered warriors. Reaching them after running off the ships, the soldiers crowded around the two Xextrum to cheer and congratulate them on their victory. Barely slowing down from her run Calea made her way past the troops to Ioxus and threw her arms around him. She stood silent as Oraien's Xextrum faded away, and he half-heartedly embraced her in his arms. For Calea, it was as if all the chaotic noises and cheering soldiers faded into the background. The only thing that mattered was the fact that Oraien was ok.

    Opening her eyes, she was embarrassed as she could feel her face becoming flushed from being so close to him. Pushing Oraien off of her, she turned to see if anyone had seen how close the two had just been before she looked into his eyes and spoke.

-"What were you thinking!? How could you be so reckless? Why didn't the two of you come up with some kind of plan or strategy?" She said infuriated. "If you two hadn't been so prideful, maybe you would be in better shape but now look at you!" She continued as she began to hit him. Fending off the affectionate attacks, Oraien tried to answer.

-"We didn't have time to do anything else but fight. Besides, we won didn't we? And as far as my condition goes, I would be doing much better if you weren't hitting me," he chuckled at the softness of her punches.

-"Glad you still have the energy to joke around, let's go," she said. "You're coming with me," Calea demanded as she pulled Oraien and Azrun back to the ship for medical attention.

The next few days that he spent lying in the hospital bed healing were among the few that actually allowed him to rest. Calea would come by often to make sure that the two of them were doing as they were told: to relax. Calea would also use force when Oraien or Azrun rejected certain treatments. The rapid healing abilities of their Xextrums allowed them to leave after only three days. As they walked down the hall of the hospital, they heard their names being called and turned around to see who was talking to them.

-"Well if it isn't Ioxus and the infamous Ferverous," a familiar voice said as he was walking into view. It was Caileb, being escorted by his sister, who was coming by to see how the two warriors were faring.

-"So how is everything going?" He asked as he walked over to meet the two. The four of them now walked to the end of the hall in unison.

-"Everything is fine now that we get to leave," Oraien said as the two laughed.

-"How is everything back on the front?" asked Azrun.

-"For now, things have quieted down. My father told me to take a break from all serious matters while I still had the chance." Caileb stated. "Oh, one more thing, take this, Oraien. It's the same thing my sister has. It's a Mobile Information

Directory Connection Extender, or you could just call them MICE for short, don't worry about the 'D'." He chuckled handing the MICE over to Oraien then stepped over to Azrun and put a friendly hand on his shoulder. "So now we're all free."

-"That's great. All I was going to do today was show Rai the greatest city in the Ring," Azrun said jokingly, "So feel free to join us. The more the merrier," He added as the group left the hospital.

For the rest of the day, they walked throughout the city, learning various histories concerning the Calfieren people. The others were in complete awe as Azrun explained the meaning and purpose behind many of the buildings. Along the way, they stopped at various restaurants, some of which served a selection of foods with tastes that were less than savory. Never had Oraien taken time to really understand the work that had gone into the magnificent fire-maroon colored city. During their time in the city Calea would often find herself looking at Oraien, remembering the hug she gave him and how it made her feel. When Oraien caught her staring at him instead of the attractions, she snapped at him questioning what he wanted, starting countless arguments throughout the day. Though he never said anything, Oraien often thought about the fact that Calea had a boyfriend and the fact that she never told him. Every time they made eye contact, Calea knew what the real underlying problem was and that she had messed up. Caileb who was unaware of the situation thought it was cute and often laughed at their quarrels and frequently elbowed Azrun to tune him in on the spectacle. Despite the tension between Oraien and Calea, that day was the most fun any of them had experienced in a long time, and it would be a day that all of them would cherish and keep in their memory for all time.

Chapter 13

Journey to Celeres

The next day came as no surprise to Oraien. He was a guardian of the galaxy, and he had work to do. Caileb and Calea left together back to the RE2 moon base, and Oraien was alone in a luxurious dwelling. The room was suspended over hot springs that gave a pleasant tangerine scent as he was enjoying the flowerbed that came standard to all Calfieren inns.

Oraien remembered the small organizer that Caileb gave, and he rose out of his bed to read what his next journey would be. He completed his mission in retrieving the power of the Fuegus-Quarton, but he had yet to obtain the power of the other half of the Quarton: the ice side. Oraien got out of bed, packed all his things, and boarded Ferra once he made it through to the surface. Once inside the ship, he activated his mission log to see what his next assignment would be and found a message.

Rai, this is Caileb. I understand that you will be headed to Celeres soon, but before you leave I need you to deliver a package that is in the city. Normally, we would send it with a group of our best troops. However, a letter of this great importance needs extreme security. Meet Calea at Novalis port C. From the city docking station C, there will be four soldiers that will accompany you and my sister to the dividing energy ring. Once you reach the barrier, there will be two guides waiting to escort you to Raveria. Be safe and have a prosperous journey.

-*Raveria? Maybe that's what they call the ice side of this planet.* Oraien thought to himself.

Oraien asked Ferra for the fastest route to port C. Immediately she began downloading the information to his organizer, and Oraien left in no time. With the destroyed ships and the smoke gone, Oraien was able to see the port in its entirety, albeit it was under reconstruction. The port of Novalis was unlike any docking station he had ever seen. Its unique design supported the two gravities alone with a middle section that had zero gravity. It was a double-sided dome with its magnificence due to its enormity. At the other end of the port were tunnel like structures for the ships to enter and exit. Oraien finally arrived at the station and sat on the nearest bench and waited patiently. He began to dose off into a dream world of his childhood; he could never remember what his parents looked like and not even in his dreams did they appear.

-"Wake up!" Calea yelled into Oraien's ear.

-"Ahhhhh!" Oraien fell off of the bench and onto the floor. Calea began to laugh at Oraien and fell down on the bench as a result. "Why? Calea! I was sleeping peacefully, and you just had to steal it from me." Oraien said as he sat there.

-"Aww, does someone need a kissy-wissy?" Calea said as if she was talking to an infant. She reached down her hand and gently grasped his face. Oraien jumped up and turned away from Calea. He then turned around like a robot and picked Calea off the ground slouching her over his shoulder. "Rai, what!? I'm sorry. Ok, ok. Stop!" Calea said while she giggled.

Oraien began to spin in circles, making Calea dizzy. Oraien had a robotic look on his face, and Calea could barely contain herself. They both had two minutes to act silly before Oraien finally placed Calea on the bench. Calea sat there quietly as she realized that she didn't smile or laugh as much when she was with Lok and that Oraien was the only person she was truly comfortable with. They enjoyed the time they spent together, but Oraien's face loosened once he settled down and came back to reality.

"So... where's Lok?" Oraien asked solemnly. Calea's face dropped when she heard the mention of her boyfriend.

-"He's was dispatched back to Nekio yesterday," Calea said as she looked towards the ground. "Look I'm sorr...."

-"My only question to you is, when exactly were you going to tell me?" Oraien interrupted, "I mean you're able to tell me everything else while trying to boss me around half the time, but those words somehow never came out of your mouth. You know... more than anything, I'm mad at the way I found out," Oraien finished.

-"I know you're mad at me, and I am sorry you that had to find out that way," Calea said softly. "I don't know what else to say."

-"What was all of that between us?" Oraien asked, "Did any of that mean anything to you?

Do you feel anything for me?" Oraien finished looking Calea directly in the eyes.

-"I.... I'm not...," she started. After letting out a large sigh she answered, "I don't know."

Their concentration on the matter was broken as the transport vessel arrived. Stepping out of the vessel was a short Calfieren man followed by a much taller Calfieren. They introduced themselves and invited Calea and Oraien aboard.

The vessel they boarded had two levels. The top level was similar to that of a sea ship, and the bottom contained four rooms. Two of the rooms had beds and an extra storage facility. Calea was the first on the ship, followed by the troops and Oraien. As the vessel slowly took off, they passed through a large tunnel that led towards the surface. Nearing the exit, a large circular gate opened to allow them passage to Evalesco. As they ascended, the only thing Calea and Oraien could see was the base of a massive mountain that stretched into the sky. As they rose above the summit, they observed the system of gates around the base of the mountain that were allocated for their corresponding cardinal direction. In between the larger gates that were designed to accommodate Cruiser ships, two smaller circular openings designed for smaller vessels were seen. Oraien gazed in awe at the complexity of Novalis as it faded into the distance.

Once it was out of sight, Oraien began to train his body. The trip to the energy wall took a few hours, and the hours flew by as Oraien performed various workout routines he learned from Retsum. Calea sat reading a book while occasionally looking up at Oraien.

-He's really mad at me...he has all the right to be, Calea thought.

Oraien left his workout to look far in the direction of the energy wall. It surged with energy from the two Quarton's separating the planets' temperatures. When the ship approached the wall, it slowed down and slowly began to enter the wall itself. The white plasma was flowing upward towards space, so the ship pushed forward towards the energy. Soon the ship was totally enveloped by the wall, and Oraien could feel the light breeze of the plasma blow through the deck of the ship. Calea was at the other end of the ship putting her hand in the plasma treating it as if it was a downy cloud. Traveling through the energy Oraien felt mysteriously at ease, as if he was a part of the planet itself.

The fire ship sailed into the center of the barrier where Oraien noticed that he could feel neither heat nor cold. The barrier was a true neutral zone for the planets' inhabitants. Towards the center of the barrier, Oraien and Calea could see a second ship waiting for their arrival. The second ship had a design that was very distinct from that of the vehicles of Novalis. The Calfieren ship pulled up next to the idle ship and allowed Oraien and Calea to cross over into the next vessel.

-"Good, it's not too big or too small," Calea said moving forward.

-"How gracious of you, your highness," Oraien responded without thinking. Looking over at Calea who would normally throw him a vicious death stare, she realized that he responded out of habit and smiled faintly.

Once on the vaguely smaller ship, Oraien and Calea saw two guides exit the captain's den and start towards them while nodding at the Calfieren troops. Oraien also looked back to the soldiers and asked, "Aren't you guys coming?"

-"We, Calfieren, cannot step foot beyond this barrier into Raveria, nor can they step foot into Evalesco," the Calfieren guide stated.

-"Why not?" Oraien asked curiously with Calea turning to face them, awaiting an answer.

-"Long ago, Raveria and Evalesco were two separate planets, with the Calfieren and Zeofieren on our prospective planets. So naturally, our bodies adapted to the two extremes. Zeofieren bodies, trap heat in which makes them very resilient to the cold, and...."

-"Calfieren bodies," one of the Zeofieren soldiers interrupted, "Rapidly release heat, which allows them to survive the heat of Evalesco. Such things went relatively unquestioned until the final battle of the Millennium War when our two worlds were nearly destroyed and were combined. Then we had to learn the reasons why our two races couldn't last very long outside the barrier. While we can visit other planets with more moderate temperatures, without the aid of temperature controlled suits there would be no way for us to enter into the extremes of heat, or the cold for Calfieren." the soldier finished.

-"Millennium War, Millennium War...why does that sound so familiar?" Oraien asked, trying to recollect his memories of the familiar words.

-"How would I know?" Calea answered. "I'm more concerned with how the two planets were combined. That's crazy, but it explains why there is such a vast difference between Evalesco and Raveria," she finished.

-"Argh! Yeah you're right, but this is going to bug me until I remember where I know that term from." Oraien said in a frustrated tone.

-"Young ones, you must leave for Celeres. The Zeofieren will accompany you the rest of the way," he said as he and his partner nodded to the Zeofieren and headed back to their ship.

-"Lady Calea, my name is Gabe and this is Umicel. We will transport you to the city of Celeres within the day," said Gabe.

-"Thank you for keeping us safe and accompanying us," said Calea politely.

The ice ship emerged from the barrier to reveal a beautiful sea of water and ice. Shortly after leaving the barrier, Umicel handed Oraien and Calea a pair of heavy coats to keep them warm against the unforgiving cold of Raveria. Oraien stood on the deck with his body leaned against the rail. He closed his eyes to breathe in the cold air, allowing his senses to relax and clear his mind. His concentration was broken once he felt the ship quake from a mysterious outside source.

-"They never leave us alone," said Gabe.

-"They?!" asked Oraien in a cautious tone.

-"The Hydra, they are giant sea serpents that attack anything foreign to their territory. Despite these Hydra, this is the safest route to port Ve3." Gabe added.

-"Calea! Oraien! Come with me to get Hecho-lasers!" Umicel commanded while rushing down the steps to the weaponry room.

  The weapons were made in Novalis. Each gun shot a solid laser stream of fire. For the next thirty minutes, the crew had to fend off the large yet stunning serpents. One beast came very close to sinking its teeth into Umicel; however, Gabe threw a smoke bomb into the monsters mouth causing it to flinch. That gave Calea the opportunity to strike one of the Hydra's eyes, and the gigantic snake fled. Right before they could safely exit the Hydra's territory, another serpent came to test its might against the ship and her crew. It would have been easy for them to drive her away, but once she broke through the icy surface and displayed her massive size and elegant form, it was apparent that something extra had to be done. The four concentrated their Hecho-Laser's at her but it was to no avail. The gigantic Hydra whipped her tail towards the ship causing considerable damage to the speeding hovering vessel.

-"This is madness," Gabe stated, "The Hydra are protective, but they have never been so relentless in their attacks. It's as if their possessed by something."

Fearing that things were getting out of hand, Oraien had no choice but the call forth Ioxus. He jumped into the air towards the serpent and transformed, quickly drawing Exus and severed the Hydra's tail before it hit the ship. Oraien fell into the broken ice, and the sea-monster dove into the water following him. From the surface, Calea and the two guides could do nothing but hope Oraien was ok.

Before Calea's anxiety could set in, Oraien emerged from the water exhausted, yet excited.

-"That was fun!" Oraien said as he leapt onboard the ship.

The rest of the trip fluttered by as the city of Celeres rose above the horizon. By this time, Oraien enjoyed looking at details of cities he had never seen. Gazing into the distant city, he could see a barely visible barrier that covered the city. It looked as if its purpose was to keep the city comfortably warmer than the surrounding landscape. The barrier slightly reflected the setting of Antares, and the look of the city sung songs of beauty. Once they were close enough and after the Antares glare disappeared, it allowed for a clear view into the city. In the center there was a massive mountain shaped cylindrically as if it were carved from the ground itself by an ice titan. Around this tall mountain were many bright buildings built to fit the scenery, and they stretched as high the tallest skyscrapers of Luna. The last thing that really blew Oraien away was the additional buildings at the very top of the tall mountain, each artistically constructed to blend in with the cold landscape. Everything about the city looked peaceful yet arctic, and once they passed through the barrier,

Oraien could feel a breeze of air flowing around him. The air was not warm, but not nearly as cold as outside the barrier. Looking into the water, Oraien could see that the barrier also continued underwater.

-*It's a perfect sphere for the whole city,* Oraien concluded in his thoughts. When they arrived, Calea took Oraien aside and began to speak with him.

-"This is where we split up. You are going to head for the east foyer. Ferra has been transported to port Ve5. Don't forget, your room is in the left wing on the thirty-fourth floor. Here is your room key. My room is next to yours, but for now I have to get going, Rai. There's something I have to do on behalf of my father. I hope you can handle yourself in the city as well as you do on the battlefield. Bye!" Calea said in a hurry as she departed after handing him the letter.

    Traveling through the city, he used his MICE to navigate to the leaders' conference hall which was located at the very top of the central mountain. Oraien hopped onto a public transport vehicle that took him to the first level of the central mountain. He entered the edifice, and before he could begin to look for a way to the top, he simply had to stop and admire the magnificence of the central mountain. The solid walls reflected the insides of the mountain and seemed to endlessly flow upward. Countless new objects and designs were intriguing him, but he could soon sense something that he was becoming awfully familiar with: the presence of a Quarton. He searched around to find the Quarton in the very center of the mountain. Not only was it in the center, it was *the* center: the internal foundation of the mountain which acted as an energy supplier.

    The plaza was filled with many designs, but it was also filled with a countless number of people. The new things quite overwhelmed Oraien, and his face was soon filled with great confusion. One Zeofieren native saw that he could not find his way around and stopped him.

-"Hey, you're from Luna aren't you?" he asked. His mist skin perfectly matched his white and blue hair as well as his eyes which also matched the cool aura of the city. "You've never seen a Zeofieren before, I see," hinting that Oraien was doing a little too much examining.

-"Oh sorry, I was actually guided here by two, but I couldn't get a good look at them because they were mostly covered up to shield themselves from the old." Oraien slightly bowed his head and introduced himself. "Hi, I am Oraien. I'm looking for the leaders' conference hall. Is there any way you could direct me?"

-"Well, you're not far. I'll take you there. It should only take a few minutes, so it won't be out of my way," the Zeofieren said as he continued to introduce himself, "The name's Leo, nice to meet ya." Leo began to walk towards a door in a pillar of the mountain plaza, and Oraien asked him a question while they walked,

-"So, what's this place called?"

-"I'll give you the short version. This is Mount Dintio, and its purpose is to conceal the Quarton. Thousands of years ago when the planet was saved, the Quarton extended through the surface and elevated the land from beneath the ice. We built this city around her, and this mountain was cut in a cylindrical shape to simulate a large building. It has dozens of levels, and the citizens live at the very top. The building you're looking for is located on the east side of its peak." They arrived at the door, and Leo pushed a button followed by a code input. "We're just going to take this suspense-elevator to the top. It should only take about five minutes."

Oraien familiarized himself with Leo and learned many things about the Zeofieren. Their past history intrigued him and made him appreciate his own planet even more. The elevator finally leveled out, and they reached the top. Leo stepped out first and Oraien followed. It was slightly colder than the ground level, and the clouds were so close that Oraien felt as if he could reach up and grab a handful of them. Snow was everywhere except on the walkways and the streets. Leo nodded to Oraien and spoke,

-"This is where I leave you Oraien." He said with a kind smile. "It was nice meeting you, Eluesian."

-"Nice meeting you too, Leo," Oraien nodded and started to utilize his Mice to show him the most convenient path to the leaders' conference hall. Oraien arrived within a few minutes. The guard immediately notified the Zeofieren Council of his arrival, and a meeting was called. The leaders entered the room and took their respective seats, but one leader remained standing to welcome Oraien.

-"Greetings, Oraien, we have heard much about you from the Calfieren. Word of your battle with Ferverous is still buzzing through the streets." He paused to sit, "My name is Proevus, head of the Zeofieren Council. I trust you still have the letter in your possession."

The letter was passed around until it reached Proevus, who proceeded to open it. Oraien watched silently as Proevus held the thin metallic letter. He removed a stylus that sat on his desk and signed it. The high-tech letter recognized his signature and allowed him access to its contents. He let out a sigh of relief knowing that he finally gained the information he needed.

-"If you don't mind me asking, what exactly does that letter contain?" Oraien asked with great curiosity turning the Council's attention from Proevus to him.

Before Proevus could answer, the door to the Council hall opened, and a beautiful woman walked in. Her tremendous aura of confidence could be felt throughout the room as she approached the Council as if they were equals. Completely unaware of Oraien's presence, she came to a halt and began to speak.

-"Has it arrived yet?" she asked, placing her left hand on her hip.

-*She's gorgeous... and powerful.* Oraien thought.

-"As a matter of fact, it has Aiya," Proevus said. "You can thank him for that," he said, looking to Oraien. When Aiya turned around to face Oraien, she was almost at a loss for words.

-"Who—who is this?" She asked trying to regain her composure.

-"Allow me to introduce the two of you. Aiya meet Oraien, the Xextrum of Lightning: Ioxus," said Proevus.

-*No way, he's Ioxus?!* Aiya thought trying not to let her face show her shock.

-"And Oraien meet Aiya, the Xextrum of Ice: Uvatuus."

-*No wonder I got that vibe.* Oraien concluded.

-"To answer your question Oraien, the letter contains coordinates."

-"Coordinates?"

-"Yes, coordinates to a hidden Niphiliem base. A few days ago during the invasion, the Niphiliem somehow managed to steal the Zeofieren Sphere. The sphere is one of two ancient devices. The other is the Zoduk sphere which they obtained when they invaded and destroyed the planet Zoduk. Together they have the power to negate the gravitational effects of a black hole.

-"What could the Niphiliem possibly do with such a thing?" Oraien questioned with anger.

-"We're not sure, but we can't afford to sit around and find out," Aiya answered. "That's why once we decipher the coordinates to the base, I am going in to retrieve the sphere. How long before I can head out?" she asked turning her attention back to Proevus.

-"We're not sure. The Council will alert you once we finished decoding the letter," He said handing the metallic case to an assistant who walked into a room behind the Elders. "Thank you for your help, Oraien."

Oraien and Aiya turned to walk out of the Council Hall together, but before they could

Echoes of Tempore: Revival of Light

exit the room, a powerful explosion shook the entire structure, loosening many large stones in the chamber walls. Realizing that the explosion came from where the letter had been taken, Aiya immediately transformed into her Xextrum. Instantly, Oraien transformed into Ioxus to support her without hesitation. Uvatuus dashed from her position to reach the back room in a timely manner, but once she got closer to the outer wall, another explosion was set off. The second explosion sent an enormous stone hurling in Aiya's direction at an incredible speed, leaving her no time to react. Using his lightning speed, Oraien appeared in front of Uvatuus and cut the stone in half with a single swing of Exus.

-*He's the real deal*, Aiya thought, impressed with Oraien's agility.

Snapping back to reality, Aiya realized that walls around them were collapsing. To prevent the entire structure from caving in under its own weight, she froze the inner walls of the chamber, coating them with a thick layer of ice. The reinforcement she provided would undoubtedly prevent them from falling even if another explosion were to go off. The two of them pressed forward into the back room after confirming that the members of the Council were safe. When they entered the room, they were shocked by the countless bodies they saw. However, a spark of hope was seen when they spotted a survivor who happened to be the only code breaker alive. However, that spark of hope was soon to be diminished.

-"Xodus," she hatefully mutter the single word and closed her eyes for eternity. Uvatuus laid her head down gently and stood up slowly. As Oraien surveyed the room, he could sense the fury of Aiya as he looked down to find her fist shaking. Oraien dashed into the meeting room and spoke quickly, "As a Xextrum, I make this urgent command. Proevus, assemble a group of your most qualified troops to lead an aerial search for the perpetrators, while Aiya and I search by land. Have them bring all the necessary equipment, and be hasty." Aiya walked back into the Council Hall and spoke, "The Niphiliem fled into the snow desert and will probably hide in the ice mountains or even possibly under the snow plains to the west. She turned to face Oraien, "We must get the coordinates back. The E.Q.O.D.A depends on it." She looked out of the hole that the Niphiliem had created from the blast. "Let's go." She ran and jumped out the large blast hole.

-"What the......" Oraien ran to stop her but found himself falling through the air.

    The two jumped from the leaders' conference hall. Oraien almost lost himself to the breathtaking scenery of falling from such a height, until he saw Aiya, determined and focused on the task at hand. She immediately positioned herself to dive in the direction of the ground outside the city barrier. Since they jumped from such high distance they were able to freefall safely for a few minutes.

    Aiya came in gently despite her speed and was able to land with her legs at pace by creating a gust of snow. Oraien on the other hand, hit the ground and stumbled into a large pile of snow. Aiya looked back but continued forward. Oraien brought himself out from the snow and noticed that she was a good distance away from him. Like a bolt of lightning piercing the air, he came to her side.

    Once they were well outside the city, they stopped briefly to plan their search. They decided to split up and meet up at a northern plain they located using their Area Information Directory (A.I.D.) programmed in their MICE. After an hour of searching, the air search party arrived and joined together with the two Xextrum. The search lasted five hours, and the two called the rest of the soldiers to regroup for the night.

-"Why are we stopping? Oraien asked. "The Xodus is still out there somewhere; we might lose him if we rest!" Oraien objected.

-"Oraien, I admire you for your diligence, but we can't leave our men to freeze to death. Even for us Zeofieren, including me outside of Xextrum form, not to set up camp outside of any of the cities is certain death against the late night air."

The recon team was in the middle of a plane of endless snow. Tents were set up, and everyone was allowed to rest. Oraien and Aiya began to analyze the information collected. Oraien noticed a strange consistency with each person's information and spoke, "Aiya, look at this pattern here," The information was displayed visually over a camp fire to provide light. "See, the heat readings here and here are faint, but when you look at this location..."

-"Oh, you're right, Oraien." She said looking impressed. "And if you look at the texture of that certain area you see that the snow is slightly raised." She sat back on the portable bench that surrounded the fire. "First thing in the morning you and I will go there while the troops continue their search. But before we rest, we should monitor the area with S.A.N.D. I'll let one of my men handle that before we call it a night." Aiya deactivated the information display of the fire.

-"I guess you and I make a good team." Oraien said looking into the warm fire. Aiya turned to him and rested her eyes on him. Oraien did not notice it until he pulled his hands out from his over coat to put them near the fire. Once he noticed her, he simply pretended not to and kept his eyes on the fire.

-"Oraien," Aiya said gently. Oraien turned towards her and put his hands back in his coat.

-"Yes."

-"So, tell me. What's it like on Luna?"

-"Well, for starters, it's not cold," he said smiling. Aiya looked down and laughed as well. "In my opinion though, Luna is very different like this planet. It looks like a moon because its soil is white." He looked at Aiya and said, "I could tell you the details, but I would rather show you someday." Aiya looked into the sky.

-"That would be nice," she sighed.

-"What, is there something wrong?" Oraien asked. Aiya took her left hand out of her coat and focused her eyes on the small pile of snow in front of her. Placing her hand above the snow, she waved it slightly, and Oraien watched as a small of amount of snow rose from the ground and slowly moved towards her hand. She began to twirl her finger and faintly smiled, and the snow began to spiral upwards. Blowing the snow into the fire, she continued, "Being a Xextrum, I'm always fighting....protecting," she turned to him and continued, "It's not like I don't like protecting those dear to me, it's just that..."

-"You never get any time for yourself," Oraien said while looking down with empathy.

-"Yeah," she looked at him with appreciation knowing he could understand her. "I guess you can understand where I'm coming from since we have the same fate."

-"I've only been a Xextrum for nearly two months. But when push comes to shove, this privilege is really almost a burden." He stood up by the fire and continued, "But Aiya, don't let it weigh you down. Just a few days ago, I met some good people on my journey and also had a great time." Oraien felt a connection with Aiya and wished to make her feel better.

-"When this mission is over, how about we have a day together in the city. You can show me around. So, don't use that as an excuse to turn me down." Oraien turned to show her a gentle face of kindness.

-"So is there anyone special in your life?" Aiya asked with great curiosity.

-"If you're talking about a woman, then the answer is....." immediately Oraien's mind flashed back to the day he met Kisca and Lok; Calea's boyfriend,

---

"Oh, him?"

"Oh so you guys know each from Nekio since your both soldiers."

"Yeah, that and the fact that I'm Calea's boyfriend,"

"So how long have…."

"About five Months now"

-"The answer is no. I'm single."

Aiya had so much to say to Oraien after hearing his response, but she could not bring herself to say a single word. Aiya realized that she liked Oraien, and she was surprised because no one could get past her invisible wall of command. Aiya stood up, and unexpectedly gave Oraien a hug. The two stood together a while.

-"Nothing happens for no reason. Thank you, Oraien Zeal. I hope I can get to know you more as we work together," Aiya left the warmth of the fire for her tent. Oraien stood still blushing and extremely surprised.

-*Well...... I hope everyone rests up. I guess I'll just keep an eye on everyone for the night.* Oraien said to himself as he took his seat by the fire once more for the night.

When Aiya was ready for bed, she wanted to know if Oraien had left for bed yet, and she slightly peeked through her tent entrance. She saw Oraien sitting firmly, gazing into the fire. Seeing him there made her feel safe, and also let her know that he sincerely cared for all his troops. She wanted him to rest, but she did not stop him from doing what he had in his heart to do. She rested peacefully as did all other troops that night, and from a distance, a small fire of hope could be seen in the middle of a cold and dark plain.

When morning broke, Oraien stood up to wake everyone but was stunned to see the face of someone he met back on Luna approaching the camp with four men of his own. It was Xan, the silent friend he found while helping the city volunteer reconstruction group. The same look crossed Xan's face as he came close enough to recognize Oraien. Xan walked directly up to Oraien to salute him and spoke.

-"Oraien Zeal," he said with a smile, "Why would a Duro like you be out here?" Oraien let his shock show as he spoke.

-"Xan?! I'm here leading a ground search for a letter. Let me think. You're the guy I found helping Luna right?"

-"Yup."

-"So what are you doing all the way over here, Xan?"

-"I'm trying to make a name for myself. So I joined the air search group. I was the only

Eluesian accepted into the group because of all my past work with other planets in the Alliance. You only saw me on Luna, but I do work all over the quadrant." Before Oraien could speak, Aiya interrupted.

-"Hey Oraien," she turned to Xan and the troops. "Finally, you have arrived. Oraien, this is the third group sent in from the city. They are going to help our guys. In the mean time, we have to go check the spot we discovered last night."

-"First things first, Aiya, just call me Rai from now on," he said easily, "And I want you to meet someone I met a while ago on Luna. His name is Xan." She looked to see the man he was talking about and noticed Xan, who responded to Oraien's comment.

-"Nice to meet you, Xan." She nodded to him and spoke, "And I'm sorry to be brief, but Oraien and I must leave soon. Hopefully we can become a little more acquainted after the search. Good luck on your part." Aiya grabbed Oraien by the hand and lead him into camp. "Oraien, we can't be wasting time. Are you ready?"

-"Yeah. I guess I'll talk to him later. Let's go."

The two traveled by ground on hovering single passenger crafts instead of using their Xextrum to conserve their energy. When they reached the designated spot, Aiya and Oraien dismounted their vehicles and approached an oversized lump in the snow. Aiya began to inform Oraien of the plan of action they should take,

-"Let's do this," Oraien said preparing to transform into Ioxus. Aiya quickly stopped him and spoke.

-"Rai, I'm not sure if you've had the chance to realize this or not but electricity and water don't mix. There are sure to be puddles everywhere, and we don't know who has the coordinates. You may accidentally spark and kill whoever has them and possibly destroy the coordinates. The same thing goes for me; I could mistakenly freeze the coordinates, destroying them just the same. So for the sake of the mission, neither one of us can transform and barge in there. I will use my latent Xextrum abilities to create a tunnel into the stronghold. When the path is created we can sneak in, take the letter, and call the remaining troops to handle the Niphiliem. If worse comes to worse, I will transform destroy the entire cave."

-"Sounds like a plan," Oraien said.

    Once they came to an agreement, Aiya began to silently create an opening in the snow. Oraien sat down patiently in the snow as he watched her. Once the tunnel was complete, Aiya notified Oraien, and they began their descent. In the air just above them, Xan's team spotted the hole that Aiya created without knowing about her plans, and they descended to examine the site. Aiya and Oraien soon found themselves in a pocket under the snow with many sleeping Niphiliem. Aiya and Oraien moved swiftly and silently as they desperately searched for the coordinates.

    On the surface, Xan and three troops entered the cave quickly. Inside of the cave, Oraien noticed that Aiya was right about him transforming.

-*There is water everywhere, no doubt that the electricity Ioxus naturally discharges would be enough to end the lives of the beasts since they're all wet*, Oraien thought.

They moved slowly through the small, wet, and murky cave since it was hard to find a dry spot to step on. As Oraien stepped softly, lightly treading his foot along the ground so that he didn't splash in the puddles; he accidentally knocked over the enemy's rifle. Oraien closed his eyes in disbelief when he realized that he had given away their position. It was the longest few seconds of his life as the rifle hit the ground but didn't seem to come to a standstill until it made sure to sound an alarm loud enough that even the people back on his home world could to hear. Immediately, he and Aiya both froze, holding their awkward walking positions hoping the Niphiliem wouldn't wake. Their worst fears came to pass as all the soldiers in the ice cave groggily woke up, completely unaware of the situation. As they opened their eyes fully, the Niphiliem were all at a loss for words as they stared at the presence of two intruders in their mists. To make matter worse, as Oraien and Aiya were standing still like statues staring at the Niphiliem soldiers, everyone's concentration was broken. Xan and his team came rushing in to examine the suspicious tunnel Aiya previously created. Once Xan and his men came to a screeching halt, they saw the two parties in the cave turn in unison to look at the arrival of the newly uninvited guests. All within the cave stood silent and motionless, with no one sure of what to do. In the mist of the awkwardness, a thin metallic object lying on the ground in his peripheral vision soon broke Oraien's attention from Xan's entrance.

When the Niphiliem commander looked at Xan's face, his eyes shot open in disbelief, but before he could say anything his subordinates began to open fire. Without hesitation, Oraien dove to grab the panel containing the coordinates as Xan's team provided cover fire. Wanting to prevent the deaths of her men, Aiya jumped overhead and ran towards the exit of the cave. Oraien jumped behind her, but proceeded to grab Xan before leaving. The Niphiliem scrambled to kill as many people as possible to prevent the coordinates from slipping away. Xan and his men mounted a defense and tried to provide cover for Aiya.

-"Xan! What are you doing? We have to get out of here before Aiya takes this place down!"

-"There's no time. Get the letter back to the Council. Run, and I will hold them back!" The three soldiers grabbed Oraien and left the cave, leaving Xan behind. Oraien attempted to go back to help Xan, but Aiya's voice overpowered the landscape, causing everyone to halt.

Echoes of Tempore: Revival of Light

-"Absolute Zero!" her voice echoed in her Xextrum form. The tunnel she created along with the entire snow dune structure was completely brought down, as if it sank deep into the snow.

-"Xan!!" Oraien yelled as his friend left him again for the last time.

Chapter 14

Journey to the Far-Flying Star

The next morning Aiya began her preparations for her mission of retrieving the Key in the Nibiru base. She was in her room preparing her mind, considering every possible outcome of her mission. Abruptly, she was interrupted by someone knocking on her door and went to answer.

-"Who is it?" she asked.

-"It's me; Rai." Her heart skipped a beat. *What is he doing here?* She thought as she slowly walked towards the door. Her silence prompted Oraien to speak again.

-"I don't need to come in. I just wanted to say that I really enjoyed our time together. And..."

-"And?" she repeated, waiting for his response.

-"I don't want you to go to the base." Oraien's last statement stunned Aiya, and she immediately opened the door. "Let me take your place, and you can take mine." Oraien stepped into the room, and the door automatically closed. He was looking at her now. "You know I'm a noob around here, but despite that, I'm good. You've seen me fight Azrun. I know you have. Give me your mission." Aiya affirmed her expression and looked straight at him assertively,

-"You came here to ask me that? Why should I let you take my mission, Rai? You're no better than I am." Before she could tell him to leave, she turned, and Oraien gently grabbed the back of her arms.

-"Because... I feel strange. It's like Ioxus, or some weird kind of energy is telling me that I need to go, and that if you go..." Oraien paused as he tried to find the right words "Look, I don't know what I'm feeling Aiya, but you have to trust me on this. It has to be me that goes." Oraien let go of her arms as she began to walk away from him. Aiya knew exactly what Oraien was talking about. She, too, had felt this energy before. It was like an instinct that couldn't be ignored, or, more importantly, one that shouldn't be ignored. That very same feeling saved her life many times before in battles, and she couldn't help but think that Oraien had the exact feeling she had felt in previous times.

-"Rai. I know how you feel," she said as she finally broke the silence in the room. "What you're feeling is your connection to the energy that flows through each and every Quarton. I'm sure you have felt it before in battle but on a much smaller scale. When a Xextrum is near a Quarton as you are now, that feeling is multiplied many times over and compels you to act on it. At this point I know I can't stop you," she paused and chuckled to herself, "Its best that I don't stop you, so make sure you do a good job." Turning around, she began to walk back towards Oraien. She stopped once she was very close to him and looked up into his eyes.

-"Rai, I don't want to put up any false pretenses. So I want you to know that even though we haven't spent much time together, I like you." Oraien's eyes shot open when he heard Aiya's statement, but strangely, he liked the way that she was straightforward with him. "So make sure you take care of yourself and come back safely. The sphere is important, but we can always come up with another plan. We can't replace you."

-"Thank you," Oraien said pulling her closer to wrap his arms around her.

-"Don't worry. I don't expect you to say anything about what I said, I just wanted you to know how I felt," Aiya said. "You should hurry. You need to make the necessary preparations," Aiya continued.

-"Alright," Oraien responded slowly pulling away from Aiya's warmth. "Here," Aiya said remembering to hand Oraien a small cube device. "The Zeofieren Sphere gives of a special frequency that this machine can pick up. Once you transform into Ioxus, your Xextrum will automatically target this signal, and that will be your guide to where it is in the base."

-"I'll come back as soon as I can," Oraien said turning to walk out of the room.

    Walking through the city as Antares was setting, Oraien knew that the time was soon approaching when he would have to begin Aiya's mission. He would have to travel to the Niphiliem base, NB4, to retrieve the Zeofieren Sphere that could be located by locking onto a special frequency it transmitted. NB4 was no ordinary base; it was the second largest that the

Alliance was aware of, as well as ranked four out of five based on its destructive capabilities.

With the passing of a few hours, the time had come for him to leave. He knew that he could not tell Calea what he was about to do, so he decided to wait until she was asleep to say good-bye. Standing over her as she slept, he saw how peaceful and serene she looked. It was hard to imagine that she was the same girl who was constantly causing bodily harm to him and starting arguments with him about everything. Standing in the large windowsill he looked back one more time, transformed into Ioxus, and then jumped off into the lower atmosphere to Ferra and embarked on his mission. Waking from her sleep, Calea thought she could feel someone looking at her only to see the trail of electricity left in Ioxus' absence.

Rai, she thought as she walked over to the window to see Ferra ascending in the atmosphere.

-*Where are you going?* she asked herself, leaning against the ledge. In the ship, Ioxus calmly sat down in the pilot seat and began to speak.

Echoes of Tempore: Revival of Light

-"Ferra, set and lock onto this frequency," he said in a firm voice. She quickly calculated the position and path of flight.

-"How long before we reach the base?" Oraien asked. *One hour*, she displayed.

-"Let's go, we don't have much time," He said as the ship went into stealth mode and blasted off.

    Not long after the departure from Igni'ice, Ioxus found himself looking at a massive stationary structure floating in between two of a foreign world moons. After stopping a safe distance from the base, Ioxus had Ferra jettison him towards the large rotating object. Taking notice to a large opening in the base, he figured it was a docking station for the departure and return of ships. Oraien took advantage of the seemingly single entrance into the base by hopping onto the back of a cruiser-sized ship by holding onto a metallic panel. The large hard door shut as soon as the entire ship was safely inside the base. Not wanting to be seen, Ioxus used his great speed to enter another part of the base through a door that a lone soldier opened.

-*Now comes the hard part,* he thought to himself as he began moving through the large, dimly-lit base.

Ioxus was fully aware of the severity of his recon mission and knew anyone who saw him could not live. As he traveled through the base, he quickly killed all the soldiers in his path by breaking their limbs and snapping their necks from behind. If there was no way to sneak up from behind, he used his incredible speed to position himself to fire his bow. His swift movement seemed to slow down his surrounding area which gave him the time he needed to perfect his kill shots and wiped out hallways of patrolling officers. Ioxus was careful to leave no survivors and to attack the next group that was completely unaware but more importantly before they could sound an alarm. Occasionally, Oraien focused the energy of his Xextrum and tapped into his internal sensors to follow the signal being given off by the Key. To further aid him in his infiltration, he would use his Neo-ray to find routes to the Key with the least amount of resistance, also saving him time. Once he cleared the first level of the base, he traveled up an elevator shaft using his lightning speed to avoid groups of Niphiliem and found a shaft that lead to the upper floor. Before exiting the shaft, he used his senses to find the best opening to emerge from, before he could continue with his mission.

Entering the new level of the ship from an overhead shaft located in a dark corner, he could hear soldiers talking about the Key.

"Hahaha, who would have thought that taking the Key from those people would have been so easy," a soldier said laughing.

-"I know, it was far easier than we ever anticipated. He shouldn't have overestimated them by thinking they could put up a decent fight," they other soldier added.

-"Have you seen it yet?" the larger soldier asked.

-"No, do you know where it is?"

-"On the fifth level. I snuck and got a glimpse of it when I was relieved of patrol duty. If you want, I'll watch things here for you until you get back. It's truly amazing."

-"Alright, I'll be right back," the little soldier said.

-"But you better hurry up. It won't be looking pretty for long seeing as how they are about to start the extraction." Watching the soldier walk into the distance, Ioxus concealed his presence behind the corner to make sense of what he just heard.

-Extraction, what could they possibly be talking about? He thought. *I see now that time is almost up, I must hurry.* He began to run towards the large unsuspecting soldier.

In the central command center of NB4, a rather small soldier had his eyes fixed on the monitor watching as an unknown presence was trailing a ship entering the base, trying to hide behind one of its panels.

-"General Feldspar, there is something I think you should take a look at," he said, "It appears to be a Xextrum, but our records show no information on this one." he added.

-"Could it really be? "Feldspar exclaimed, "Has the Fifth Xextrum finally emerged? Lord Cyranus will be most pleased with this news," he said laughing.

-"Should I sound the alarm, sir?"

-"No, let him think that his presence is concealed to allow us time to capture him," he said, watching as Ioxus used his lightning speed to disappear from sight, leaving nothing but electricity from where he once was.

Rushing to the fifth floor through a staircase, Ioxus could see a light seeping from underneath the door. Realizing that he didn't have the time to play Mr. Invisible any longer, he blasted though the doors and was greeted with the sound of a gunshot and terrible pain emerging through the debris.

-"How do you like that, my mystery Xextrum? It's still in progress but I think it works perfectly fine," Feldspar proclaimed. Oraien felt as if he was dying, like all the energy was being drained from his body.

-"What did you shoot me with?" he managed to ask feebly as he fell on his hands and knees.

-"It's just a little something you may have heard of, only in myth," the general said standing over Ioxus, "dark matter."

-"Impossible," Ioxus said as he hit the ground.

Chapter 15

Capture and Seize

Calea woke up the next morning and realized that it was not a dream that she had that night. She could not find Oraien or Ferra. Calea had no choice but to return to RE2. Once she arrived, she thought back to the day she treated him harshly when they met Kisca and Lok.

-*Is he avoiding me because of that?* She questioned. It burdened her and made her feel uneasy. Calea wished she had the strength to stop him, but he was too fast for her. She began to worry about Oraien, and it greatly distracted her from her duties on base.

Meanwhile, Oraien had been captured on NB4 and taken to a holding room. The room was enormous and housed two gigantic dematerializing generators. They stood fifty feet high in length and width. Each was placed at the ends of the room so anything in the middle could be targeted. Unconscious, Oraien was placed on a vertical table, and they bound his arms outward. The soldiers left the room and turn all the lights off except one that shined over the captive Oraien. When Oraien woke, he noticed that Ioxus had faded away. When he attempted to summon his Xextrum, not a thing occurred.

      Back on Nekio, Retsum was making his final preparations with the council to assemble Grigori's defensive division troops and merge them into the offensive division. Grigori took over the second level fleet while Retsum lead the first. Luna had already sent one third of their fleet to Nekio to assemble within the water atmosphere and await orders from the Alliance. Soon, they would move to join with Igni'ice to increase their chances of victory against the Niphiliem. As the two walked back into the office after watching the formation of troops from the terrace, Retsum spoke.

-"This long life has always sustained its own, good and bad. But there comes a time when fate itself must be changed," Retsum said to Grigori while reading a large map on a wall of the Antares system.

-"Life sustains life, yet do we also fight to defeat death." Grigori replied.

-"My, my, must you people always be so cryptic?" a female voice spoke from the shadows. As she moved into the light, her identity was exposed. "What does that even mean anyway?" she continued.

-"We were beginning to assume Ioxus had gotten the best of you Vexia, glad to know your ok," Retsum spoke.

-"Barely. That guy almost killed me, but rest assured; he has no idea that it was all a part of his training. You sure went out of your way for him," Vexia replied rubbing her hands on the furniture in the room in a seductive manner before she took a seat.

-"Good, so everything went according to plan," Grigori stated.

-"You were able to advance your own quest for the Scrolls, right?" Retsum asked.

-"Yeah, the Demitian unknowingly helped me find a few clues to the location of the closest scroll."

-"So, what news do you bring us on the front?" Grigori asked.

-"Well, I can tell you this. Nibiru is planning an all out attack on your planets to gain access to the Keys and Neo-Quartons of the Xextrum. They are sending forty-five percent of their entire fleet in this next wave."

-"That's less than we expected," Grigori said with a small hint of excitement.

-"I don't mean to burst your bubble of hope, but I need for you to understand what I mean by sixty-five percent," Vexia quickly interjected. "For the last thirty-three years, the only thing Nibiru has done is prepare for war. From the time you are born, you are placed in military school. From there, you become a soldier, and all you want to do is kill by the time you reach that stage. Economy-wise, the entire planet is fueled by the making and distribution of weapons. Every single Niphiliem that isn't in the military serves Lord Cyranus by working in energy plants. For every planet they destroy, they make sure to take a few million slaves back to the planet to work at the plants as well. And to preserve that balance of power, they mass murder a group of older slaves after each new world they conquer. That means every day, all day, all year, the only thing Nibiru does is build up and enhance its military arsenal and capabilities. So know that when I say that they are sending sixty-five percent of the entire military, that could mean that they outnumber the entire Alliance by four to one." Standing up she continued,

-"I sure hope you boys are packin' something special."

-"We have a few surprises, though we hope you will be in place," Retsum stated.

-"Oh don't worry, I'll be in pocket. After, what they did to my family, I'll do everything in my power to destroy all that they stand for.

Feldspar was in his office reviewing the readings of Oraien's Xextrum. NB4 was not a base to be underestimated, and Oraien had done just that.

-Wow. So it was this boy that destroyed NB2. Interesting, Feldspar said to himself while reading the military reports. Feldspar had many thoughts of admiration towards the captive Xextrum while all Oraien could think about while in the dark room was his home. Oraien knew that Luna was not his only home now, but home was also with his friends: Caileb, Azrun, Aiya, and the one that made him feel safe, Calea.

Chapter 16

Feldspar's Manipulation

Conserving his energy, Oraien decided not to waste his strength trying to transform. The only thing he could do was to await his fate. He would not have to wait for long however, because someone had just made their way into the enormous room. The blinding light overhead distorted his vision and he could not make out the figure that was closely approaching. A physical identification of the unknown being was not needed as he spoke as Oraien instantly knew who it was. Feldspar came and stood just outside the range of the light beaming down upon Oraien.

-"Are you enjoying your stay, mystery Xextrum?" he asked sarcastically.

-"For the record, the name is Ioxus," Oraien stated as proudly as he could.

-"But of course you are, the Xextrum of Lightning, right? You see, we have no record of you or your power, but after single-handedly thwarting our plans on Luna in Vicero, Sarren, and then going on to destroy our hidden base, our soldiers now fear the name."

-"Glad to know I have fans. Release me and maybe I'll even sign a few autographs," Oraien said sarcastically, smirking. "But speaking of Sarren, what could you monsters have possibly wanted in that forgotten city?"

-"Has your memory failed you so quickly? Don't you remember what I shot you with?" Closing his eyes, Oraien thought back to the terrible pain he felt earlier before responding.

-"Dark matter? But what does that have to with Sarren?"

-"Sarren… that city is just a holding place of our freedom," Feldspar said.

-"Freedom? Freedom from what? The E.Q.O.D.A. is fighting for freedom from your people's destructive nature." Oraien became riled with anger, and questions began to emerge. "What is your purpose!?" Oraien only let out that one question, and he knew it to be the only question he needed answered. *What is the purpose behind all the killing?* Oraien thought as he let his head down.

-"Purpose?" Feldspar said looking up towards the high ceiling of the large dark room. He let out a deep, murmuring sigh and continued to speak. "It's been so long since I've thought about purpose. Even thinking about it now makes me feel strange... Before the war began, we, Niphiliem, desired to follow in the footsteps of the Shudo'mitian, and we ignorantly proceeded down a path that would ultimately lead to a drastic change in our way of life. It was seventy-four years ago. We wanted to unlock to powers of dark matter to build a better society for ourselves. We progressed slowly due to the limited amount of energy we had, so we attempted something dangerous. Quartiio energy, as you know it, is the combined energy of theoretical light energy and dark energy. Our planets' Quarton flows with the same quartiio energy as all do, and they flow with that energy because within each Quarton, there is a light gate and a dark gate that intersect at a high pressure point to create quartiio energy. We wanted to seal the light gate within our Quarton to allow dark energy to flow on its own because we believed that dark energy is the more powerful of the two." Feldspar put his hand on his forehead, "Because we did not have enough power to seal the light gate, we asked the Xextrum to help us, but we were denied. The Xextrum told us that history would repeat itself if we were to proceed. Without the Xextrum we decided to create our own Xextrum. Our planet's Neo-Quarton was not ready to choose a Xextrum, so we sped up the process by forcing it off the Quarton using our own methods. The Neo-Quarton was put under immense stress and shattered once it finally gave in. We thought that all was lost until scientific research discovered that the fragments held its properties and energy output. With the fragments ready for use, we created our own 'Xextrums' which we called Xodus. Little did we know that such power came with an inconceivable consequence. Before that foolish incident, our people's life span was roughly three hundred years, but after the Neo-Quarton shattered, it plummeted dramatically. Millions died within the first ten years, but some managed to live upwards of forty years, making our average lifespan that of a mere thirty years. You see, the Quarton plagued our people with an invisible disease, and even if you were older than forty, you only lived for forty more years." Oraien's face at this time had completely changed, but he did not allow Feldspar to shake his beliefs. "We no longer had the time to explore dark matter, our extinction was upon us. So we began to search for a cure. Entire planets went extinct before we figured out a cure." Feldspar paused, "The cure was the disease. A doctor took the last fragment of our Quarton and grounded it to a powder, and created ink that could be tattooed onto the body. The ink sustains us as long as it doesn't fade away, but as you know, Neo-Quartons are small. We did not have enough for everyone, so we began destroying planets to get their Neo-Quartons." Feldspar let out another sigh, "This is where we really lost it. In the beginning we only destroyed desolate empty planets in the Caligo system, but soon we realized that the Ink from dead planets faded too rapidly. After more and more of our peoples died, we were driven to commit a great horror. You remember the Zoduk Genocide, right?"

-"Yea, you destroyed the planet and killed all the inhabitants. You exterminated an entire civilization to save yourselves..." Oraien said looking Feldspar directly in the eyes, trying to make sense of what he was hearing. Although the story being told was coming directly from the enemy, Oraien couldn't help but feel that every word Feldspar spoke was the truth.

-"Let me ask you this, Xextrum, since you are so quick to judge. What would you have done if it were your people in our situation? If all the Eluesians were on the verge of extinction, honestly, what would you do?" Oraien's eyes widened. He couldn't find any words to counter his captor's question.

-*What would I have done*, Oraien questioned himself. He was unable to answer or rather he didn't want to answer. He didn't want to face the fact that he may have done the same.

-"We destroyed Zoduk by accident. Our experiment was never meant to go that far," Feldspar had his chance to finally twist the meaning of his words. We only wanted to stay alive and end our suffering as soon as possible. After ten years under the rule of Lord Cyrano, we had destroyed twelve planets with inhabitants, but Zoduk was supposed to be different. After we failed, we resorted back to our previous methods of extracting a planet's Neo-Quarton and decided to continue forward with Luna. However, you stopped us."

-"So you want to kill me and take my Neo-Quarton right?" Oraien took the realization hard, and it made his stomach feel uneasy.

-"Not if you choose to join us, maybe with a Xextrum on our side we could stop destroying planets and release the full potential of dark matter to not only save our people from extinction but to right all the wrongs that we have caused for so many years," Feldspar was attempting to deceive Oraien by telling him half-truths and half-lies, and he knew that his words were sinking into Oraien's mind.

    The fact that Oraien had only been a Xextrum for a few months made it harder for him to make his final decision. He did not know what to do at this point. He was thrown into war and responsibility so unexpectedly that his mind at that moment had too much to process. Oraien closed his eyes and thought back to his training with Retsum as well as his time with Calea, Aiya, Caileb, and Azrun. Everything was so overwhelming for him and he shut down. Feldspar watched as Oraien had lost his conscious and let an evil smile creep across his face.

-*This is it. We will have our Xextrum now. Or else we will kill him and have one of the strongest Neo-Quartons we have ever possessed,* Feldspar thought. Feldspar did not notice that Oraien had seen his smile and made up his mind.

-"Looking at you and thinking of my friends," Oraien knew in his heart what was right and just let it flow from his lips, "You are not asking for my help, Feldspar. You want me to serve as your weapon, and no one is ever going to use me unless I say so. Be on your way Feldspar. My answer is no."

-"How unfortunate, I guess you'll have to serve us in another way," he said approaching Oraien and touching his chest where the Quarton was located. "So, I will take this soon. Oh, and I guess I owe you one more thing before I kill you. The Demitian lead us to something that will help us, but I doubt that we will stop our reign of terror even after we find a permanent cure." He looked at his hand and made a fist, "Once you have power, it's too hard to let it go."

-"That's what you needed Ms. Emery for!" Oraien said as he suddenly realized what was going on.

Echoes of Tempore: Revival of Light

-"You're not the brightest Xextrum in the group, but you're catching on nonetheless," Feldspar exclaimed. "While she has virtually no knowledge of the ancient ways of extracting dark matter, the ancient paths lead to their secrets within the city walls, one of nine Anteeo Scrolls. Allow me to educate you." Feldspar stood at ease, preparing himself for the telling of a history, "Long ago, the ancient Demitians were among the most advanced civilization in the universe. They had a countless number of achievements yet to be rivaled or recreated even after thousands of years. Allow me to tell you of their greatest achievement: the discovery and manipulation of dark matter. It is a mystery how they harnessed it, but it didn't take long for them to realize the overwhelming power it yielded. It was this tremendous power that allowed such legendary accomplishments. Ironically, it was the same power that ultimately lead to their demise. Before the discovery of dark matter, the Demitians lived peacefully as they ventured into the realm of quartiio energy. Once they found the existence of dark matter though, society literally split with the dark energy users calling themselves the Shudo'mitian. Following centuries of experimentations and new innovations, a vicious war erupted which later resulted in the emergence of a being from the dark universe. Society was nearly wiped out as a whole, but in the end, the Demitians won and banished the Shudo'mitian and all knowledge pertaining to dark matter to unknown worlds." His facial expression changed with his anger, "So as I was saying before, without the guide, finding the secrets of your people will be virtually impossible in that city," Feldspar said with anger. "Our methods of Dark matter experimentation, as advanced as they have become recently due to the dark star Caligo, are nowhere near what the ancients were capable of achieving, but with the Anteeo we have a good chance." Feldspar looked at Oraien once again and said, "This is your last offer; join us or die, Xextrum, or..."

As Feldspar began to approach Oraien in his weakened condition, the door opened, and the surrounding soldiers dropped to one knee before Feldspar himself turned to see who it was. Straightening his posture, he placed a hand on his chest and bowed his head, as the unknown figure continued walking not saying a word, allowing only the sound of his footsteps to break the fearful silence in the room. When the silent leader came into view, Oraien's eyes shot open in disbelief and only one mystified word could escape his lips.

-"Xan?"

Chapter 17

Xan's Revelation

-"A weapon that powerful will only cause division between our people! Jovan, think about what you are asking us."

-"I am, we must all stand for one cause, to defend ourselves from the Xodus. Ever since the Niphiliem mysteriously discovered how to divide their Neo-Quarton, all they have done is destroy planet after planet in search for more of them. It has lead to their high efficiency facilities and to stronger commanders in their military. They are following the path of the Shudo'mitian, the original practitioners of dark matter itself. So we must rely on the technology of our good ancestors, not the evil."

The meeting was fierce, however, the need for a weapon of protection found favor within the group, and when the vote was passed, the preparation immediately began. Soon the people began to build a large cylinder shaped generator that had an empty sphere in the middle. The sphere would convert the quartiio energy into the theoretical Light Matter.

-"The Shudo'mitian unlocked the mysteries of dark matter long ago. In theory, if there is dark matter, there should also be Light Matter," Jovan informed.

After the enormous tool was complete, the notice of the Channelir completion was delivered to an office high above in a skyscraper. The messenger shared an immense pressure since Luna and the entire E.Q.O.D.A. were under concerning the growing Niphiliem threat. He eagerly desired that the Channelir bring them hope, no matter which form it came in, and all of the E.Q.O.D.A. sat still that day in anticipation of a miracle. The messenger reached Jovan's office and walked through the door. As he looked through the room he saw Jovan sitting at his desk with his eyes closed and his arms crossed,

-"Sir Jovan, here is the notice regarding the Channelir." Jovan opened his eyes and peered at the courier through the steam of his coffee as he was handed the piece of paper.

-"Thank you. Tell the troops that we activate tonight, while Vicero sleeps," said Jovan.

-"Yes, sir," the messenger saluted and went his way.

Jovan was head of the Assembly of Vicero as well as one of three members of the Luna Legislation. His status was hard earned through his life, and he was earnestly loyal to his people. Jovan thought of his life as he stood from the chair and walked to the balcony of his office. He could see the Quarton glowing with energy in the distance, and the Channelir was so large itself he could see it clearly from where he stood. Soon, the message would reach the ground, and its initiation would be activated.

As Jovan leaned against the soft rails of his veranda, he looked into the stars and closed his eyes, at that moment a loud deep knock echoed throughout the city. The noise came from the Channelir, and very soon the weapon began to channel neon-purple energy from the Quarton into the glass sphere. All went well as the sphere began to glow with a bright light. The Quarton's symbols began to pulse, alerting the ground units, and immediately the sphere was at its capacity.

Five men disconnected the sphere from the Channelir and transported it to an outside base. Jovan followed behind the transporter, and they all entered into a lab dome once they all arrived. The sphere was attached in the center of the room. The top of the glass ball had a latch where an engineer placed a large cable.

-"I will now prove to you that Light Matter exists by letting it flow through this laser upward towards space. Oddly, Light Matter does not give off light, yet the energy it produces can be seen by the naked eye. It should appear to be almost clear, faintly white," The scientist spoke and began to activate the laser. At that instant, cracks began to forge all around the sphere.

-"Turn that laser off! The sphere is going to explode!" Jovan yelled as he jumped for cover. All the glass from the sphere dropped straight to the ground, yet no energy was visible.

-"This is our weapon after all that money and time?!" asked a commander.

    Everybody within the dome began to argue over the seemingly foolish decision they had made. It appeared that Luna's hopes had sunken into hopelessness as the clamoring became louder and more hostile, but out from all the noisy chatter, leaped the cry of an infant. All the discussion ceased, and the leaders looked in the direction of the sound. No one could believe their eyes, for what they saw was a baby laying in the middle of the glass from the sphere.

    Months later and after several studies, a conclusion was made. The mysterious powers of the Quarton caused a phenomenon to occur in the attempt to create Light Matter as a weapon, and the quartiio energy was directed into a life.

The infant was a baby boy, who had horizontal markings on his abdomen that matched many symbols found in the ancient Demitian alphabet and on the planet's Quarton. Two years later there was a second attempt to create Light Matter, but this led to the result of another life. It was another baby boy, and he had vertical markings on the right side of his chest. They could not explain how or where the two children had come from, but they decided to change a few specifications and re-launch the Channelir. It was tested again a third and fourth time, but these attempts did not produce any results at all. So the leaders of Luna began to pursue another avenue to increase their defenses.

    The first child was named Xan; he was kept at the South Luna Base, while the younger child was sent to Vicero to live a normal life. Xan grew up in a military school with the knowledge of his birth, but it never made him feel any different towards anyone. In many cases, he exceeded not just the children in his level, but also those older than him, even his superiors' had difficulty keeping up with him. His body was faster, stronger, and he learned at a miraculous rate. All his excellence was explained to be a part of where he was from his birth, and his parents. Theory after theory was thrown at Jovan as to Xan's purpose. Many thought that he came from another universe while others believed Xan and the other boy were the Quarton incarnate, but what did resonate with them all was the strange eerie feeling they experienced when they were around either child.

During Xan's upcoming, the far away Niphiliem planet Nibiru, was watching. They never took eyes off of Luna, and they had many spies hidden within their ranks. One Nibiru spy that participated in the Light Matter Project witnessed the birth of Xan. The spy immediately knew that she needed to report her discovery to her superiors. While the spy attempted upload the information to Nibiru, she was discovered and imprisoned, but the information had already made its way to the planet. Months passed as Luna continued their project of future defense, but they did not know that the Niphiliem finally deciphered the information sent to them by the spy.

With the knowledge of Xan's birth, they infiltrated the base in which he was schooled. The Niphiliem had everything they needed to make a swift mission; blueprints, and staff schedules. They kidnapped Xan at the age of six, and by the time his warden figured out what happened, the Niphiliem had already departed and exited with the defense satellites disabled. They never saw the second child because he had been dispatched to Vicero without record of his connection to the project. Soon after the event, a brief meeting was held between Jovan and key leaders of the E.Q.O.D.A.

concerning the kidnapping. The meeting continued for hours, but it was only when Retsum arrived that the meeting really began. Entering the room, he sat down next to all the other leaders and cleared his throat to speak.

-"I am here on behalf of the Xextrum. I have spoken with Charrio Megas from the Noali Quadrant." The leaders began to speak amongst themselves at the mention of the name.

-"So what did he have to say?" asked Jovan.

-"Jovan, even though your intentions were right, the project may have brought the Niphiliem more power. We don't know what the children can do, what their powers are, or their purpose." Retsum lowered his head and rested his chin on his crossed fists. "Where is the other child?"

-"He is safe, no one knows about his involvement other than me and the Demitian Tarria. She is personally watching over him now."

-"Well, the only thing left to do is wait, and have hope. Have you taken care of your security?"

-"We've already taken care of that; the system is run directly under my control. Now with a new and improved cryptogram structure, we have already found all ten of the Niphiliem infiltrators."

-"So you had spies within the government?"

-"Jovan, you have no choice but to increase security, not everyone can be trusted," said Retsum.

-"True, but you live and you learn. We found a Niphiliem female spy hacking the satellite system. It seems that she not only disabled the system, but she also uploaded information written in a code we cannot decipher. It's too late to get him back, but while we build our forces for the attack, we must also defend ourselves. I can't wait till this war is over, ending in a complete victory in our favor," said Jovan with a silent sigh.

-"Well said," Retsum agreed, "Jovan, old friend. If the people of Luna ever need aide, you know who to contact. I wish you and your people safety." After Retsum finished talking, the meeting ended within the hour.

    Security on Luna increased, and their defenses were soon believed to be impenetrable. They created a satellite patrol area that implemented two satellites to orbit the planet at parallel locations. The energy used for the satellites came from lasers that were located on the ground that channeled the quartiio energy of the Quarton to each satellite. Once the system was perfected, other planets around the Great Ring began to follow in their footsteps.

After the meeting, the Niphiliem arrived with Xan at their home planet Nibiru, and immediately began to run test on him. The Niphiliem desired to explore his potential, and why his birthright made him such an asset to Luna. They concluded that he could live much longer, heal faster, and become stronger than any living race. The Niphiliem saw that they indeed had a weapon; a weapon that could think, strategize, fight, and conquer. Xan was taught the ways of Niphiliem politics, economics, wars, and beliefs in a military institute called Leadus.

Naturally, as Xan aged he began to believe the prospects of Nibiru. *To have peace, order must be forced upon the weak from the strong.* Nibiru viewed themselves as the stronger race, including Xan into its ranks due to his roots. Xan also had one major attribute that set him apart from the rest of the Niphiliem; he did not have to depend on Neo Ink to survive. He wanted to end their struggles so they could continue in the Shudo'mitian's path. At the age of nineteen, Xan rose to the fourth highest rank and was the future successor of Cyranus who was the head of all the divisions of Nibiru and its people.

Being at his position and having his advanced intelligence, Xan lead the Niphiliem to much advancement in technology. When he proved that he could change their existing energy, the Niphiliem introduced him to their secrets experimentations with dark matter. Xan was mystified and taken by the potential he saw, but not even he could unlock its secrets. Eventually, Xan and members of his command discovered through ancient records that the Shudo'mitian had much of their power come from activating the Quarton of a star named Caligo. It seemed impossible to Xan, but the records did not lie. With firm determination Xan lead a team to find the Caligo star, which by that time was no longer a star, but a black hole. No one knew what to think, or do, but Xan decided to go in search for more ancient records. Cyranus and Absalon decided to promote Xan to third rank, and Xan took Feldspar's title.

By the time Xan was twenty-one, and he had made history in the Niphiliem government. He had done more than any single person had ever done, but he had much to learn about the Niphiliem people. After serving his duty on the planet, Xan was granted a Warus Battle Ship, but there was one more mission Xan also wanted control over. He spoke with Cyranus about becoming a spy in the E.Q.O.D.A., and there was no debate about it. Xan was

Eluesian after all, and it would be nothing for him to build his reputation. Never did Cyranus realize how powerful of an ally Xan would become when they kidnapped him so many years ago, and he knew that he would use Xan till the bitter end.

    Occasionally, Xan would receive orders from Cyranus and Absalon; the most recent of his orders instructed him to travel to the Fourth Niphiliem Base to learn about the progress they had made and to also pick up the Zeofieren sphere. When Xan arrived at the base he was greeted by Feldspar and five soldiers.

-"Hello Xan, I see you've finally become my superior."

-"Yes, and from now on you'll be calling me Lord Xan, and now that I am here, Feldspar, let me inform you of my orders. Absalon requires that I personally deliver a report on your progress as well as the sphere you obtained from Igni'ice."

-"Come to the office, you should relax. We can discuss this matter somewhere else other than the docking station, Xan. Oh, and I have some interesting news for you." said Feldspar.

    Xan entered the base and was escorted to the upper level. He reached his private quarter and prepared himself for the next day. Xan dressed in uniform and realized that each day of his life, everything followed the same order. The only time of the day that Xan ever thought of anything but his mission was the five minutes he spent looking at himself in the mirror while brushing his teeth. It made him uncomfortable because deep within his own conscience, he did not know who he was. Exiting his room at the third hour of the day he headed for the meeting place Feldspar had prepared for him. Feldspar awaited Xan in the room at the end of a large hallway designed for a transport ship. A few soldiers directed Xan and his men towards the black doors leading to the dock. When the doors opened, all Xan could see was darkness, and in the far center of the room stood two soldiers and Feldspar. Feldspar was speaking to a captive held under an interrogation light, but he stopped once Xan was seen entering the room. The soldiers bowed before Xan and Feldspar gave his respect by bowing his head.

-"The attack on Igni'ice failed since they had three Xextrum protecting them, two in Evalesco and one in Raveria. Luckily, the Sphere was located in Celeres, and with our numbers, we were able to grab the Key and make a swift getaway. This Eluesian came here to take back the sphere, but even better, he is Ioxus in the flesh."

-"Ioxus." Xan whispered. Xan was surprised to find Ioxus here. Walking into the light, Oraien got a good look at his captor's leader, and it was none other than the soldier that sacrificed himself for the mission back In Raveria.

-"How is this possible?" Oraien stated.

-"I could ask you the same Ioxus. Or shall I say Oraien", Xan replied laughing, "Who would have thought that the second child would become Ioxus?" he continued. "It's almost poetic in a sense."

"Second child? Just what the hell does that mean and how is it that you're still alive?!" Oraien asked.

"Well, I had to ensure that one of you Xextrum came here." Xan said.

-"What?" Oraien said in confusion.

-"How is it that you think the Alliance obtained the coordinates to this base?" Xan said smiling devilishly. "I leaked the coordinates to ensure that one of you fools would come and be captured, but things took a turn for the worse when my idiot subordinates stole them back. So to guarantee my plan was executed, I helped in the search to recover the letter by merely playing my role as a spy. Once the coordinates were back in your possession there was no longer any need to keep up my false facade, so I volunteered to stay behind and make it appear as if I had been killed by that woman's attack. But to answer your first question, didn't you ever wonder why you had no parents, no family at all growing up? Well let's just say that you and I are what people call brothers," he smiled. "Brothers born from the same mother, Luna. Didn't Tarria tell you anything?" he asked bitterly sarcastic.

As much as he wanted to deny it, Oraien could feel the truth. All his life he felt different from others, and in a time of chaos, when there must have been millions of others asking for help and the strength to fight back during the invasion, the Quarton chose him, proof that he was connected to it. As Xan was encircling Oraien, Feldspar interrupted,

-"I tried to persuade him all night, and he does not want to join us, Lord Xan. He is blinded by the ways of the Xextrum! Lord Xan, please allow us to use him as bait to..."

-"Silence, Feldspar," Xan said.

-"Join us or die here, now, Oraien; that is the reality of the situation. Make no mistake, our common origins mean nothing to me. Regardless of whether you live or die, I will destroy all that you know and create a galaxy without needs. Everyone will have what they need; limitless energy." Xan paused and looked directly into Oraien's eyes, "When I walk outside of this room and the door is shut, it will also shut all hopes for your survival. So make your decision now or be destroyed along with everything else." Xan said as he turned and started walking. Feldspar joined him and so did all the Niphiliem.

-"Xan! Wait! Tell me more about our parents!" Oraien screamed. Xan stopped half way to the exit and turned,

-"Our parents? There is no us, Oraien there is no you and me. Don't ever think of me as family, you Duro. Besides... I told you everything I know," he said as he turned and continued walking. "It doesn't matter anymore though, you are dead." The light went out, and Oraien could feel his whole life flood his eyes for the first time.

-What am I?

Chapter 18

New Found Power

All alone in the dark room, Oraien was left in solitude. He couldn't see nor hear anything except for his tiresome breathing and the creaking of his restraints every time he tried to break them. Being in the dark for so long, he lost track of time and could no longer tell how long he had been held captive.

-How long have I been here? A week? No, at least two.

His concentration was broken as the lights in the room suddenly turned on, blinding Oraien momentarily. It was a group of Niphiliem who came to feed him. They fed him scarcely and very cruelly every chance they got, often beating him while in his helpless state. Once the soldiers left, days went by before he heard or saw anything but the darkness that enshrouded the room. Without warning, Oraien began to hear a buzzing sound coming from the generators located on both sides of the massive dark room.

As the sound became louder and louder, he could feel something was terribly wrong with him. The buzzing sound soon faded into very strong vibrations that shook the entire room, putting Oraien's body under stress. More and more, he could feel the inside of his body being pulled to the surface of his skin. Eventually the pain became unbearable, and Oraien let out a terrifying scream of pain. He was being tortured to death, and on top of that, he could feel the vibrations pulling on the Neo-Quarton within his body, trying to take it out of him.

-*Am... I... going to die?* The words could barely enter his mind, *Have I... come all this way... for nothing? There is still much I have to do!* He forced the words into his mind. Oraien let out another roar of pain before attempting to hold himself together. *There's no way... I can let it end like this!* And with yet another mysterious explosion of determination, Oraien managed to say a few words,

-"There are still people I want to protect!"

With the howl of resilience, the faces of his friends found their way into his mind. He was not sure why, but as he continued to think, all the people back on his home world came into his mind as well. They also needed his protection, and soon, he could feel a strength building within him once again. Now two forces fought each other within his body, each with the goal to win over his Neo-Quarton.

-I promised I would protect you, and I will! He remembered the promise he made to Calea and all the people of his home world, all while Xan's ruthless words kept festering in his mind.

Through all the pain, he could once again feel the pulsing sensation he felt back on Luna. Although he self triggered the pulsing with his desire to protect, it was fueled by his anger. The anger painfully manifested itself inside Oraien's being and almost became its own entity. The pain he felt inside combined with the outside agony began to drive him to the brink of throbbing insanity. Oraien would do anything to prevent his fears from happening, and when that fear finally developed his mind, it shook the foundations of his very being; then the impossible happened.

A violent light exploded from within Oraien. It was the mystical implosion that drew forth his Xextrum, but this explosion was much larger, completely destroying everything within a fifty feet radius. He blew out the power in the room, and the base resorted to emergency power, barely lighting the room. Oraien floated in the center of the exploded room, and electricity filled the ambiance, circulating and traveling from his entire body. He had transformed into Ioxus, but his Xextrum was now much stronger and faster. It also had more armor for protection, and when jettisoned, the great sword Exus had been altered. Oraien transcended his Xextrum to its next level: the Deo phase.

    Oraien noticed that even in gravity he was able to float. The alarm sounded. Oraien dashed through the air towards the door and released a discharge from his sword, completely demolishing the wall it was attached to. Exiting the room, he quickly found himself being engaged in combat with the Niphiliem. With the frequency of the sphere still embedded in his suit, he began making his was way through the ship until he reached its location.

-"XAN!!!" Ioxus yelled. Anger still surged through his veins, and the new power made him feel capable of wreaking much havoc.

Chapter 18.5

Ioxus vs. Feldspar

-"This is quite the surprise, Oraien. Lord Xan left long ago," Feldspar said turning to get a good look at Oraien. "I see that you even managed to transform into Ioxus, though... you do look a little different," he said ending his statement in confusion looking at his appearance.

-"Yeah, let me show you just how different I am," Ioxus stated as he unsheathed his sword from his back and began approaching Feldspar.

As the fight began, six Niphiliem dashed to intercept Ioxus. The two on the outer corner released beams of dark matter from their guns while the two in the middle threw quantum grenades to disable the atoms around Oraien and prevent him from converting them into his own usable energy. Instantly, Ioxus side-stepped into a handstand and threw himself over the two beams but suffered heavy damage from the quantum grenades. Landing just thirty meters from the six

Niphiliem, Oraien looked into the eyes of one, readying his counter attack within his mind and striking fear into the eyes of the loyal soldier.

    Locking onto Feldspar's subordinates through the eyes of his Xextrum, Ioxus quickly charged up a single discharge and released it from the palm of his hand. As the ball of powerful electricity traveled towards them, it separated into the corresponding number of enemies he locked onto and obliterated them on impact. Their bodies fell to the ground limp and burned by the high voltage energy that surged through their bodies. Caught off guard, Ioxus was once again shot by Feldspar with dark matter, but in his new form, that only weakened him. Oraien dragged himself to his feet and spoke.

-"Typical Niphiliem Duro, hiding behind your twisted ways of power. You're too weak to fight me head on." Oraien began to provoke Feldspar hoping he would take the bait and fight Oraien fairly. Feldspar stood straight and let the gun rest at his side. He then looked up as if he was thinking and smiled.

-"I'm not stupid, Xextrum. Remember that I am a Xodus, and you should know by now that we are smarter than these mindless soldiers you have become accustomed to," He lifted his dark particle cannon and aimed, "This fight will not be fair. I have more power than you do, and as far as I can see, I have the upper hand. On your guard, boy!" Feldspar yelled as he let out a dangerous shot of black energy towards Ioxus.

    Oraien had the time to dodge the shot but was hit directly by the next, and the next, and the next. Oraien was used to his new abilities only to the extent of the first level of his Xextrum, but now that he had transcended to the next level, he did not know how to control it. However with his anger accumulating, Oraien noticed that he had better control of his new limits. With that knowledge, Oraien pushed himself to control his anger and sharpen his focus when receiving massive damage.

    The energy bullets pierced Ioxus's defenses and clouded his vision in blackness. He lost massive amounts of energy but stood strong and firm, walking towards Feldspar step by step. Quickly he thought back to his teachings on Nekio, remembering that his Neo-ray allows him to see in the darkness. Feldspar could not see or sense Oraien's energy approaching him due to the energy of dark matter covering the entire passageway, but he could hear a noise coming from the direction where he last saw Oraien. The noise sounded as if their surroundings were being destroyed and absorbed into a vacuum. Once the noise stopped, Feldspar convinced himself that he had totally destroyed Ioxus. As he dropped his guard, a metal fist emerged from the darkness and struck Feldspar in the chest. Immediately after, he fell to the ground but continued to slide across the floor and through the wall at the end of the corridor. By the time Feldspar came to a rest and tried to pick himself up, Oraien was already standing behind him. Ioxus grabbed his face and lifted Feldspar to eye level. Ioxus then punched Feldspar's head out of the grip of his hand and into a wall over to the side. Blood shot across the wall as his head beat against the solid metal barrier, but Oraien continued his pursuit. Oraien jumped straight into Feldspar with his knees pounding the flesh out of Feldspar's body through his armor. Feldspar could not counter because of Oraien's speed, but through the terrible agony he was in, he noticed how Ioxus's eyes were focused; frightening. Oraien grabbed Exus and separated the swords, lounging both tips threw Feldspars armor, his body, and the wall behind him.

-"War is life, commander." Oraien said not directly looking into Feldspar's eyes. "War is death…" Oraien pulled out one of the swords and turned and walked a few steps away. "War is real and never will it not exist!" Oraien was blind by anger, and Feldspar was barely alive, but a crazy idea came into Feldspar's mind at that very moment.

-I might as well try it. I'm dead either way. Feldspar looked into the Xodus Fragment located on his broken left arm and looked over the Dark Particle Cannon in his right hand. He lifted the gun with one fluid motion, jammed it into his fragment, and pulled the trigger releasing dark energy through his body and broke off the gun handle to keep the flow of energy surging.

    Oraien finally snapped out of his blind rage and controlled his anger once again. He let out a breath of victory but was too late to sense the dangerous force behind him. He turned to see what the source of the power was and was knocked into the next room by Feldspar. Ioxus crashed through the wall and was buried by rubble, but knew that Feldspar was approaching fast. Oraien jumped from the debris and put his hand out to catch Feldspar's blows at the point of impact.

"How are you still alive?" Oraien asked, but Feldspar could not speak. It was as if he had changed into an animal.

Oraien could barely hold his ground against Feldspar, but fought hard enough to notice the cannon was surging dark matter through Feldspar's Xodus Fragment. The battle waged on until Oraien could no longer spare any energy due merely to his bleeding body underneath the Xextrum armor.

Feldspar had the upper hand and took his revenge on Oraien tenfold. With several loud cracks Oraien's entire right arm was shattered beneath his armor, disabling him greatly. Feldspar advanced again but hit Oraien head on this time shattering many of Oraien's ribs and causing him severe internal bleeding.

All was lost, and Feldspar stood over Oraien ready for the last attack. The dark energy at his command, and a legend at his feet, Feldspar always wanted to feel utter victory, but it came at a high price. The dark energy began to reject the Xodus Fragment, and it burrowed further into Feldspar's body to escape the control of the fragment. Feldspar fell face-first to the ground and could feel his very life energy being ripped apart from the conflict of the opposing energies in his body. After just a few minutes,

Feldspar exploded into nothingness and the battle was over. Oraien witnessed the entire event but could only conclude that it was the dark matter that killed Feldspar. Oraien used his ability to defy gravity to stand against a wall.

-I can't waste any energy, Oraien thought to himself

He saw a hallway burned by dark matter but could only think of one thing, *I was created by man*. Oraien could sense the reality if he would allow it, but it would drown him in questions that he did not have time to think of. Fearing that he missed the opportunity to complete his mission, Oraien used the last of his energy the speed towards the energy remnants of the Zeofieren Sphere. When he reached the end of the room, the Key was not in sight. He began to scan the entire base but found that the Key was no longer in the facility.

Interrupted by two Niphiliem soldiers, Ioxus split his swords and threw them into his enemies. He then used his palm of his left hand to attract the swords. Knowing if he didn't escape soon he would be captured again, he used his anger, his pain, and all his strength combined to let out a single attack. He lifted his left arm and let all his energy escape upward causing a colossal surge of lightning to blast a hole straight through every floor of the fortified base. The lightning left the base and continued on into empty space. Oraien then jumped into the path of destruction with the last fibers of his strength and allowed the suction of space to pull him into its void. Ferra spotted Oraien and immediately picked him up. Once aboard, tired and wounded, Oraien ordered Ferra to head back to Igni'ice. With enemy ships in pursuit of Ferra, she blasted off into the distance in stealth mode, completely outmaneuvering and outrunning all enemy fire.

Chapter 19

Basium

When Ferra neared the space area around the RE2 moon base station, Oraien did not wake up. All he could envision in his mind was the truth of his birth, his close encounter with death, and that the only person he could call family was his dark brother, born of the same planet as he. He also felt the pressure of failure because he was not able to retrieve the Zeofieren Sphere. The weight of the entire situation along with the failure of his mission proved to be too devastating for him to handle, and sleeping helped him stay detached from reality.

Port operators soon noticed the sedentary ship, and tried communicating with the vessel. When no answer was heard, a low level alert was called. Some officials demanded that the ship be destroyed and others requested a scan, but a scanning procedure could only be done near the ship, so it made that option more dangerous. After a decision could not be made a message was sent to Caileb.

Echoes of Tempore: Revival of Light

The report of the ship reached one of Caileb's subordinates, who eventually informed Calea and all other commanding officers. Calea then told Caileb that she would handle the situation. Calea went alone, knowing that her brother and father would be busy discussing battle tactics for the Alliance. When Calea arrived at the moon base port she was greeted by the port chief,

-"Commander Calea, was your brother not able to come?"

-"Chief, is there something I cannot do for you?!" Calea asked firmly. "My brother is busy, and this is only a level one situation. So if you don't believe I can handle this, then please..."

-"Sorry, Commander," the chief bowed his head. "As you can see there is a ship that has just entered the RE2 space area. The code matches our authorization, but there is no response." Calea could see the ship through the V.D. in the port traffic control center.

-"Zoom in closer to the ship. It looks a little familiar." Calea requested. As the chief gave an operator the signal, the image of the ship became very clear to Calea. Her voice changed into a controlled excitement.

-"Get me a scanning team and a stand-by medical crew. I'll be heading the scanning team personally." Calea said.

-"You know this ship, miss?" The chief asked.

-"Yes, it is Ferra, the ship of Ioxus." Immediately the chief called for the two groups and Calea to head down to the port.

 Knowing she would see him soon made her anxious and excited. He had been gone for almost three weeks. As Calea entered the ship, she almost let out a scream. Oraien was not asleep on the healing bed of Ferra; he instead was sitting still, almost lifeless. Blood colored the floor, and Oraien was unconscious in the corner of the ship, his Xextrum kept him alive by preventing massive blood loss. He did not have anything left inside him, no will and no strength.
 Calea, who had become strong through the devastations of war, fought her shock and pushed it aside. She struggled to get Oraien on her back. She put each of his arms around her and carried him off the ship to the shaken team. Rushing out to the sound of an alarm, the

medical team came and took Oraien away, assuring Calea that they would do what they could.

      Entering the RE2 moon base from the southern port, Aiya arrived a few days ahead of schedule to attend the meeting between the Alliance Council leaders. The mission she handed off to Oraien was starting to weigh heavily on her mind and soon she started to get a bad feeling regarding his well being. As she traveled through the corridors of the moon base to rendezvous with Azrun, she could hear chaos throughout the facility. Soldiers were rushing about franticly trying to make their way to the port. Aiya stopped a passing soldier to find out what the commotion was all about.

-"Hey, what's going on, why is everyone rushing around like this?"

-"Lady Aiya, guess you haven't heard? Oraien Zeal has returned from his mission but has suffered great injuries and is at the brink of death. He's being rushed to the infirmary as we speak."

When the news was conveyed to Aiya, she felt as if her heart dropped to her feet. Her doubts had become a reality and she could feel the tears begin to well in her eyes as she began to expect the worse. Oraien fell into a trap that was meant for her. Leaving the soldier behind, she dashed off from her position, leaving an icy mist in her wake. When she arrived at the infirmary, she was not allowed to enter the room due to the doctors performing operation on Oraien's wounds. The only thing she could do at the moment was wait as she took a seat across the hall. She was sure of only one thing; she would not leave his side.

Asleep and lost, days meant nothing to Oraien. He could not feel them pass, much less feel himself. Calea and Aiya both would often come and check on him with Azrun stopping by twice, hoping that he could pull himself through. When the doctor spoke with the two women, she could empathize with their pain.

-"I'm sorry, Oraien is physically fine, yet it seems that something traumatic has caused his mind to protect him by locking out his senses, causing him to sleep. Oraien must find his path before his body permanently shuts down. Sadly, it's something that he has to do on his own since he cannot hear us."

The news struck them hard and cold as neither one could bare to look at Oraien. Aiya could not bear the reality that she might never get to let her feelings out to him, and Calea could not believe that she may never feel his protection again, never hear him laugh or see his smile again. Later that night, Calea went back to see Oraien. She sat next to his bed and while in deep thought, Calea remembered a song that her mother would sing to her during her childhood. Calea's mother told her that the melody and the words could make someone feel stronger within themselves. Calea closed her eyes and tried as hard as she could to remember the beautiful song. The melody caught her tongue first, and the words soon after revealed themselves to her. Looking at the stars and planets through the window in Oraien's room the magical song began to flow...

The weight of hope is great yet great. Ten guardians carry universal sustenance, ten corners embrace weariness. Oh my guardian, Oh my seraph. You cannot bear the burden on your own, therefore my guardian, allow love into your sanctuary. There is a star knocking at your hearts gate. Listen closely.

Tears rolled down her face at the end of the song, but her voice was steady and affectionate. She rose from her chair and gently kissed Oraien on the cheek and departed. Oraien could hear a beautiful voice echo through his mind, and the words swam through his stillness. He also felt a tender connection to the real world. Oraien wanted more of this connection; however, he could not bring himself to reality. Oraien struggled and fought, but it was all in vain until he remembered whom that connection came from.

-"Calea," Oraien said as he woke up. By the time he got up, Calea had already left, and he saw that Aiya had her arms around him. Aiya let him go, surprised, and her eyes began to glaze as tears built up behind her pride.

-"Oraien-you-you're ok!" Aiya threw her arms around him and Oraien braced himself for the pain her weight would cause him. Once she was done holding him Aiya sat down on the bed and spoke.

-"It was my mission…" She looked away from him with guilt, "I should have never let you take my mission." Oraien put his hand on top of hers.

-"It was meant to be Aiya; nothing happens for no reason. You told me that, remember," Aiya gave him her full attention. "If you would have gone, there was a possibility that you would not have made it."

-"That same thing could have happened to you."

-"But it didn't. See me now; I'm here," Aiya looked down at Oraien's hands.

-"It's because of that song Calea sang to you," Oraien knew that it was Calea, even though she was gone when he woke up.

-"All that matters is that your here," Oraien said pulling Aiya closer to embrace her.

-"No, you come here," she said as they hugged each other.

    The next morning Oraien began his search for Calea. He tried contacting her using his MICE but could not get through to her. Oraien was on the RE2 moon base that orbited the Stegeton Igni'ice, and he was not at all familiar with its layout. Oraien searched for the port and finally found it. Looking even further, he found Ferra at the furthest docking station down the west port hall. He entered his ship with the hope to figure out where everyone had gone. As he walked through the ship, he thought back to his miraculous escape from NB4 and remembered that it was Ferra that rescued him and brought him back to safety.

-"Thanks, Ferra, you got my back don't you," he said rubbing the control panel. "Update me on what is currently going on regarding my mission." She displayed text informing him that a meeting concerning the Niphiliem's possible plans with the Zeofieren and the Zodok sphere was coming to order at the conference room of the base. "Ferra, where is the conference room?" She displayed a large gathering of people in a conference hall in the east wing of the facility, so Oraien left the ship and went straight to the meeting.

While Oraien made his way through the base, lingering thoughts of Xan crept into his mind. He cancelled them out, however, by focusing on what he needed to do at the meeting. Nonetheless, Oraien found himself looking at the walls of the base and seeing illusions of dark matter appear as it did on the Niphiliem base. Oraien hit the wall of a hallway and closed his eyes. He wanted to forget about everything.

-"Are you ok?" A soldier had surprised Oraien while his eyes were closed. Oraien immediately grabbed the solider by the neck as electric sparks were emitted from his fists and forearms, but when he saw that it was just a fellow trooper he let him go with his sincere apologies. Oraien finally made his way to the room and stood before its entrance.

As he opened the door, all the chatter stopped and focused on Oraien. All eyes were on him, yet he did not notice any of them other than two sets of eyes that he knew from Luna: Tarria Emery and Assembly Leader Jovan. As the entire meeting body looked at him in astonishment, Oraien could feel the sickness of his terrible experience fade. He stood before people that needed to hear his words, and he spoke without bond.

-"E.Q.O.D.A.. I bring you information pertaining to the plans of the Niphiliem." As Oraien told the accounts of his near-death experience, the assembly became riled and troubled.

-"The Niphiliem will not hesitate in using the two Keys to unleash Caligo." Ms. Emery stood and said. Oraien's eyes squinted in confusion of her comment.

-"For all we know, they probably already have." Said Jovan.

-"Please, there must be something..." Oraien was cut off by another presence entering the room. It was Aiya, and she had her eyes dead set on Oraien.

-"There is more hope than we think," her attention shifted to the group. "Azrun, Oraien, and I are only three Xextrum. Master Retsum makes four, but have you forgotten of the other that resides within the quadrant as well? Avius. Have you also forgotten of his planet, Arius? Oraien has fought and seen the new power of the Niphiliem, and their dark matter. E.Q.O.D.A, we Xextrum need your support. Will you agree to a meeting with Arius?"

-"If we send out a delegation to Arius, we will receive nothing from them, just as in the previous attempt. They do not care about what is going to happen to us." Proevus spoke.

-*Proevus? Is everyone here?* Oraien asked himself. He scanned the room to see if anyone else was there he knew and found Caileb, Calea, Retsum, Azrun, Kilm, Nolus and the Calfieren leader Maltoris, all together for one monumental meeting of the E.Q.O.D.A.

-"Yes, true, but we are not the type of people to let a helpless planet be conquered or destroyed by the enemy. Otherwise, we are no better than the Niphiliem," said Aiya.

-"What is this you speak of, Aiya?" demanded Maltoris. Retsum interrupted and kept Aiya from responding.

-"Our sources informed us that the Niphiliem are planning on attacking Arius and they will succeed if we do not help them." Immediately the room began to chatter about what they had just heard. Let us go ahead of the Niphiliem and sway them to join the E.Q.O.D.A." She spoke to everyone as a single unit. "In war, customs are ignored, rules are broken, and only those who are determined to lead can prevent chaos." The assembly began to debate amongst themselves. Aiya looked at Oraien and grabbed him by the arm. She then touched his forehead as if she was checking to see if he had a fever and touched his chest near his heart.

-"Your Neo-Quarton is responding well to my touch," she said. Azrun was making his way down through the group of people to confront Aiya. The people began to slowly quiet down in anticipation of a decision.

-"Stop touching Rai like he's a baby, Aiya. He can handle himself. Believe me, I know," said Azrun. Aiya dropped her hands off of Oraien and gave him a flirtatious wink while turning to face the crowd. Standing next to Caileb, Calea raised her eyebrow in witnessing Aiya's advance,

-"The Alliance has decided to allow a mission to Arius, with permission to materials, supplies, and people to accomplish the mission. The delegation will consist of Aiya, Oraien, Calea, and Azrun," said Retsum. "The open meeting is now over, Xextrum, and Alliance soldiers feel free to caucus amongst yourselves as the council members must now speak in private." Before Retsum left with the other Leaders, he walked over to Oraien and put one arm around him.

-"We only have our comrades around as long as they are alive! So remember that your life is a victory in itself."

The meeting room immediately turned into a social event, and everyone began to chat and laugh as they exchanged war stories. Oraien wanted to enjoy himself but could not bring himself to forget what his brother Xan revealed to him. Oraien walked out to a large deck that overlooked the stars of night sky. He pondered his near death experience. The thoughts brought his face down in sorrow for his brother, and Oraien could almost not endure the undeniable evidence that pointed to the cold truth. Oraien placed his hand over his heart, feeling for the warm resonance of the Neo-Quarton within him. Mourning was the only thing he desired to do at the moment, but he felt that he had a duty, and feeling too many emotions was out of the question. Nonetheless, he felt it in his knees and reality, and at long last it pierced his steadfast heart. He could hold them back no longer, and let out a many tears, but did everything he could to hold back the rest. In the party, Aiya realized that Oraien was not around, so she began to look for him. She found him alone on the large observation deck and started to approach him. Walking closer, she realized that he was troubled.

-"Are you going to just stand there?" Oraien could sense Aiya's presence, and she came to his side. "Aiya, have you ever wondered if stars are alive?" Oraien said. She then gazed out at the stars.

-"The ancients say that they are. Why?" she asked.

-"If I did not have a mother or a father," Oraien looked at the stars as if he was part of them, then he looked into Aiya's eyes and continued, "Don't ask me how because I don't understand. It could be possible but, if I was born of a planet, would you feel differently about me?" The abruptness of the question took Aiya but surprise, but she answered Oraien by shaking her head while still keeping eye contact.

    Aiya had grown to adore Oraien since their first meeting, and his sensitivity made her desire to comfort him. Aiya told Oraien before how she felt about him, but the situation was not the same. She wanted to let him know that she was sure, and that she wanted him. Aiya was a woman, decisive and strong. She knew what she wanted, so she hugged him softly. Her body felt warm against his. Her arms did not want to let him go, and Oraien could feel all the tension slip away.

-"Rai, I want to help you carry your burden. I want to be by your side because, Oraien...because..." She stopped her words and turned him around. "I haven't felt this way in a long time. It's been so long I don't even know what to say so I'll just show you." She grabbed his hands and kissed him with all the gentleness she could ever show. For the first time in years, she did not think of herself as a guardian Xextrum but a loving woman. The kiss was so tender and innocent that Oraien could barely keep himself up, but her soft lips kept him connected.

-"There's nowhere else I'd rather be," Oraien whispered into her ear.

Calea was still in the conference hall discussing and enjoying the momentary peace. Soon she noticed that Oraien was not in the gathering, so she began searching for him. Calea wanted him to tell her about his mission. She wanted to be alone with him for a few moments because even though she wasn't too sure about the matter, she felt as if she was finally ready to tell him something, anything about how she felt for him.

-*I wonder if I waited too long to say anything...* she thought.

Calea knew that Oraien had gone through many moments with her that brought them close, but she was too uncertain of what she wanted. She kept hoping that it was not too late to tell him how she felt; too late to open herself to him. Calea had never trusted any man besides her father and brother, and she realized that it was her unyielding spirit that held her back from his affection. Calea finally walked to the large balcony and saw Oraien standing against the vibrant panoramic view of space, gazing at the stars as if they were priceless jewels. She could feel an ocean of truth build up behind her wall of uncertainty.

-"Ra..." Before she could call his name, Oraien turned, and he had Aiya in his arms as the two gently kissed one another.

Calea's feelings broke through her last bit of immaturity as she left her last bit of pettiness behind. The ocean of sorrow flowed deep within her and even manifested itself as tears from her beautiful eyes. Her heart plunged into a sea of remorse. She watched them only for a second but felt as if an eternity had gone by. Her face was wet from her tears yet the night still showed no concern. Calea turned and walked away, trying to conceal her state of emotion.

Chapter 20

Ignorant Refusal

The next day came quickly as each member of the delegation woke up early. There were soldiers at the docking station loading Ferra with fuel and supplies. Oraien was the first of the group to arrive at the docking station. He began to help the troops with their job until the others arrived, and when Aiya arrived, she called Oraien.

-"Rai, I forgot to tell you something," Aiya said as she waved her hand to signal him to come to her. Oraien walked slowly to her, waving Caileb and Azrun morning greetings, but Calea was not yet there. When Oraien reached Aiya she began to speak, "Remember the purpose of the Zeofieren sphere?"

-"Good-morning to you too, Aiya."

-"Oh, yeah. Good-morning, Rai. But really we don't have a lot of time, so you remember?" She asked. Oraien was still in his morning state of mind and wished he did not have to think. With a reluctant groan, he answered, "Not really. All I remember is that it was very important and that I needed it to progress my Xextrum's development."

-"True, but the sphere serves two purposes. One is that it is a Key to our Quarton: the Alsius Quarton. The other purpose is only known by the Niphiliem, and that is why we did not want them to have it."

-"So my chances at acquiring the enhancement of Alsius is gone," Oraien said as he let out a sigh of defeat.

-"Not exactly," Aiya said looking at the troops readying Ferra. "There are two ways to have access to a Quarton, Rai, you should know; you're a Xextrum, after all." Rai could not remember what she was talking about, and his confusion was apparent through his countenance.

-"Aiya, just tell me. I can't remember it right now. I'm definitely not a morning person."

-"A Xextrum has access to his or her respective Quarton. Meaning you have access to Luna, and I have access to Alsius," she said with a sarcastic, yet flirtatious smile. "It's going to take the men a few hours to finish loading the ship. I'll let you into the main body of our Quarton so you can have your upgrade. However, you have to ask me nicely," she said as she turned her back to Oraien.

-"Wh-What? Let's go Aiya. We don't have time to waste." Aiya did not move a single muscle, and with yet another heavy sigh, Oraien gave in. "Can you please take me to the Quarton, Aiya?"

-"I would love to, Rai," Aiya turned and lead him out, but before they exited, Oraien asked one last question, "What about Calea?"

-"What about Calea? She's not a Xextrum! So she has nothing to do with you and me right now. Let's go," Aiya said in a slightly demanding tone.

    The two left the port and quickly made their way into the Dintio Mountain base. Once inside, Aiya lead Oraien down a flight of stairs that took them to an underwater section of the city that was protected by a large dome. They came to a large field of sand that surrounded the

Quarton's bottom section, and the turquoise color from the planet's water amplified the radiance of the Quarton's own striking light.

-"It's beautiful, isn't it, Rai," Aiya said looking at the Quarton in awe.

-"The feeling I get from it reminds me of the Luna-Quarton. It's like it wants to talk to me," Oraien said as Aiya looked at him with serene peacefulness.

-"That's why I'm here, though I doubt you'll ever hear it talk to you. It can't speak, but it will definitely help you," Aiya approached the Quarton and placed the palm of her hand on the Quarton's base. Light lined around her hand, and soon a door appeared. "Come on, Rai!" Aiya entered the door and went into the Quarton. Oraien followed her inside, but kept his suspicion at a safe level. Soon the light from the outside faded, and the door closed itself in the distance. Total darkness covered him as Oraien stood still, careful not to move in the wrong direction.

-"Aiya," Oraien whispered. He could see nothing and hear nothing. "Aiya," he called a little louder this time.

-*Don't be afraid*, Oraien heard a voice in his head,

*Aiya has lead you here for your gift. Take this, Oraien
Zeal, and make our Luna proud.
You are her son, born of her womb.
The legacy will be relived, as has Luna's Love,
And now her little love.*

As the voice faded away, Oraien was surged with a sensation of tranquil power. He noticed that every time he came in contact with a Quarton, he felt at ease, but he wished that the voice could tell him more about his family, or better yet, his purpose. He had so many questions, but he just stood in peace knowing that he had to find them on his own.

-*This must be it: the gift*. Oraien had received the power to execute a new attack that allowed him access to the corners of his limits. *I can't wait to try this out*, he thought. A light broke the darkness, and Oraien could see Aiya at the entrance door waiting for him.

-"So, how did it go?" she asked, but Oraien decided not to tell her that he had heard the Quarton speak. He did not know what her response would be and decided not to gamble on the chances of her assuming him to be a strange fellow.

-"It was nice in there," he stretched his arms up and let out his morning yawn. "Excuse me. I had to get that out."

-"I see that," Aiya responded. Oraien looked at her sarcastically in retaliation of her comment.

-"Now that I'm officially awake, we can finish loading up everything," the two then returned to the port, and this time Calea and the group were impatiently waiting the two.

Oraien, Calea, Azrun, and Aiya situated themselves into Ferra. The ship gently lifted off the ground and headed towards the exit of the base. Caileb watched as they took off with high hopes that they would have a successful mission. The E.Q.O.D.A. relied on it.

-"Ferra, plot a course for the planet Arius." After a few moments the ship displayed the calculation of the distance as well as the longevity of the trip. *The targeted destination was seven planetary regions away and would take ten hours till docking at Arius,* Ferra displayed.

-"Then let's get started," Oraien said as he sat down in the pilot's chair. "We need to get there before they do."

    Ferra built up power within her engines and took off into the Emuli quadrant towards their possible new ally, Arius. Shortly after leaving the base of the RE2 moon base, they passed by the planets of Nekio and Luna, Oraien and Calea's home worlds, and realized that they were now leaving the safety of the E.Q.O.D.A. and moving into less familiar territory. As they headed to Arius, they passed by some of the most amazing planets they had ever seen. They marveled at a rather large planet with hundreds of jet streams that traveled both horizontally and vertically, intersecting to give off vibrant neon colors. Soon after, they reached a pair of planets that shared a crossing ring of asteroids. They traveled through a mystical planet museum of their quadrant in the Antares system.

    Four planetary regions away from Igni'ice, they came across a planet that emitted a very large spectrum of colors from both of its poles as it spun in very strange unstable rotations. They were overwhelmed with excitement and awe at the existence of such wondrous planets. Their smiles soon faded knowing that the survival of the E.Q.O.D.A.

depended on the war against the Niphiliem. Despite the joyful astonishments of these wonders, they questioned how long these planets would remain unharmed to present their wonders. The four young warriors knew that if they were to fail, they would be annihilated or enslaved for the sake of malevolence.

    Oraien walked over and joined Aiya and the two began to converse. He was extremely comfortable with Aiya and enjoyed seeing her smile as well as the cute expressions she made after one of his humorous anecdotes. Even though he liked being with Aiya, he had trouble letting go of Calea. From their experiences and times together, he grew to like her, or at least the vulnerability that she revealed every once in a while. Oraien looked over to Calea and caught her looking straight at him. He did not look away, and the two stared at each other with an amorous connection. With a sensor on the control panel beeping, their connection was broken from their planetary observation. They had reached Arius, and they were not in the least bit prepared for the marvel that stood before them. Approaching the planet, they saw that Arius was a golden planet of clouds, encased in a dazzling display of six asteroid rings all rotating in different directions. Inside the rings, they could see the planetary defense system had been integrated into them.

-"Whoa, now that's a defense system for ya!" Azrun exclaimed.

-"Ship identification, please," stated a voice over Ferra's intercom.

-"Ship name Ferra, we are members of the E.Q.O.D.A. Forces, sent here on a mission to speak with your leaders," Oraien said in response.

-"Port in the capital city of Astreus," the operator informed.

As they entered the atmosphere, they took notice of the enormous clouds of the upper atmosphere and then suddenly reached open space with large structures among the clouds. The light of Antares reacted with their cloud composition to give off a distinct golden array of light. As they made their way through one of the large clouds, they couldn't believe their eyes. The city of Astreus was yet another wonder Oraien had never seen before. The city was made up of five islands: one central island, and four smaller islands that were spread out in cardinal directions. Connecting the islands was a massive network of bridges. The larger bridges were located on the upper level while the smaller series of bridges connected the upper levels of the city to the lower levels beneath the floating islands. The young warriors found themselves looking down in silence until Oraien spoke.

-"From here, the inner bridges resemble a leaf. Don't you think?"

-"Well isn't that poetic, a leaf on the wind," Azrun said as the others began to chuckle. Reaching the port, they were greeted as if they were tourists.

The planet was mystically striking. Even the Visiean natives had a peaceful yet powerful appearance to them. Their features resembled the planet they lived on. Their hair was like fibers on a bird's feather; which varied in color amongst the people. Their eyes were gray and their skin was a sandy auburn.

-"Welcome to Astreus, city of the Four Winds," the greeter stated, "Follow me," she continued as she led the group onto a massive staircase leading into the city. Astreus was a floating Metropolis supported by four major jet streams; maintaining a perfect balance that allowed the large islands to float unmoved.

When they reached the top, they were amazed to see the carefree life on the planet; ignorant to the possible hectic life they could have. The four of them looked at each other in confusion and asked the soldier why the city was not prepared for an attack. After walking throughout the city, they came to a large tower that rose into an upper cloud section joined by the other large towers. Walking through an extremely large archway, they soon found themselves face to face in front of four seated people.

-"We were beginning to wonder when you all were coming," a rather large figure spoke.

-"You knew we were coming?" Calea asked.

-"Of course. We knew it would only be a matter of time before you came into our territory wanting to spread your war upon us," he said in response. Oraien looked at Calea to see her reaction, but her face remained steady.

-"Our war?" Calea asked. Aiya began to approach the floor to speak only to be cut off by the leader.

Echoes of Tempore: Revival of Light

-"The answer is no, we don't want any part of your war," he said firmly. The four warriors stood in shock, as they had not even asked their question. Feeling anger building within him, Ferverous lashed out at the Visiean Council.

-"Our war? Are you insane?!" he yelled out, "This war affects you just as much as it affects us. Just because the Niphiliem have not reached this planet yet doesn't mean they don't have their sights set on it," he said as Oraien held him back.

-"He's right," Oraien interjected. "The only reason your world hasn't been affected is because of the distance. The Niphiliem plan to destroy and enslave all and won't stop until they do," Oraien said. He then changed his composure to that of a true leader and continued, "We must all come together to stop them," Oraien said as he walked into the middle of the large room.

-"Our answer is final." Oraien looked back at Aiya and Calea, then back to the leader.

-"Well, since we are here, can we Xextrum do anything for you?" Oraien was waiting for him to mention his name.

-"You may address me as Ovim. If you want to help, you can recover the four hidden gate Keys of our Quarton to bring back here for safekeeping. If This Nonly, my first in command, will be in charge of the mission, and Ventus here will accompany you on your journey." Everyone was surprised at how fast Ovum had put them to work despite his ignorant refusal.

-"Ventus?" Azrun said wondering who he was, "I've heard a similar name before haven't I? It's probably because the stories about your journeys have been told so much that they changed your name."

-"Vento is my nick name."

-"Vento! Oh, the Wind Xextrum, Avius." Azrun walked to him to shake his hand; "I finally get to meet you in person." Oraien began to walk up to greet the Xextrum as well but stopped when Ventus refused to respond Azrun's greetings.

-"We have work to do," Ventus said as he turned walked away. Azrun stood, completely disrespected but reserved. Oraien patted him on the back and whispered, "They just don't understand, don't take it personally."

-"I know... Let's get out of here and do this mission," Azrun responded. Leaving the great room, the four of them walked in silence, not fully comprehending what had just happened. "Something about that meeting didn't feel right," Calea said as they left.

Chapter 21

Four Paths, One Phoenix

Together with Ventus and the crew from the E.Q.O.D.A., Nonly came up with a plan to get all the Keys within the day. Each Key was located on four floating islets located along the middle circumference of the planet. Eight jet streams covered the planet, and four individual streams led to four different floating islets. In his plan, the four Xextrum, Avius, Ioxus, Ferverous, and Uvatuus would ride each wind stream to retrieve the keys. Four paths were taken to reduce time. Azrun took the east wind while Vento ventured through the west. Oraien pursued the north and Aiya took the south. Oraien was the fastest traveler so he made it to the middle of the northern jet stream in no time. Oraien only had one chance to hit his mark the small floating islet that had a stone tablet in its center. The small island was much smaller than he had expected, no bigger than a small boat.

Oraien channeled the wind around him using his arms and steered his way to the distant islet. Shortly after, Oraien made contact with the island but was torn off by the pressure of the jet stream. He would not fail again, yet by the time he was able to react he was almost a mile away from the Key. Oraien exploded the energy of Ioxus, and time almost stood still as he traveled like a bolt of lightning towards the stone table that held the Key. Oraien took less than one second to snatch the Key, also remembering to grasp it tightly. He then traversed the stream peacefully until it reached the opposite side of the planet where all the wind streams intersected. The intersection of the four winds then plunged into the center of the planet like a massive whirlpool.

    As Oraien dove into the depths of the storm he spotted Azrun, who was just coming over the tops of the windfalls. His body was flailing, and he was screaming in fear like he had been on the wildest ride of his life. Oraien let out a laugh as he saw Azrun in the distance, but soon Azrun disappeared from sight as Oraien was sucked deeper into the planet until he could no longer see the sky. The combined speed of the jet streams actually gave Oraien a rush. Even though he usually traveled faster himself, the air resistance and turbulence in the stream was exhilarating.

The wind began to slow down as Oraien approached a large triangle shaped land mass, and within it he could sense the Arius-Quarton. He could soon see two people waiting on a large peninsula on the floating continent. Avius and Uvatuus awaited him and Azrun. Ioxus landed smoothly on the rock and waited with the two for Ferverous. With a blast of fire, Azrun flew out of the stream towards them dangerously fast and out of control.

-"I can't stop!" yelled Azrun as he rocketed in their direction.

-"Jump!" yelled Aiya. Azrun hit the meeting spot with his rear first and smoke quickly diffused throughout the area.

-"Azrun, why can't you control yourself. What happened?" asked Vento as he entered the smoke. As soon as Aiya knew that Azrun was fine, she let out a small laugh of relief.

-"That's almost all Azrun's good for, entertainment," said Aiya.

-"And what the heck is that supposed to mean? That jet stream could have made me go to the wrong place or maybe worse," yelled Azrun heatedly.

-"You ok, Azrun? I know you were scared, but wasn't it fun, man!" Oraien said excitedly.

-"Rai. I don't enjoy having my insides jumbled around like you. Ok? All of you are crazy for not feeling weird after that," Azrun exclaimed.

-"We have to hurry. Let's go," rushed Ventus.

Uvatuus, Ferverous, and Avius handed their fragments to Ioxus. Oraien then slowly combined them together. Suddenly, when he finished, the Key began to glow, and the immense Quarton began to react. Gigantic gates opened on the six corners of the Quarton, and energy began to flow freely through the ambiance. Oraien was pulled into the Quarton and found himself standing before a beautiful Visiean with phoenix like features. Her hair appeared to be glowing red with energy like fire. She approached him and gently touched his forehead. Oraien's conscience then involuntarily opened and reached out towards her...

Oraien, your fate is shaped by your decisions. The responsibility you now possess is your willingness to choose your power. The abundance of power allows a truthful guardian to handle burdens lightly." The Quarton spoke to Oraien. *"My sister was alone, and she could not protect her children. Please, Oraien, find it in your heart to forgive us for giving you this life. In return, we promise to do all we can to allow you to live that life. Your mother, go to her Oraien, and protect her.*

Instantly Oraien felt Ioxus interact with Arius. The power that she gave him was now surging through his body. He wanted to talk to her, but the connection was already broken. Oraien was back in the real world lying on the ground, with the other Xextrum crowded around him. He could hear the others calling his name, so he stood once again.

-"Hey, Oraien, I don't know what the heck you were dreaming about that could have taken two hours, but we've been waiting for you. We can hear explosions coming from the surface, we gotta go," said Azrun with a concerned tone.

-"Oraien, can you fight?" asked Ventus. Oraien stood up as he felt Ioxus's new powerful abilities.

-"I hope the Niphiliem are as ready as I am."

Chapter 22

Enlightenment

Oraien was the first to reach the city of Astraeus; the other three did not make it until a few minutes later. All around them, buildings were coming down; people were screaming and port ships were being bombed. Yet the only thought on Oraien's mind was Calea. He knew that she could take care of herself with the ELX, but he also knew that if there was a Xodus with the invading group she would not stand a chance. Looking high into the upper atmosphere, the group could see a Niphiliem force unlike anything they had previously seen. It was a massive assault, and the very thing they intended to prevent. Now that it began, they knew they had to intervene.

The four of them spread out into the city. Oraien used his Neo-ray to find Calea. He finally spotted her in bewilderment on the east island. Once he located her, he immediately made his way to her. As he got closer he noticed that the bridges that kept the island attached to the central island were being destroyed, so he tried to speed up to reach her before it was too late. Ferverous was enjoying the thrill of the battle as he destroyed as many of the ships and soldiers as he could.

    Uvatuus was using many of her special attacks to defend the city from the onslaught. If she couldn't freeze the enemy due to civilian interference, she turned to her terrifying double-sided lance. Its beauty was only matched by the deadly skill in which Uvatuus used it to plow though all who stood against her. Avius, now fully ready to do what he must, used a combination of wind and melee attacks to blow ships into each other. Azrun was able to see why Avius had so many stories told about him. Avius was ruthless and his eyes showed no mercy. Even his weapons were legendary. They were two large metallic morphable spheres that he shaped into different weapons using the immense air pressure he controlled. And once Avius caught you in his sight, it was over.

    A massive explosion caught everyone's attention as it had destroyed an entire floating island section of the city. The force of the explosion threw Oraien back. With the balance of the land mass and the ever-flowing air currents beneath disrupted, the island floated out into space. Space immediately claimed the lives of all the Visiean people still on the island. Oraien could not believe his eyes, Calea was one of the people on the landmass that had been sent into space. Shock gripped Oraien's body as he felt reality set in once again; he could not protect her.

-"Not again! NO!" he yelled. He broke his promise to her, and Calea was now dead. He fell to the ground full of rage, hatred and sorrow. He punched the ground, each time creating a larger crater underneath him.

-"Rai, get to the Council Hall and protect Ovim," Avius yelled out. Oraien stood straight, and followed Avius' order. He blocked his mind, and held the simple objective of killing every enemy in his path.

As he fought his way into the Council Hall of Arius still gripping the reality of Calea's death, Oraien found himself looking face to face with Ovuim, the leader of the Visiean Council. Ovim desperately grabbed onto hold of Ioxus.

-"Help me!" Ovim said as the horrific images of his dying people in his head overwhelmed him.

-"This way," Oraien turned around to lead him to a safer spot.

When Ovum thought Oraien had let his guard down, he took out a long metal hex-cylinder sword and viciously plunged it towards Oraien's head. The sword went through his skull, and Ovum had killed Oraien. Little did he know that Ioxus trusted his instincts and disappeared from Ovum's sight so quickly that it left behind a faint image of Oraien as a decoy. The image faded leaving Ovum confused and most of all: afraid.

-"I'll have to thank the phoenix for the new ability. Just who are you?" Ioxus asked, now a safe distance from his attacker.

-"The name is Omadox. I am high ranking Niphiliem Xodus, and it is I who has brought all of this into order," he said as he began to shape shift. "Although I must thank you and your foolish friends for finding the hidden pieces of four, I could never have found them without you. But I guess I can't give you too much praise since you fools never brought them back!"

-" Glad we didn't, Where is the real Ovum?!" Ioxus demanded.

-"Oh, that old fool has been dead for quite sometime. I killed him after I arrived since his obstinacy didn't allow him to tell me how to recover the Keys without riding the jet current. I was going to figure out another way of retrieving the information, but who knows how long that could have taken. However, as fate would have it, you all showed up on the day of the invasion. I knew that you would do anything to help these pathetic people ensure their survival, and you could do it in a timely manner. Why do you think I was so quick to ask you to go in search of the Keys? Though I must tell you, the Visieans really didn't want your help. They honestly thought that we wouldn't reach them." he said laughing to himself, completely amused at the situation. As Omadox finished laughing, his form stabilized to that of a Niphiliem Xodus General. "Oh, and Calea, lucky girl. I saw the look on her face before she died. I gave her the best show I could, you know: fire, explosions, and space. Frankly, I don't think she enjoyed it."

-"Enough!" Ioxus yelled out as he dashed towards Omadox, ignoring the many explosions around them.

Oraien saw the person responsible for Calea's death right in front of him, and he would not show the least hint of pity. In an attempt to throw Oraien off guard, Omadox changed his form to that of Atrum; the very first Xodus Oraien had faced after gaining his Xextrum. Ioxus would have stopped due to the revival of his past memories, but he did not care. Omadox began to attack using the same attacks as Atrum, yet they were not as effective against Oraien. Every blow Oraien threw at Omadox, he was barely able to block. Ioxus was more powerful; giving him the upper hand.

The fight continued with Omadox blocking every advance Ioxus made which filled Oraien with more rage. Omadox smiled as he thought he was exhausting Oraien's energy. After several minutes and Omadox shifting into several different people, the fight had reached a stalemate. Omadox knew it was soon that he would get the upper hand, so he slowly made his transition into offense. The very first attack that Oraien saw was his opening. He finally slipped past Omadox's defense and started changing the tide of the fight.

Once he felt himself losing the upper hand, Omadox changed into Terrus and began to use his speed to counter that of Ioxus. Omadox had a great disadvantage due to his ability. Even though he was able to change his appearance and use different attacks, the attacks were extremely underpowered. With little tolerance, Ioxus powerfully thrust his leg into Omadox's chest, followed by a crippling blow to the face. Never had Oraien attacked so viciously and dangerously. He attacked Omadox with enough power to defeat him, but not enough to kill him; Oraien wanted Omadox to suffer. Omadox lost consciousness and helplessly fell to the ground.

    Oraien walked over to Omadox and grabbed him by the neck. He then sat Omadox up against a rock and walked a few steps away. He turned and gently slapped him in the face using Exus to wake Omadox. Immediately he released an immense amount of energy through Exus into Omadox's body, disabling his ability to shape shift. Omadox screamed in excruciating pain as the electricity gripped his muscle. Oraien then implanted Exus in the ground with his right hand and started towards Omadox.

-"It's a shame that you can only use the strengths of others, but then again I guess that's because you have don't have any of your own," Ioxus said as he approached the wounded commander.

-"Mercy! Please!" he cried out. Looking around at the beautiful city once more and thinking of Calea once more, Ioxus replied, "Frankly, I don't think you'll enjoy this." The words reverberated in his mind.

Oraien dashed into Omadox, knees first, crushing him deeper into the massive rocks behind him. Ioxus then jumped back and used his hands to channel lighting into the pile of rocks. The lightning grabbed Omadox from rubble and pulled him out. Oraien began to lift him high above the ground while electrocuting him. Oraien let him fall once he was satisfied. To add on to Omadox's suffering, Oraien gave him a nice kick in the back and a large snap was heard. Oraien had broken his spine. At this point, Omadox could not yell in pain anymore.

-"Looks like I caused your body to go into shock with all that lighting I zapped you with." It would have been a joke, but not even Oraien could laugh. He felt like an atrocious monster, but he wanted to avenge Calea with such ferocity that he wanted to continue torturing Omadox.

-"P-please...no mor...e," Omadox struggled to plead. The battle over Arius was nearing an end in the Xextrum's favor. Ventus saw Oraien's battle but could not sit by while he tortured Omadox, so he jumped in-between the two looking straight into Oraien's eyes.

-"That's enough, Oraien." Ventus said. Ventus looked over to Omadox and used one of his morphable spheres to crush Omadox' skull, thus killing him. Ventus wanted to end his pain.

-"We've won. It's over," Oraien turned without response and walked away. He felt no victory, he felt no consequence. From the distance, he could see Aiya looking at him which slightly brought him comfort. At the same time though, he felt a piece missing within him: Calea.

Chapter 23

A New Friend

As the light of Antares peered through the clouds, all who were alive stopped what they were doing to observe the sunrise. It was not physically different from any other sunrise, but it was by far the most cherished. The Visieans cherished it because it could have been their last, if it was not for the Xextrum sent there by the E.Q.O.D.A; their world would have been lost. Waving his hand, Avius stood proudly as he had defended his home world. Standing in the middle of the open space between the islands, both Ferverous and Uvatuus combined their energy to create a dazzling victory explosion, which sparked a cheerful celebration from all the Visieans' who had survived the attack. They all abandoned their neutral viewpoint on the war and realized that they, too, were in danger of being wiped out. Their leaders held their heads down realizing just how wrong they really were.

    The only person not fully satisfied with the outcome was Oraien, who stood in place showing no signs of joy. He saw the person he cared most for die, and it was tearing up his insides. Looking towards the sky to stop his tears from falling, he overheard a familiar voice.

-"This way little ones," she said with a smile on her face.

It was Calea, standing across on the Northern Island. After the children crossed the bridge, she turned around to see Ioxus looking directly at her. She smiled and let out a sigh of relief to see that he was alright. The smile slowly faded from her face when she could see Ioxus speedily making his way to her. Jumping from the floating pieces of the ruined bridge, Oraien took a giant leap quickly approaching Calea. His Xextrum dispersed as he swept her into his arms. At first he did not say a word, he just held her, lifting her off the ground. Calea also held him tightly. Her face began to turn a bright red because she loved every moment of him holding her like that.

-"What happened? How is this possible? I saw the explosion. I thought I lost you..." Cutting him off, she placed a finger on his lips.

-"Hurry, hurry, we don't have much time. Take your children and go," Calea yelled as she began evacuating the last of the eastern portion of the city. "Hurry across the bridge and into the lower sections of the Northern section of Astraeus."

Nearly everyone had been evacuated as she fought off the Niphiliem who were taking the island by force. An explosion above made her look up only to see an entire ship heading her way, locked on a deadly collision course with the floating island. After killing a few more enemies, she turned and ran for the large bridge connecting the two land masses. When she was halfway across she could hear and feel the large explosion behind her, destroying that end of the bridge. Running for her life, it turned into an uphill battle as she ran up the bridge as it was falling. Barely making it across, she could see the ships retreating. They did not expect to encounter four Xextrum on one planet. After a valiant effort, the Niphiliem were defeated.

After the explanation of events, Calea placed a hand on Oraien's face and reminded him that she was not going anywhere.

-"Hey. I'm ok." Calea then gently pulled Oraien as she kissed his forehead, and both felt all the stress of war fade away. Oraien, however, felt as if he should not betray Aiya's trust and separated from Calea,

-"I'm glad... you're ok Calea," Oraien then looked up to notice the people of Arius rushing about.

Shortly afterwards, all the remaining Visieans' began making their way to the Northern Island. Oraien and Calea bewildered with curiosity also began to make the trip across the bridge. In the center of the city, Avius as well as Nonly, now the highest-ranking member of their council, was giving a speech. He explained to his people that the time for neutrality had long since past.

-"We must fight not only to protect our own world but to help save the worlds of those who sent aid when we were too foolish to accept," he paused and then continued, "We cannot fully express our gratitude for saving us from the invasion, but most of all, we thank you guys for saving us from ourselves. You have our full support in the war against the Niphiliem; now that we have seen what those monsters are capable of we can't just sit idle and do nothing. Like you, we must stand and fight for our world as well as those that do not have the strength to do so. Tell the E.Q.O.D.A that they have yet another ally."

Accomplishing their mission, the four warriors turned and headed for what was left of the Astraeus port. Waiting for a little while, Ferra ascended from the lower atmosphere. As the ship doors opened, the group turned to say their good-byes.

-"We will send back all the information regarding our plans, but as of now, know that you have one month to prepare your troops. " Aiya said as Nonly nodded firmly.

-"Alright, we gained another ally!" Azrun yelled merrily.

"No, you've gained another friend," Ventus said as he shook Oraien's hand.

"We'll see you again when the time comes," Oraien said as they boarded the ship and blasted away into space.

Chapter 24

Gathering at Space Luna

The month since the mission to Arius had allowed time for more and more ships of the Alliance to accumulate near Luna. From a distance, the combined fleets of the E.Q.O.D.A. appeared as a planetary metallic disc. Deep within the fleet, the Xextrum, Calea, and all the troops under their command were settled onboard a special ship. Oraien could feel the pressure building up within himself as more time passed. Aiya tried her best to make him feel better as the two meditated, but she too could barely bring herself to stop worrying about the upcoming battle. Nevertheless, she knew their duties and their abilities, and it would be up to them to lead the E.Q.O.D.A. to victory. In the gathering at Luna's space territory, everyone's true colors began to show as they prepared for the Emuli's long awaited resistance.

Azrun was sparring with Ventus in order to keep his nerves on the edge. Each fought with little restraint as they traded jabs and counterattacks. Calea was meditating in a room alone that was on a different level than the others. She had to prepare herself for the best leadership she could execute as well as the worst possible situation that could come her way. The final person that was not yet with the four guardians was Retsum. He finished making the last necessary arrangements concerning the joint plans of the Xextrum with the E.Q.O.D.A. He arrived from Luna and entered the preparation ship of the Xextrum. Once he made his way through the ship, he came to Oraien's room and knocked.

-"I'll get it, Rai," said Aiya as Oraien looked attentively to see who was there. When she opened the door, the two were greeted with a surprised look from Retsum.

-"Aiya? I did not expect to see you in Oraien's room, but I guess it was true what Azrun said about you two," Retsum said smiling.

-"What exactly did he tell you, Master?" Oraien asked while turning off a simulation program.

-"Well, he noticed that the two of you are very fond of each other's presence. Oraien, you because of her decisive will, and you Aiya because of his protection and the connection you enjoy sharing with him."

-"He told you all of that?" Aiya said blushing.

-"No, that much I can see for myself," Retsum replied.

"So Retsum, I'd expect you haven't come here to check up on us for this. What are you really here for?" asked Aiya.

-"Ok you two, I am here to gather the Xextrum. The five of us need to talk. Start making your way to the meeting room. There is something you all must know," Retsum said.

He left the room and delivered the message to all the other Xextrum on the ship. Everyone was to report to the private Xextrum lobby on a sealed off level of the ship. Calea said her farewells to Oraien and the group before they left, and she boarded a small transport that would take her to her own battleship. After Azrun, Oraien, Aiya, and Ventus entered the lobby; Retsum sat down and began the meeting,

-"This floor has been locked for our private meeting," Retsum looked around to make sure everyone was present and continued. "Several plans have been made. It's up to us to choose the best one," he said as the others moved closer to hear. "Don't allow fear or anger to make you do anything rash or dangerous," he spoke looking at Azrun. "Countless lives depend on the outcome of this battle."

-"Ok, so what are the plans?" Azrun asked.

-"I have a special member of the team you should meet." Everyone heard a door open to the entrance of the room. Retsum looked over and spoke, "As usual, she's right on time." He said leaving a look of determination on their faces. Oraien gave Aiya a soft stare of assurance.

The energy they all felt alerted their senses, and they slowly began to tense up. Slowly raising their energy to transform, all four of the young Xextrum were ready strike the figure emerging from the darkness of the room. Once the figure walked in to the light, all but one of them relaxed as they laid eyes on a female soldier dressed in an Alliance uniform.

-"I've felt this energy before," Oraien spoke still staring at the woman suspiciously.

-"Looks like somebody has a good memory," the woman spoke as her appearance became distorted. Once the image of the Alliance soldier faded, the woman's true form was revealed.

-"Vexia!" Oraien yelled out. The other Xextrum stood to their feet ready to strike at any moment.

-"Wait!" Retsum commanded as he raised his hand to reinforce his plea. "This is the reason I gathered you all here," he continued.

-"What do you mean? She's the enemy!" Azrun yelled.

-"That may be true when looking at her outward appearance, but aside from the Xextrum, she may be one of the greatest allies of the Alliance." Breathing in deeply, he lowered his hand signaling to the others to calm down.

-"So are you telling me that she's a Niphiliem spy?" Oraien asked forcefully. Ventus and the other Xextrum redirected their attention to Retsum and awaited his response.

-"Yes, I was trying to say that as quickly as possible before you all killed her."

-"Then what was that back in Sarren? What about that whole protect the Demitian mission Grigori sent me on? What was Ms. Emery doing there?" Oraien questioned angrily.

-"That was all his idea," Vexia stated, throwing herself in the conversation. "And as far as the Demitian goes, she didn't have a clue about our arrangement. She was simply helping me in my own search for the ancient scro...."

-"Arrangement? " Oraien questioned in confusion. Turning quickly to look at Retsum to verify Vexia's statement, he found Retsum with his hand on the back of his head looking away into space, trying to avoid making eye contact.

-"Is this true? Oraien asked.

-"Indeed it is," Retsum said turning back around.

-"Just consider our meeting another part of Retsum's training for you. My job was to keep everybody safe while making it look as real as possible, although had I known that you were so handsome under that armor of yours, I promise you it wouldn't have been all business between us," Vexia said flirtatiously winking at Oraien.

Echoes of Tempore: Revival of Light

Oraien slightly jerked his head back from the shock of her last statement.

- "Tell me again why I shouldn't kill her right here, right now?" Aiya asked.

- "Because, it's all thanks to her information that we even know of the Niphiliem blitz," Retsum said. "With her being on the inside, it positions the Alliance to have an advantage over the enemy.

- "How do we know we can trust her? More importantly why should we even consider the notion of having a Niphiliem ally that could betray us at anytime?" Ventus asked.

- "Your suspicion is more than understandable, but she has been a spy for over four years. She has kept us informed on a great number of the Niphiliem's advancements within the quadrant. Although logically she cannot relay the enemy's every move, she has been an irreplaceable asset to us," Retsum spoke.

- "Look, I don't expect to win over anyone's trust anytime soon, if that was to ever even happen, but know that I have my own reasons for doing this and If it wasn't for my involvement in the upcoming event, you all would still be unaware of my presence within the Alliance. However, you all need to be informed of the multiple roles I will be playing."

-"Calea, darling," Kilm said as he embraced his daughter. "Take a deep breath," he advised. Calea had just reached the vessel that she would be in command of. Kilm was traveling to some of the Anekie fighter ships to check on the morale of his men, and more importantly the state of mind his daughter was in. This would be her first time being in control of a vessel in a major battle.

-"Thank you," Calea said gratefully. Even through all of the meditating she did while trying to prepare herself for the battle, she forgot the most important thing to do: breathe.

-"Don't worry. According to your brother, if you command your troops the same way you try to boss Oraien around, then you will be just fine," he said jokingly. As the two stood, Calea could feel the stress lifting from her with every breath she took. Their reunion was cut short as the alarm on board the ship sounded.

-"It's time," Kilm said firmly looking into Calea's eyes. "I must head to the command ship."

With the alarm onboard sounding, all the Xextrum stood to their feet. They were all speechless, not really knowing what to think about Vexia. All but Oraien still looked at her fiercely and without an ounce of trust in their eyes. Oraien made eye contact with her and spoke firmly.

-"Even though I'm still not too sure about the situation, you managed to earn the trust of master Retsum, and that's good enough for me." Retsum raised his head proudly as he heard Oraien speak. "I will give you the benefit of the doubt, based on his faith in you. The plan is solid, and it should work if we execute it with perfection. Does anyone disagree?" Oraien asked looking around at the other thee Xextrum. Vexia was shocked by Oraien's comment, and her face became flushed the more she looked at him. Her concentration on Oraien was broken as Ventus made his way over to her to speak.

-" It's because of my respect for Retsum that I'm going along with this, but know that if you cross us, I will kill you," he said walking past her. "Let's go, we need to get in position if we are to carry out Retsum's plan," he finished.

All the other Xextrum got up quietly and walked out to head to their perspective battle zones.

-"Well, that went better than I thought," Vexia said

-"Just give them time, actions speak louder than words."

-"Yeah, but that Oraien is something else," she said remembering his words to her.

-"That he is," Retsum replied with high esteem.

Chapter 25

Beckons War

A siren was lifted across the communications of all the E.Q.O.D.A. ships. News that the Niphiliem began their movement reached Kilm in the Nekio central command ship. Kilm had Calea in charge of the third section fleet which was comprised of all Nekio defenders that stayed behind the lines. Calea had arrived at her ship and immediately began commanding the fleet. She wanted to make sure the planets did not stay without protection in case of a break through the front offensive lines. Oraien controlled one of five Xextrum aid groups that specialized in optimizing the capabilities of the Xextrum by handling the small obstacles around each guardian to allow them to hit the targets that they were designated to destroy.

Once the entire body of the fleet had moved into position every single operating section shifted into their active states. The Xextrum spread out evenly in a spherical area to create a safety zone. The rest of the fleet alignment took place within the safe zone. Once everyone was in place, the final steps commenced. Unfortunately, a Niphiliem attack started and grew from south zone of the battlefield before they could finish. The Niphiliem then reigned down from all directions, attacking the entire fleet as a single unit.

The Xextrum immediately scattered and began attacking until Caileb could finish the final configuration. After ten minutes of heavy fire, Caileb and his father Kilm finished, and the ships moved into the offense. The sphere had been sliced like a fruit, with each wedge of organized ships positioned for a perfect opening to attack. The battlefield was set, and Calea watched, preparing herself for the wave of enemies that would soon meet her.

Azrun was having fun disabling ships, and his team effectively helped him make his way quickly to the infamous Niphiliem Warus, one of the most powerful Niphiliem battle ships. Uvatuus was assigned the mission of knocking out all of the communication relays that the Niphiliem had. Retsum lead the front fleet from space and sent back strategic plans to Kilm according to what Retsum could see. Ventus was in charge of keeping Niphiliem bots and troops from entering any of the front line war ships.

All went well on the battlefield, and victory seemed inevitable. The Niphiliem had a backup plan however, their new unit. This unit was only a fourth the size of the first wave, but it would soon prove to be ten times more powerful. The E.Q.O.D.A. suffered very few losses compared to the near annihilation of the Niphiliem's first offense. Retsum knew that the Niphiliem would bring in another group soon, but he had no knowledge of when it would come. Soon, space sentries began to detect small groups of large ships coming from distant space. The news reached Kilm, and a new plan was made to counter the Niphiliem' surprise tactic.

The small groups tore through many of the Alliance ships and fast became a class one priority. There were only eight groups, four of which were led by a Xodus. The new plan was to have each Xextrum and their troops divided equally with each guardian engaging the four groups lead by Xodus. O'navus was sent to the group that was tagged the most difficult, Uvatuus, Avius, and Ferverous went to take care of the rest of the other groups. Ioxus received orders to counter an extremely small-unknown group that was ripping their way through the front lines. As soon as Oraien and his group finished their current mission, they immediately headed for the path of the unknown group. When they arrived the only thing left was the leftover pieces of the Alliance's entire first offense fleet.

-"Who could do this? This is not an ordinary group. Let's go. We have to hurry. They are headed for the third defense fleet!" yelled Oraien, knowing that Calea was its leader.

Oraien's troops could not travel fast enough to make it on time so he informed his soldiers to continue as fast as they could. Oraien traveled using his lightning speed and made it to the fleet to witness a devastating battle. Ioxus was only in Emu-Xextrum form, and once again, his anger forced him into the second form, Deo-Xextrum. His senses locked onto all enemies and also detected the use of dark matter. He let an explosion of energy escape from his Xextrum in the form of thousands of thunderbolts that pierced half of the group. Only three Alliance ships remained, and Oraien saw the starship that Calea was commanding. Calea was in her ship with a stern look on her face. She knew that they were only a few steps from destruction, but her face softened when she saw Ioxus appear through the debris, bringing a small ray of hope and comfort in her mind.

Ioxus did not stop to give the group a chance and began his merciless slaughter. He made sure to avoid the dark matter and combined his swords at the handles to create a double-edged sword to slash through the rest. Ioxus's aid group finally arrived, and everything seemed to go well. A nearby moon began to approach and attract much of the debris with its gravity. More Alliance troops finally came into view. However, an explosion and a black implosion destroyed most of the ships in one shot. Oraien looked through the smoke and saw a black figure standing with his arm extended and hand opened towards the dead soldiers.

-Look at his markings... this aura and the energy... he's definitely a Xextrum, but what's wrong with him?

Chapter 26

Power of the Void

As Ioxus looked at the mysterious Xextrum, Oraien was disturbed by what the dark Xextrum had left in his wake: a path of absolute destruction. Oraien feared that if he did not engage the unknown foe, the powerful Xextrum would destroy the remaining ships on the third line, including Calea's. Using his lightning speed, Ioxus bolted into the Xextrum, sending him rocketing towards the nearby moon. Crashing into the moon and creating a large crater on the moon's surface. Oraien followed by driving his legs into the Xextrum, pushing him even deeper into the moon. Ioxus then jumped out to see what damage he had cause his opponent. Slowly emerging from the debris, the dark Xextrum stood and rose out of the crater landing parallel to Ioxus. On the moon's surface, the two warriors stood as they drew their weapons preparing to attack.

-"Who are you!?" Ioxus asked.

-"My dear brother, don't you recognize me?"

-"Xan?" Oraien silently stated in confusion.

-"Yes, but now that I dawn the alpha Xextrum, you will call me Caligus," Xan said as he prepared to strike.

In a flash of darkness, he appeared next to Ioxus, kicking him, causing him to slide along the surface of the moon. Regaining his composure, Ioxus used his lightning speed to counter his attack only to find that his blow had been blocked. He was taken aback by the fact that that he could match his speed. Using his leg to free himself, Ioxus retreated to a safer distance and released a lightning fence from Exus. Holding out his hand, Caligus summoned a small black hole that absorbed the attack and disappeared soon afterwards. With the battle waging on in the background, Ioxus knew that he would have to give it his all if he wanted to defeat Caligus.

Gathering all the energy he could, he dashed towards his opponent. After a fearsome barrage of attacks from Ioxus, it seemed as if none of them were fazing Caligus. Jumping into the air, Ioxus changed Exus into its Arcus form and began to fire a string of lightning bolts. In return, Caligus only took delight in dodging all of them. Landing back on the surface, Ioxus showed no sign of weakness. Moving closer and closer, Caligus made his way through the attacks and engaged Ioxus in close range combat, traveling at lightning speed. Dodging and blocking attacks, Ioxus still managed to release shots from his bow hoping to land one that would allow Oraien to unleash a quartiio energy attack.

With no avail, Ioxus soon found himself depleted of energy, struggling to defend himself against his opponent. The lightning emitted from Exus soon faded along with the hope of Ioxus' survival. Caligus grabbed Oraien from behind and connected a violent blow using his right leg that sent Oraien rocketing into the same crater created by Caligus when he crashed into the moon earlier. Lying on his back looking up at the powerful Caligus, he could only await his fate and death seemed certain. Xan gripped Ioxus' leg and threw Oraien towards Antares. The heat of the star would undoubtedly kill Oraien who was now completely motionless.

Chapter 27

Awakens Caligus

Xan sat back in his chair waiting to reach his home. Within himself only a small light of his youth survived. He remembered the warmth of friendship and the kindness of people, but the harsh teachings of the Niphiliem made sense to him; absolute leadership was the only way to attain true happiness. Even if he had to kill to become the leader of all, he would.

Xan's eyes shut to the passing stars and the silent bridge of his ship. He wanted to have the title of absolute leader. Currently the leader of the Niphiliem was a ruthless tyrant named Cyranus. Xan conformed himself to be four times as ruthless to show his leadership capabilities to the people of Nibiru.

Soon the large ship arrived on the planet of Nibiru. The planet had many moons that were positioned to keep the planet in the darkness of a constant series of eclipses. Boarding another vessel, Xan was transported to the head military base in the capital city of Nocto. Absalon, Xan's superior, met him there.

-"Xan, you have arrived sooner than expected. Hand me your report as well as the Zeofieren sphere," said Absalon. Xan signaled the troops with him to hand the report and the case that held the Key. Absalon's eyes became wide and glazed, "This is the key to our victory."

-"I will take the two Keys to Caligo myself and see that the process of activating its Quarton is done properly," said Xan.

-"You must have known that Lord Cyranus would trust it to you because that is your mission."

Cyranus entered the room from the entrance.

-"Did someone say my name? Absalon?" said Cyranus. Xan looked at Cyranus without patience, and Absalon began to smile.

-"Lord Cyranus we have the Keys to the universe. The forbidden territory of the Shudo'mitian is now ours to grasp."

-"Absalon, I am surprised that this is exciting you. You are starting to annoy me. Stop talking." Cyranus turned towards Xan. "You have not greeted me, Xan. Are you too good to say hello?"

-"Lord Cyranus, we do not have time to socialize. We have worlds to tame," said Xan in response. Cyranus then looked at Absalon.

-"That is the response that I expect to hear from you, Absalon. Don't ever make me have to comment on that again. Do you understand me?"

-"Ye-Yes Sir," said Absalon with his pride broken before many men.

No time was wasted as Xan retrieved both the Spheres and entered a warship. Caligo was an entire system away, and the trip took one week. Nibiru had already set up an asteroid base nearby, yet far from the black hole. Xan stood and gave the Keys to the activation teams that would fire the two Spheres at both ends of the energy poles of the black hole Caligo. When the Keys were thrown into the energies path, they both reacted and began to channel the energy around Caligo. The Spheres gave off two distinct colors, blue and purple. When they connected, a complete field covered Caligo and disabled the massive gravity inside the field.

Xan commanded two soldiers to take him into the field. However, they hesitated because they feared certain death. Xan drew his gun and pointed at them both.

-"Don't you forget who is in charge around here, soldier. If you fear death then allow me to rid you of it," Xan discharged the weapon killing one of the soldiers. "Because he feared death, death instantly came to him. Still afraid?" he asked pointing at the remaining soldier and without hesitation, they departed towards Caligo.

Other ships followed into the field once Xan made the move. To everyone's amazement, there was no gravity within the barrier. Xan quickly dressed in a space suit and opened the door of his ship. But he soon realized that the darkness of Caligo clouded his vision. No stars, no planets, and no sign of life of any sort that were visible outside the barrier could be seen with in the temporary sphere. It was as if he was in another plane altogether.

"You are the alpha, Xan." Xan could hear a voice in his head. *"Take my power and you can make your visions come true. I am the dark energy; I am the fabric of creation, technology and life, given life by the Shudo'mitian, my purpose-Balance- but you can have my powers. I sense you were born to rule. Allow me to help you. I am the Alpha Xextrum of darkness, Caligus.*

Xan thought back to the teachings of the Shudo'mitian civilization and remembered that they attempted to use the core of a Black Hole to unlock a Quarton. The Black Hole they used was called Caligo, and it was discovered to be of the most powerful energy.

-"Caligo! Give me your power!" Xan roared as he jumped into the darkness.

Immediately Xan felt excruciating pain, and he let out a cry so agonizing that the men listening through his communicator stepped back in horror. His body began to fuse with all the dark energy from his surroundings and his mind became clear as night. Xan no longer felt his pleasant memories of his past burden him, no longer did he feel emotions of sorrow or compassion. It was as if Caligo entered his mind and made him pure evil. Xan's eyes shot opened, and he felt the power of the Xextrum flow through his veins. The darkness still occupied the dark star so he warped out of field leaving his troops. Xan wanted to test his new powers and spent hours destroying his own base exploring the possibilities of his Xextrum. With the fire and destruction reflecting off the pitch black metallic suit he had, he began to speak.

-"The universe has waited many a millennia for return of such power! I will remind them of the name CALIGUS!!"

Xan then travel to Nibiru in only one day with the speed of Caligus.

Reaching the planet, he entered the base and let the Xextrum fade as he walked through the Nibiru Council Hall. Entering a chamber deep within the fortress, he found Absalon.

-"Absalon, where can I find Cyranus?"

-"Xan? What are you doing here? You are supposed to be heading the Dark Project. And what happened to your eyes?" While the white of Xan's eyes remained the same, his iris was now black and his pupils were now light grey. His freighting cold eyes were accompanied by markings that ran down his cheeks.

-"That's not what I asked," Xan quickly transformed and charged towards Absalon. Once he reached him, Xan grabbed him by the neck, lifting him off of the ground with one arm. He chuckled softly as he watched his mentor dangle in the air, completely helpless as he kicked and screamed for his life. And without any warning Xan snapped his neck by quickly twisting his wrist to one side, killing him. Cyranus witnessed the murder and hurried to the security room.

-"Cyranus! You have lead the people of Nibiru on a slow path. Now it is time for me to show the Niphiliem the true course of power. Xan teleported behind Cyranus, withdrew his sword and sliced through the legs on which his leader stood.

-"Sorry to make you suffer before you die, but I owe you for all the troubles you put me through." Xan slowly killed Cyranus and soon took over the planet.

His speeches were motivating and within a month he was able to gain the support of all the Niphiliem. Preparations to attack the allied planets neared an end, and Xan entered the war as their commander and leading soldier.

Now, after defeating Oraien, Xan threw him towards Antares so that he could die by the heat of the Nova Star. Xan quickly made his way to Retsum and confronted him.

-"You're Caligus.. How can this ..." cutting Retsum off, Xan knocked Retsum out on the first hit and began to decimate his group. Azrun and Aiya arrived and began to fight him, soon Ventus joined the battle, and Retsum joined after he awoke from his blow. All four fought, and all four Xextrum fell by Caligus' mighty hands.

-"Enough games! This ends now!" Xan clapped his hands, and when he separated them a small black hole emerged. The four of them, along with a large number of his troops, were mangled by its power. Soon afterwards, Azrun, Aiya, Ventus, and Retsum lay defeated and motionless, floating in space with the rubble of their troops ships surrounding them. Xan then turned and faced the remaining opened fleets of the Alliance.

Chapter 28

Awakens A'ethus

With his body moving towards Antares at an incredible speed, Ioxus found himself floating lifeless through space. He knew that the others had engaged Caligus in battle, but he had no idea how they were faring. His mind shifted to Aiya, Calea, and the other remaining ships.

-*Aiya, Calea*, he thought. *Please be all right.* He felt himself accelerating due to the incredible gravity of the star. Slowly he could feel his Xextrum's armor begin to peel away from his enclosure due to the extreme heat of Antares. Powerless, Oraien gripped onto reality. He was deteriorating. It would not be long before his body was destroyed completely by the solar flares of their beloved star.

Amidst the rubble and destruction caused by Xan, the four other Xextrum were entirely drained of energy. The explosion caused by the dark matter took the allied forces by surprise as they witnessed all five of the Xextrum defeated. Tears rolled down Calea's face as she watched Ioxus float towards Antares, and she knew that there was nothing that could be done. Kilm let out a deep sigh of defeat as he watched their final and best hope to defeat the Niphiliem get tossed around, as if they were nothing. They had won the battle against the enemy ships, but they would undeniably lose the war against the powerful Caligus and his group.

    While floating in space Retsum was able to remain conscious. Never in his experience as a Xextrum had he been so badly beaten, but he realized it was unavoidable due to the mysterious awakening of the ancient Caligus. Unknown to him, Aiya, Ventus, and Ferverous were barely holding on to their senses. While each of the five warriors fought the critical state of their damaged Xextrum a thought ignited within their minds simultaneously, *Oraien*. With all the pain and suffering that each of them were experiencing, they realized that Oraien had a much dimmer fate, and all they wanted to do was save him, protect their comrade.

    Four bright lights illuminated the screens of the E.Q.O.D.A. ships. The Xextrum began glowing, pulsing as if life had been restored to them and as if they were trying to awaken something. Soon after, each Xextrum released small lights from within their Neo-Quartos, small mysterious fragments. Ferverous released his from the back, Uvatuus from the shoulder, O'navus from the chest, and Avius from the abdomen. Each light from the Xextrum had a color that corresponded to its Xextrum's element. The five did not realize that once their minds synchronized on Oraien, they released an ancient power dormant within their Xextrum. With a great explosion, their fragments were fired towards Antares. When the soldiers onboard the allied ships adjusted their screens, they could see Ioxus release the same type of light from his head. Once the lights neared Oraien, the five pieces began to encircle him, spinning rapidly, creating a white sphere of light. Caligus was puzzle by the brilliant display before him. He was certain that they were dead and that Ioxus would soon follow. With great speed, Ioxus was thrown into the massive star. Calea quickly put her hands over her mouth, not fully knowing what was to be. For a few moments, Caligus too watched with great anticipation, not fully understanding the situation, but Caligus soon turned and announced;

-"Sorry to say, but he is dead! And so comes your turn! E.Q.O.D.A.!" roared Xan.

*A'ethus is inhibited, inhabitant is hero.
We, the universe, choose the chosen.
We, the light, fight, protect, and end the night.
Against Caligus, he who owns the shadows.*

A ballad was heard in the minds of all Xextrum.

Just before Xan was about to Attack the E.Q.O.D.A., a blinding light in the form of a large solar flare was emitted from Antares and all covered their eyes from the brightness. Once the brightness subsided, there was another large explosion from the star, and almost immediately they saw something flying at incredible speed. It was using the gravity of the star to increase its own speed to catapult it towards the war zone. Behind the unknown figure, space itself seemed to be bending, unable to keep up with the speed that the mysterious figure was traveling. Unable to react fast enough, the unknown warrior made contact with Caligus. The light warrior kicked Caligus with enough force and momentum to send Xan flying out of control on a collision course with a moon. Reaching the small moon, he crashed into it so violently that the small moon nearly split in two. After a short while,

Caligus blasted back to the surface and up into space to face his new opponent.

-"Who are you, and how is this possible? There is no one who can challenge my power. I am the alpha Xextrum the ruler of darkness, Caligus!" he yelled out to the unnamed warrior.

-"I am that which cannot be destroyed. You may be the alpha but I am the omega, the bringer of light: A'ethus."

Chapter 29

Alpha vs. Omega

The two titans glared into each other's powerful eyes, Caligus with wrath, A'ethus with defiance. The longer the two looked upon each other, the more Xan wanted to eliminate that which stood before him. Xan reached for his sword that was attached to his back and pointed the end at A'ethus.

-"I'm tired of waiting. That's what made Cyranus a poor leader. Too slow, not willing to push the people to better themselves. A'ethus, you will not stop me. I am sorry if you do not understand my reasons, but because you stand in my way I will fight you. I will kill you." Without saying a word, A'ethus then reached for his bright sword.

-"I can hear the universe speaking to me. Long have your people shrouded innocent worlds in darkness, and the people desperately want things to return to the way they were before all of the pain and destruction carried out for your name.

Xan, you have selfishly taken planet after planet, city after city, but this is the end of the line. No more talking, no more chances."

    Oraien was still, his sword ready with his senses locked. He thought back to all the battles he had experienced. He remembered the pain from losing; he remembered the agony of failing. He could not help but remember the lost comrades he had to let go in the name of war. He let his mind expand, reaching out to the universe, and it filled his consciousness with so many memories; he was able to fully understand his mission.

    Caligus dashed towards A'ethus and disappeared. Spreading his arms, A'ethus charged the vicinity with light energy atoms. Caligus pushed past the energy wall and fell for Oraien's trap. A'ethus was no longer inside the barrier, and it allowed him time to catch Xan off guard. Oraien split the Antares sword, equipping the two blades to his arms; he then began to heavily deliver blows upon Xan. Caligus blocked as many hits as he could but suffered severe internal injuries. Oraien grabbed Xan by the feet and flung him out of the gravitational field of the moon. A'ethus then began to power up, but Xan regained his ground and shot towards Oraien. Xan foolishly opened a black hole and shot it at

A'ethus, but Oraien bent space to deflect the black hole back at Caligus. The next step A'ethus took was to use the energy he just gathered to destroy the outer armor of Caligus by flooding the inside of the suit with light energy. Oraien drew a symbol in space, and it quickly turned into a small bright light. Oraien grabbed the small light which was now absorbing the ambient energy of space. Soon the light turned into a large atom of energy with countless electrons flowing brightly with a distinct pattern.

    Xan saw this as he recovered from the damage he received. Oraien activated A'ethus' energy and dashed towards Xan, his wake creating ripples in space. Once he reached Caligus, he fused the energy particle from his hand to his sword and began to break each of Caligus' block attempts. The blows were not only unimaginably heavy but unpredictably fast. After A'ethus attacked with several hundred blows, he charged another light atom and forced it into Caligus' face causing it to explode; finishing his devastating assault. This attack was done in the blink of an eye, so fast that Xan's mind could not keep up with the damage his body was receiving. Caligus' mind was dazed and shaken but soon gained his composure.

As he stared furiously at A'ethus, he, for the first time since his awakening, could see his vision of dominance and order slipping away and grew evermore determined not to let anyone stand in his way. The two warriors stood silently as they glared upon each other. Simultaneously, they took their battle stances and began to absorb the ambient energy around them. The auras created by their energy struck the allied forces along with the other four Xextrum who drifted silently, and all were completely stunned by the display of power before them. Suddenly, as if space itself screamed out in agony from the clashing of their opposing energies, the two blasted off from their positions, disappearing from sight. The two of them were moving so fast that only the clashing of their powerful weapons alerted the surrounding forces of their presence. On the enormous battle field, the remnants of their energies could be seen in the wake of their collisions.

As the two sped about the battlefield, A'ethus fought with an unusual calm ferocity that threw Caligus off guard as he tried to gain the upper hand on his opponent. A'ethus, anticipating a direct thrust from Caligus, blocked the oncoming sword with an agile kick using one leg to bring the other around with freighting velocity to connect with Caligus' face, sending him speeding towards the small moon once again. As he neared the surface, Caligus executed a succession of back flips to slow himself down before landing. Immediately after reaching the surface, Caligus jumped back towards A'ethus, creating a small crater beneath his feet from his powerful takeoff. A'ethus braced himself as he expected Caligus to make contact, only to be taken aback when Caligus disappeared from directly in front of his sight, leaving nothing but a dark mist. Quickly using his senses, he positioned his sword to the left side of his body to block a devastating attack. Immediately, A'ethus performed the same feat and vanished from in front of Caligus leaving only a white mist in his place.

    The other Xextrum, more than anyone else watching the fight, understood the gravity of the clashing superpowers. They desperately struggled to keep up by using their Neo-rays. One thing that each of them could not help but notice, was that even though Caligus and A'ethus were battling, the remnants of their energies were battling to dominate one another's space.

-"Unreal," Azrun said, staring wide eyed as he watched nothing but the energies distort the fabrics of space every time they came into contact with one another. "It seems like there are two battles being waged right now," he finished.

-"Yeah, I see it too," Vento added, "But I'm not sure what is happe..."

-"The two energies cannot occupy the same space at the same time or they would destroy each other. The light cannot live without erasing the shadows, and darkness cannot thrive without extinguishing the light. Every time they try, the distortion of space itself will inevitably be the final result," Retsum explained.

-"They are even destroying the rest of the Niphiliem battle ships in the process, it's like the only thing they are concerned with is destroying each other," Aiya spoke.

With the possibility of loss in Caligus' mind, he resorted to self inflicting measures. Xan allowed dark matter to escape from around him into the area, causing the light to fade away. He then swung his sword towards A'ethus' head and released more dark matter to disable his sight temporarily. With the upper hand, Xan grabbed hold of the space around him and began to fold and twist the energy in hopes that he could implode a gigantic amount of energy into his

Neo-Quarton. He foolishly absorbed it into himself in attempt to stabilize the overwhelming power. The only thing that helped Xan to stay conscious was the power of the Caligus-Quarton within his body.

A'ethus was now able to see, and at that very moment, he knew that Caligus was planning on absorbing all the ambient energy. Oraien began to pull light energy from Antares using every fiber of his strength, ever so fluent with each decision he made about A'ethus' actions. It had only been a few minutes since the fight started yet Oraien quickly learned that his new form required the utmost wisdom to wield. Gently closing his eyes, calm, he channeled his collected energy into Caligus' area of energy absorption. With the additional energy, it became too much for Xan to handle, so he released all of the energy he was gathering so that his Neo-Quarton would not suffer further damage. In the interest of self-preservation, the only thing he could think of was to escape to the Caligo Black Hole.

A'ethus did not want to give Caligus the upper hand, so he chased Xan through warp space. At the speeds they traveled they both made it to the Caligo Star jointly. Xan had already arrived inside of the barrier created by the two Spheres, but when Oraien came within range of the barrier an implosion took place within the field. Xan recovered and received a boost from being near his Xextrum's Quarton.

Xan then appeared in front of Oraien, and the two withdrew their weapons and began to battle once again. Each connection of their swords resulted in a distorting explosion, and the power was equal between them. Neither one could gain an advantage over the other. In the end the two had proven themselves equal in all strengths but one; the mind. Caligus held A'ethus' sword with two hands but could not move unless he desired to meet his end. Xan looked into Oraien's eyes and saw a new person. He saw a fixed emotion of binding contrition through his Xextrum's eyes. Xan finally drew back and quickly began to open the dark gate within the Caligo Star Quarton.

-"This comes from the realm of darkness itself!"Caligus yelled as the dark hole began to rapidly expand.

-"Don't be stupid, Xan! You'll kill everyone if you do that! If it expands too far you won't be able to control it!"

"Not everyone, just you," Xan replied laughing hysterically.

Oraien quickly dashed towards Xan realizing that he had complete control of his creation, and tackled Caligus, throwing them both into the wormhole.

Chapter 30

Fraudulent Peace

Floating in space, Oraien opened his eyes, nearly drained of energy. He had accomplished his mission; he finally destroyed Caligus. He did not however, dwell on the events that happened within the dark realm or how he was able to escape. Only one thought emerged from his mind, as he was still shocked by how things played out.

-If it was not for her aid, I would still be stuck with Xan.

Using the last of his energy, he traveled back to where his friends and fellow Xextrum awaited his arrival. Coming to a halt, he felt the power of A'ethus fading away as he saw the other Keys returning to their perspective suits. Soon he was back in the form of Ioxus with all the damage he had sustained before. Looking up he saw the other Xextrum huddled together bracing each other happy to see him. Behind them was a surprisingly large number of remaining ships of the Alliance. Without knowing it, he and Caligus destroyed the remaining Niphiliem ships in the course of their devastating battle.

On the front line he could see Calea's ship, safe and fully intact. On board the ships, there was a mighty celebration at hand as they relayed the news back to all the worlds within the quadrant. All the planets rejoiced at their accomplishment. They were able to overcome their differences and unify under their common interest: to defeat Nibiru who were driven by their selfish hunger for survival. Everyone could feel the balance, and everyone on Luna, Nekio, Igni'ice, and Arius exhaled in relief.

Quickly giving out instructions, Calea ordered the pilot of her vessel to pick up the Xextrum. Once on board, they were overwhelmed with cheering soldiers. The Alliance had mounted a successful counter strike, and the five Xextrum were the backbone behind the entire operation. Calea moved the soldiers aside as she made her way through the crowd. Reaching the center she was just in time to see them release their Xextrum. She walked over to Oraien who was being held with his arm around Azrun and gave them both a hug. Once Aiya was able to make it through the joyful crowd, she walked up to Oraien and held him close and told him how proud she was. Shortly afterwards, a V.D. opened aboard the ship with General Kilm addressing the Xextrum, "We are proud of all of you, without you all, the five guardians of light, none of this could have happened," he said smiling, "Pilot, fire your engines, let's go home."

———————————

Back on the planet Nibiru, a Niphiliem soldier gave his weekly update from a report,

-"Lord Syprine, it seems our troops in the Emuli Quadrant have been defeated."

-"Well, that's too bad, I let Cyranus have a little power, and this is how he repays me," he said letting out a sarcastic laugh.

-"Master Xan apparently gained the power of the legendary Caligo star. He was presumed to be dead after being thrown into the Caligo Black Hole."

-"Presumed?" Syprine said with curiosity.

-"Yes sir, that was until his body was found in a cryogenic state at the excavation site on the ancient Shudo'mitian planet of Deseris."

-"Does he live?"

-"Yes my Lord, but it appears he's been there for nearly three thousand years."

Terms Information Directory (T.I.D)

Antares
- The largest star in the known universe.
- The Antares solar system is so large it can be mistaken for a small galaxy.

Caligo
- The largest dark hole in the known universe.
- The Caligo hole is the only star known to have increased in gravity, thus resulting in the destruction of its planets.
- System information incomplete...

Eximetus (Exus)
- Ancient sword inherited by Ioxus. Original name; Eximetus.

Energy Types
- <u>Atomic Energy</u>: energy used when tapping into the power of atoms.
- <u>Electrical Energy</u>: energy mainly used to produce, amplify, or trigger other forms of energy.
- <u>Heat Energy (Fire)</u>: energy that increases the temperature of atoms it reaches.

- <u>Quartiio Energy</u>: Mysterious energy that can only be directly used by Xextrum, and indirectly channeled from a Quarton.
- <u>Light Energy</u>: System information incomplete. The energy given from light and theoretical Light Matter.
- <u>Dark Energy</u>: System information incomplete. Energy that makes up twenty percent of the universe.

Ferra
- Ancient ship assigned to Ioxus.

Jeno-Ray
- a scanner that detects not only life, but also energy through a visual spectrum.

Neo-Quarton
- a type of Quarton
- a small fragment of the larger scale Quarton.
- used to power the legendary Xextrum guardians.

Neo-Ray
- an extra sense provided by the Xextrum.
- the ability to sense life in an area.

Quarton
- an activated core of an energy planet.
- mainly used to channel the massive energy output of the planet
- only ten percent of the Quarton is ever harnessed.

Ship Types
- Warus: Niphiliem battle ship.
- Cruiser: Nekio travel ship.

Stegeton
- Planet with an activated Quarton.

Tetra
- Distance Measurement Unit of 5×10^6 miles.

Xextrum
- Ancient Guardians of the ten corners of the *Antares Ring*.
- Each Xextrum specializes in the use of a form of energy.

Xodus
- Niphiliem soldiers that use a Xodus-Quarton to power a manufactured suit with extreme abilities.

Xodus-Quarton
- a Neo-Quarton that has shattered into many smaller pieces.
- Invented by the Niphiliem.
- Only has the ability of an atomic energy.

Zodok
- First planet destroyed by the Niphiliem.

Made in the USA